RESCUE ME

Christopher Hart was born in 1965 and educated in Cheltenham, Oxford and London. He works as a freelance journalist and lives all over the place.

CHRISTOPHER HART
Rescue Me

ff

faber and faber

First published in 2001
by Faber and Faber Limited
3 Queen Square London WC1N 3AU
This paperback edition published in 2002

Typeset by Faber and Faber Ltd
Printed in England by Mackays of Chatham, plc

A CIP record for this book is available from the British Library

ISBN 0–571–20630–1

2 4 6 8 10 9 7 5 3 1

For Rowan and Annie

Description of man:
Dependence, desire for independence, needs.
Pascal, *Pensées*

But oh, what a cruel thing is a farce to those engaged in it!
Robert Louis Stevenson, *Travels with a Donkey*

'I think I hardly need to tell you that you're fired.'

'No,' I sigh. 'I suppose not. But it would be nice to be told, all the same. Just to make things crystal clear.'

Oliphant's eyes bulge at me. He looks like a nuclear reactor about to pop its pile-cap.

Today Oliphant is fetchingly attired in a lychee-pink double-breasted corduroy suit, no tie and a huge-collared, kiwi-green shirt. His hair is severely greased and parted fore, but aft there hangs a fluffy little ponytail. It must be prosthetic. His hair is dyed pineapple yellow. All in all, he looks like a bolus of half-digested fruit salad sicked up by Godzilla.

His lips quiver with anger. Behind his non-prescription image-only plum-purple plastic specs, his eyes glimmer and seethe. But Oliphant is not a man of violence. His fat white hands lie motionless across the desk like bleached seaweed. And it is noteworthy, too, that he is *sitting behind his desk*. I've never seen Oliphant sitting behind his desk before in my life. Management style nowadays is all about perching deftly on the corner of the desk when talking to your lackeys, or, even more grossly, having an equal-to-equal heart-to-heart sitting beside each other on the Habitat sofa, sipping espressos and kissing buttocks.

In truth, I am aware that Oliphant has never liked me. He considers me fundamentally unsound: I lack bottom. 'The business of advertising is not all five-hour lunches and co-*caine*,' he is fond of saying, rubbing his fat, white, coke-streaked hands and grinning like a retard. 'It is a great deal more about catching the clients and balancing the books.' Balancing the books has never been my forte. Whereas five-hour lunches . . . So I am aware that Oliphant has never liked me. He just hasn't the balls to say it out loud.

'To be perfectly frank, Swallow,' he blurts out, 'I never have liked you.'

Y'see?

I can't even get that right. Cunt that I am.

OK. Here's what happened.

One day, a few weeks back, I'm sitting at my modest desk at Orme, Odstock and Oliphant, Europe's leading advertising agency ('Say it with an OOO!' etc.). I'm doing no one any harm, sorting out my paper-clip pot while softly humming '*O mio bambino caro*' to myself and brooding over Miranda and my non-existent love life and the problem generally with bloody women. You know the My Fair Lady song, '*Why can't a woman . . . be more like an inflatable doll?*' Doesn't talk, and after sex you can just roll her up and shove her under the bed until the next time.

Then the phone goes, and it's Lisa on Reception putting through a call from someone called Terence, a tin-voiced middleman ringing on behalf of JACKAL TV.

JACKAL TV is an exciting new wildlife/docusoap/horror/daytime-porn-by-subscription-only cable channel. One of JACKAL TV's more radical or 'zeitgeisty' ideas is a daily late-night programme called *It's a Bloody Knockout*, in which volunteer contestants armed with rubber coshes, knuckle-dusters and lengths of bicycle chain will inflict considerable injuries upon each other's person, in a kind of jokey, fantasy, Teletubbies-style landscape, until the last man (or woman) left standing will get to win *ONE MILLION POUNDS*. To circumvent legal problems, it will be filmed in the Ukraine.

'And it'll piss on Chris Tarrant,' a senior creative there assures me.

Despite having all these brilliant, zappy, zeitgeisty ideas, however, JACKAL TV still feels it needs to go on our books.

That's what happens at Orme, Odstock and Oliphant. People ring us up and ask, and *beg*, to go on our books.

Less than a month later, I'm standing in a totally bald, windswept field on the Essex/Suffolk border with a television crew and a catering crew and medical crew and a technical support crew and three minor but much-loved television personalities and one enormous fucking balloon. The balloon is a deranged red/orange/purple, straining enthusiastically at its guy ropes, desperate to get on with the job. Touching, really. All around it, camp production assistants and girls called Katrina are twittering joylessly at each other and punching their mobile keypads and moaning that they are so far from London and civilization that they are *off network*.

And I'm circling around on the periphery like an absent-minded electron, uncomfortably aware that it is I who am actually responsible for this fiasco. It is all my big idea. And already I have a Bad Feeling about it.

The three minor but much-loved television personalities are taking it all remarkably well, considering. They grin and wave from the creaking basket with childlike optimism (and childlike faith in adult competence, the poor *fools*). Andrea Jolly, the fast-rising black star-weather girl of JACKAL TV, and hotly tipped to be the favourite weather girl of the entire nation in the near future – Andrea Jolly is taking it especially well. The other two TV-people are both male, Caucasian and wearing boldly coloured fluffy jumpers that clash badly with the colours of the bouncing balloon over their heads.

As a result of a quite incredibly complex series of contractual negotiations, Andrea Jolly herself is wearing not a boldly coloured fluffy jumper, but a dazzling white T-shirt emblazoned with the legend *Cut Loose, Be Free!* This is a promotion for the new brand of True® Tampons. As it turns out, with hindsight, the legend has the most darkly ironic connotations and becomes the butt of many a cruel joke on the more tasteless satirical television programmes.

3

And where is the jackal? you may be wondering.

We couldn't get hold of a real jackal in time. But instead, when the much-loved trio get airborne, they will pull a wire and a panel will open up in the base of the balloon basket beneath their feet, through which a calibrated orifice will dispense over middle England exactly 10,000 free televisions over a period of five hours. Not real televisions, obviously. Heavens to Betsy, that might kill a kiddie (and there is something especially tragic about the death of a child). Oh no, these tellies are tiny, the size of postage stamps, and made from imperishable foam rubber. And each one is stamped with a cute little brown jackal-type mutt ('a jackal crossed with a kind of cocker spaniel' is what I actually asked the designers for). Genius, hunh? We had some trouble from pollution protesters, and had to get air-traffic permission, because apparently if by some freak enough little foam-rubber televisions were to get together to form a mid-air cluster, they could make a 'significant appearance' on radar screens. But it's OK, we're cleared for take-off. And then – this is my masterstroke – once the TVs have landed, anyone who manages to find and collect a hundred of the buggers will win a FREE GIFT! as the popular pleonasm has it. *A brand-new wide-screen digital TV all for themselves* – subject to the usual contractual agreements, JACKAL TV awards ceremonies, publicity appearances etc.

The kids'll love it.

(Can you die of cynicism? I'm beginning to wonder. Save me, someone, lest I perish of pointlessness, die of dearth and lack of I know not what.)

Balloon in field, three minor but much-loved television personalities and 10,000 foam-rubber TVs. It may all seem rather far-fetched, I grant you, rather *unrealistic*. But you don't need me to tell you: nothing is realistic nowadays.

So now the JACKAL TV cameras are lumbering forward,

each one mounted on a human torso, anurous Anubis, blind muzzle like a dead eye, devouring our every move as we take up positions. We are going to cut the guy ropes dramatically with machetes. Just for the cameras, mind. The genuine anchor rope will be released only after final safety checks and the crucial installation of the trained balloon pilot. But he's not sufficiently telegenic – mottled visage, tremendous gut, riotous nostril hair – so we'll do a fake take-off first with just the three lovely, fluffy, made-for-television television people. After a little back-room editing it'll all look perfectly authentic and immensely exciting.

I catch Andrea Jolly's eye. She smiles down beneficently upon me. The cameras roll, we slash at the fake guy ropes, the main anchor rope uncoils like a malevolent serpent and, before we know what has happened, the balloon is 30 feet up in the air and rising, the distance between us filled with anguished cries, thinning out fast.

'Pull on the vent line!' yells the non-telegenic balloon pilot beside me. 'Let the gas out!'

But the three minor though much-loved TV personalities are already out of earshot. Apparently the conditions are all wrong for this kind of thing anyway, cumulonimbus clouds = thermal conditions, and soon the balloon hits a warm current that whisks them up giddyingly to 10,000 feet in a matter of seconds, like a ping-pong ball on a fountain of water, and then, the temperature already down to 2°C or something, it encounters a contrary airflow that shouldn't have been there and is blown in precisely the wrong direction, away over East Anglia and out across the mutinous, grey North Sea . . .

As PR stunts go, OK, I admit that it wasn't as successful as it might have been. But I can't help feeling that everyone made rather a fuss about it. I mean, it's not as if it was Noel Edmonds in the fucking basket, is it?

All the same, it caused a considerable *esclandre*. Last night on the news, it was implied that the PR whiz kid behind the stunt was effectively responsible for the deaths of three Jill Dando-type national icons. I am not a popular man. I'll never work again, not even ankle-deep in pig fat frying beef-flavoured burgers for scurvy teens. But then again, every cloud has an etc. Orme, Odstock and Oliphant are in deep shit too, and JACKAL TV is almost certainly finished. At the very least it'll have to change its name.

So I stand with dignity and button my jacket and shake Oliphant's fat white hand, farinaceous with co-*caine*. He tells me that I have fifteen minutes to clear my desk and he does-n't suppose he'll be hearing from me again.

There's nothing I want from my desk – not even my beloved paper-clip pot. Instead I take the lift two floors up to say goodbye to Clive. People pause for me in the corridor, standing well clear, terrified of catching the contagion of failure. (AIDS, CJD, Ebola, they could live with, but *failure* . . .) I favour them all indiscriminately with a winsome, vacant, Andrea Jolly-type smile, and pray desperately that I don't get an attack of the hiccups, as I usually do in moments of extreme emotion. And then I find Clive, standing by the new temp's desk. The new temp is Amrita: long haughty nose, gold bracelets, scarily clever. Talks with amazingly precise enunciation, in perfect sentences, if not paragraphs. Sounds like a *Times of India* editorial. Clive is besotted with her. The fool. He'd have more chance with Andrea Dworkin.

They both turn towards me. Slightly awkward, but at least they don't treat me as if I'm a virus in human form. 'So,' says Clive, 'you got the boot?' I nod. 'The *bastards*,' he hisses, holding the back of his hand to his mouth as if to muffle the intensity of his own voice. 'It was an *accident*, for Christ's sake, anyone could see that.'

'An accident that resulted in the deaths of three minor but much-loved TV personalities,' I point out. 'Not good PR, not good at all.'

'It is not the people they mind about,' says Amrita, 'it is the money that went up with them.'

They're silent for a while, then ask me what I'm going to do. I shrug. 'Get pissed. Watch daytime TV – though maybe not JACKAL. Then find another job, I suppose. Or maybe sell the car and go travelling for a bit.'

Clive nods broodingly. 'Well, stay in touch.'

'Are you sure?' I say, voice rich with self-pity. 'Everyone else in this place is doing their best to avoid me. Odstock won't even shake my hand.'

'*Wankers*,' he hisses, then says much louder, 'They're all wankers. Ignore them.' He stands tall, all 5 feet 7 of him, maybe to prove something to Amrita, I don't know, but I'm touched anyhow. Rolls his shoulder back, booms, 'There are still some of us here not so mindlessly shallow as to ostracize a friend just because he's killed three people.'

The Hon. Clive Spooner. I could hug him. I don't, of course – I'm English, for God's sake. But . . . the *Honourable* Clive Spooner.

Amrita shakes my hand. A jangle of bangles, kohl-rimmed eyes, her smile firm and serious. 'Shantih shantih shantih,' she says. 'Meaning: do not let the buggers grind you down.'

The Hon. Clive Spooner is the third son of Lord Craigmuir. His parents are separated. His mother, Olivia, resides in London and is a highly respected dealer in nineteenth-century topographical art. She often travels. Lord Craigmuir speaks in a clipped, violent tone of voice, and his John Lobb brogues are always polished to an insanely high degree, as are his burgundy cheeks. He has a little grey moustache and is often known to shout.

When his four sons were younger he would line them up in the ancestral hallway and inspect their shoes – at least, on those rare occasions when they were home from boarding school. Clive, like his three brothers, Hector, Hamish and

7

Dougal, was sent away to boarding school at the age of seven. On his eighth birthday he received only one present, postmarked Braemar, from his father. Inside was a tin of brown shoe polish. No note, no birthday card. Just the shoe polish.

His mother sent him nothing.

Except the next day she drove straight into Old Quad at 8 a.m. in her clapped-out Alfa Romeo, 'The Girl from Ipanema' on tape, tooting her horn, wearing a silk headscarf and wraparound shades, demanding of Clive's flustered housemaster that she wanted to see her birthday boy. His housemaster said that Spooner-3 was in breakfast and anyway this wasn't an exeat. Lady Craigmuir paused to light a cigarette in a long black holder and then told the housemaster that she wasn't moving until her darling boy was released into her custody, and that if this didn't happen by the time she had finished her cigarette she would start to take her clothes off.

Spooner-3 was installed in the passenger seat of the Alfa Romeo in under a minute.

Clive and his mother spent the next two weeks driving very fast around Europe, swimming in various seas and eating ice cream.

When Clive returned to school he wept and begged to stay with her. His mother sighed and said it was quite impossible. She lived in a shoebox in Pimlico. Behind her wraparound shades she cried too, but she never let him know.

As she drove back into London, the headlights of oncoming cars blurred and enormous through her ungovernable tears, she smoked furiously and repeated to herself a mantra that went *Heartless bastards. Heartless English bastards.*

How do I know this? Because Olivia told me, in a moment of intimacy.

Read on.

*

One last thing, before I depart the accursed precincts of Orme, Odstock and Oliphant for ever: an illicit cigarette.

Smoking is strictly forbidden at Orme, Odstock and Oliphant, and we even have a full-time Personnel Welfare Officer, Ms Gwenda Dear, to enforce the ban. So on the way out I slide my pack of Camel Lights from my inside jacket pocket and flick a single, blissful cigarette loose. Pause by the door. Light up. Inhale that good aroma. Lungs thrill with pleasure, alveoli sigh and shudder, my eyes turn dreamy and serene.

And then all the alarms go off.

Chuckling like a bad schoolboy, I head for the door, waving a last goodbye to a laughing Lisa on Reception.

And then I'm out into the streets – *a free man*.

It feels good. I step out rangily. The streets are mine, time is mine, go where I want, do as I please. A true free-lancer, ranging the warm London streets, the air perfumed with Turkish cigarettes and dry martinis, among the floods of beautiful people, hands in my pockets and a debonair lilt in my step, free for a while, back in the game, to rendezvous with some girl with endless legs and a forgiving smile.

Or, failing that, Indajit in the corner shop at the end of our street in the Bush.

Indajit is in one of his horribly ebullient moods.

'Daniel, my fren', have you seen this story that is in the newspapers today? It is really very funny!' He thrusts a *Daily Mail* under my nose. 'Do you see this man who has killed these three lovely telly people – do you see what they are saying his name is? *Daniel Swallow*! The same name as your name! Isn't that very funny now?'

I can barely reply for mirth. I buy a lunch-time *Standard* – it's a page-three story for them – but mercifully no one has tracked down a mugshot of me.

'You take care now, Daniel, my fren', or maybe some bad luck has been put on you!' Indajit calls after me cheerfully. 'I do not like the feeling of it at all!'

How wonderful it is to live in such a classless, multicultural society as ours, to be on first-name terms with your local newsagent, and to feel so relaxed and fraternal with each other that he takes the piss out of you at every possible opportunity.

2

When I get home, I find Kate sitting at the kitchen table with her hippie little sister, Jess. Kate is drinking camomile tea, Jess is smoking a spliff. Kate is my beloved landlady, thirty-four, eight years my senior, unmarried, keeps falling for wankers called Tom. Sometimes I could even imagine marrying Kate myself – if I believed in such a fatuous, deluded institution as marriage, that is.

'Fired?'

I nod. 'Fired.'

'Cool,' says Jess. Strokes back her long, preternaturally glossy hair.

'Inevitable, I suppose,' says Kate.

It must always be something of an embarrassment, I would imagine, chatting with one of your tenants who has just been on last night's news, and then again in today's papers, on account of having killed three minor but much-loved television personalities. So instead we swerve the conversation towards the eviction of the latest Tom from Kate's life.

While Kate has a thoroughly modern, post-feminist attitude to life as a single, free, independent woman with a full and demanding career in PR and a healthy salary, and while she jokes that she really has no time for relationships, she gets all the company she wants from her friends, and while she likes knowing that she can go out to a bar or club any night of the week and pick up a man of her choice, men all being such big tarts and Kate being by no means unattractive, and the following morning just kiss him and tell him sweetly, *Thank you and goodbye, I have to go to work now* – all the same, after the second bottle of wine or so, when she's having dinner with me and/or girlfriends and/or her hippie little sister, Jess, *in vino veritas* – she will sort of admit that what she really wants is a decent man.

But are there any left?

Despite the solitary pleasure she derives from running her bath after a long day's work, and choosing which bubble-bath to use from her considerable collection – dewberry? orange blossom? herbal aromatherapeutic? – and running the hot tap at only half-speed so that the bath takes longer to fill and she can spend more time faffing around her bedroom in her dressing-gown sorting out which clothes she's going to wear afterwards – despite the solitary pleasures of such baths, safe in the knowledge that they will not be interrupted by some beery male voice at the door demanding to use the loo (assuming I'm around, that is), and despite being able to spend as long as she wants in there, twiddling the hot tap on and off with her big toe, and despite pleasures such as eating *exactly* the food she likes, including serious chocolate binges and a banana intake of almost obsessive levels – six a day was about average, eight or nine not unknown . . . Despite Jess making unkind jokes about the Freudian significance of such a fruit, despite the voluptuous sensation of cool, bare sheets on her double bed, entirely her own, still, I know very well that there are nights when Kate would rather share that cool and solitary space with the musky, hairy, even *beery* sprawl of a male body. And all she gets is boys.

The most recent, Tom, was thirty-six. And still emphatically a boy.

At first this had been part of his appeal. She loved his boyish enthusiasm for her collection of colourful and unusual egg cups; and his boyish laughter at the first joke she told him; and his boyish delight when his exploring right hand first discovered that she was wearing stockings and suspenders.

(Amazing how much my landlady tells me about her love life, now I come to think about it.) And his good looks were boyish too: slightly wavy light brown hair, which he insisted was blond, and bright blue eyes unsullied by time or disillusionment; a slim boyish waist and hips, and a casual offhand sexiness when he was dressed in nothing more complicated than a T-shirt and jeans.

They had got together swiftly and easily. And stayed together. I always thought he was a wanker, and he ate one of my Biopot yoghurts once and never replaced it. Still, the weeks and months went by, and Kate and Tom seemed set to last. And although she couldn't quite put her finger on it . . . *nothing happened*. She tried asking him once or twice, with extreme delicacy, prefaced with a pre-emptive joke or two about how obviously she wasn't suggesting *marriage* or anything so ridiculous, but, all the same . . . did he feel that their relationship was *going anywhere*? At which he would look genuinely puzzled and say, What do you mean? Where is it *supposed* to be going? And at the end of the first year, she dared to identify what it was in her own unwilling mind that she had until then studiously avoided. What she meant by *nothing happening* was that Tom wasn't growing any older. Except physically, of course. Physically, yes, little signs were appearing more obviously as the days and weeks went by. That wrinkle across his forehead remained just visible at all times now, whether he was raising his eyebrows or not. Tiny laughter lines were appearing around his eyes (which themselves were, admittedly, still the same – unsullied, unhurt). And certainly that neat circle of thinning hair on the crown of his head had grown over the past year, had extended the borders of its evil dominion, deforesting slowly but surely in all directions, his skull becoming more palely visible through the sparse thatch, despite the vastly expensive lotions that he applied twice daily with unsmiling faith and optimism. Once she had been foolish enough to tickle this sensitive zone with her fingertips as he lay half

13

sleeping on a Sunday morning. In an instant Tom was wide awake, leaping out of bed and marching towards the privacy of the bathroom, incongruously outraged and insulted in his cotton M&S boxer shorts.

Wrinkles, laughter lines, male pattern baldness – yes, Tom was getting older in that way, the way we all grow older, sulkily following the path of slow decay that nature mapped out for us all aeons ago. But Tom wasn't *growing up*. The years would come and go and Tom would mature no more. Like some mediocre wine, he had reached his point of maximum maturity fairly early on – in his late teens, maybe – and there would be no more improvement. Drink now. Ahead, there is only sour regret, the vinegar of aged petulance, childish octogenarian complaint.

Kate never seriously thought that she would spend her whole life with him. She found it hard to imagine spending her whole life, her precious one and only life, with any one person, all the way to the bitter end – though some couples did, so there must be something in it. (Yes, I explained to her: there's *fear* in it. Fear is what keeps it all together. Nothing else.) But now she began to think that she couldn't stand Tom much longer at all, however pretty and boyish he might be. If he was boyish about egg cups and jokes and stockings, he was also boyish, rather more infuriatingly, when it came to the need to sort things out, to discuss things, to listen to one another's dissatisfactions, to compromise, to forgive.

'Tuh! Men!' I would sympathize helpfully with her.

But Kate was still prepared to forgive – though she wasn't quite sure why – when, only a week ago, she came home unexpectedly early to find Tom sitting on the edge of the bed with his trousers round his ankles and a goofy look on his face, jiggling a naked teenage girl up and down on his lap. It wasn't the girl who annoyed Kate – she recognized her from the 7-Eleven down the road – so much as the goofy look, one moment semi-orgasmic, the next shocked and shamefaced;

but goofy either way. Even more irritating were those stupid bloody boxer shorts, nestling atop the trousers around his ankles, the same ones she always pictured him in, with the grinning, bouncing tomatoes, which he wore to show what a crazy, fun, young-at-heart guy he still was.

It was pretty much the end, although Kate tried to talk about it, gave him the chance. It was like asking for meaningful communication with a pocket calculator. Tom gave predictable answers – $2 \times 2 = 4$, $3^3 = 27$ – and then switched himself off to save needless consumption of battery power. After that, Kate told him she thought he ought to leave. He left.

There are times when she seriously considers:

    a) a vow of lifelong celibacy,

    b) lesbianism.

Apparently she recently turned to her little sister for advice and moral support. The conversation went thus:

'Nah,' said Jess. 'Tried 'em.'

'You've tried *lesbianism*?'

'Well, at school – you know . . .'

'Oh, *that*. That doesn't count. No, an *adult* lesbian relationship, you know – a proper partnership. And I also find it hard to believe you've ever made a vow of lifelong celibacy.'

'Well, it wasn't for life, it was just *for the time being*, when I made it. A resolution, not a vow. A New Year's Resolution, in fact.'

'Made at midnight?'

'Yep.'

'At a New Year's Eve party?'

'Yep.'

'After a drink or two?'

'Yep.'

'And, let me guess: it lasted . . . two hours?'

'Er – about one actually,' said Jess cheerfully. 'I can't remember the exact timescale. It was at uni. That was the night I met Stefan.'

'Right,' said Kate. 'You little trollop.'

'Strumpet,' agreed Jess.

'So,' I say, 'Tom's gone.'

'Yesterday. I told him to pack his bags and bog off.'

'And he didn't object?'

Kate struggles with her pride and then admits, 'No, he didn't.'

Jess puts an arm round her. There is nothing to say.

'He was a jerk,' I say anyway.

'A pillock,' says Jess.

'I think that about sums him up,' says Kate. 'So – what about you? What are *your* plans?'

Um . . .

3

I'm lying in bed one morning, dozing my way through the *Today* programme, when I dream briefly that the three much-loved telly people have been found alive and well and living on an iceberg wearing pyjamas. I wake up and find that it is half true: they really are alive and well, having been spotted by a Norwegian trawler, bobbing along in their basket with the deflated balloon trailing along behind them like a monstrous amniotic sac. They are now recovering in Trondheim, being force-fed schnapps and soused herring.

No doubt the mega-book deals plus telly rights will be announced next week. *All at Sea* by Andrea Jolly. *An Ill Wind. The Moon is* Not *a Fucking Balloon.*

Still, at least I'm not a murderer. Maybe somebody will employ me again now. Though God knows who.

And then, a few days later, just when I am beginning to accustom myself to the lifestyle of the long-term unemployed – late rising, daytime telly, penury, a lot of tea drinking, frequent though listless manstupration – somebody *does* employ me.

I'm squatting on the can, leafing through the latest *Private Eye*, when I come across the following ad:
Followed by a mobile number.

> GENTLEMEN REQUIRED
> To accompany ladies to days out at the races, nights out at the opera, or just to share a candlelit dinner for two.

So, having completed my leisurely act of matutinal defecation and fortified myself with nicotine, I ring.

An answerphone instructs 'lady callers' to press 1, while 'gentlemen' should press 2 and then leave their address after the beep. Further information will be sent out. I press 2, leave my address, replace the receiver and then, after a decent pause, I redial and press 1.

Immediately the phone is answered by a female voice horribly afflicted with some weird, faux-Kensington accent.

'Good morning, Grosvenor for Ladies,' she says. 'Can I help you?'

I try to fake a female voice but manage only a strangulated squawk.

'Good morning?' she repeats.

I drop the receiver down and collapse in a fit of uncontrollable (and unattractively high-pitched) giggles.

I cannot be serious.

But it seems I am.

Two days later a very proper-looking application form arrives, requiring full personal details of prospective gentleman: age, height, weight, hue of hair and eye, career history, education, interests, plus a photograph at least 5 x 4 inches – *head and shoulders only*, it italicizes (like I'm about to send in a Polaroid to some vicious old procuress of myself sprawled butt-naked on a bed in a state of priapic abandon – they should be so lucky).

I don't have any 5 x 4 pics of myself, only tiny, gnarled photobooth images of a Baader-Meinhof member distantly resembling how I used to look about eight years ago. So when Kate gets home that evening . . .

'You're looking very smart. What's her name?'

'I don't know yet,' I say slyly. 'But – do you think you could take a picture of me?'

And so Kate shoots off half a dozen Polaroids while I sit in an armchair, freshly showered, shaven, sprack and spright-

18

ly, spruce, besuited, and smiling in what I fondly imagine is a rugged, mysterious and just *slightly* cruel fashion.

'Dan, could you stop – I mean, your mouth's curled up all weird. Could you try to look a bit less like Mr Bean?'

So I abandon the attempt to look rugged and settle instead for vapid.

Kate scrutinizes me and then sighs, 'OK, that'll have to do.'

Of the eight photos she takes, one is just about acceptable. She wants to know what they're for. I'm evasive. 'Just a job,' I say. 'Rather glam, actually.'

'JACKAL TV presenter?' she suggests. 'OK, OK, I was only joking. Um, male model? Rent boy?'

'Tuh! Rent boy indeed.'

That night, I scrutinize myself naked in the bathroom mirror and wonder if I really cut the mustard as a gigolo. The reflection gawping back at me is no Richard Gere.

Daniel Swallow . . . Tall. Average-looking. Bushy eyebrows. Dark eyes, good nose and mouth. Receding hair. A little hirsute. Awful flamingo legs and bony knees. Asymmetrical ears. Tendency to hiccup in moments of heightened emotion. Keen smoker. Never voted. Educ. public school, Oxford, then advertising/PR, before branching out into an exciting new career in prostitution. Vague, disorganized, idle and poorly motivated. Promiscuous, greedy, but thin. High-pitched giggle. Terrible driver. Once cautioned by the police for indecent exposure. Once trod on Jeffrey Bernard's toe. Can juggle while standing on one leg and singing '*O mio bambino caro*'. Favourite film, *Kind Hearts and Coronets*. Would like to be practising Xtian but never believed a word of it, really: bad faith. Not only hopelessly promiscuous but also hopelessly romantic: a tricky combination. Loves opera, music and crosswords. Penis 6¼ inches at full turgidity, which is ¼ inch or 4 per cent over the average, according to Dr Desmond Morris in *The Naked Ape*.

*

I've almost forgotten about Grosvenor for Ladies when the phone goes about a fortnight later and that same faux-Kensington voice invites me over for 'a little chat' somewhere in Covent Garden.

The following morning I find myself sitting in an immaculate, claustrophobically tiny office talking to Caroline – my procuress, my bawd. She seems pleased with our little chat, deigns to describe me as 'a nice boy – just our sort', and asks when I would be free to work. Straight away, I tell her. She takes my mobile number and says that I should have at least a day's notice. Clients might choose me just from a description, or they might find me on the Grosvenor website.

'To be upfront with you, love,' says Caroline, 'I'd have thought you might really clean up.' (Faux-Kensington accent and idiom slipping fast now.) 'The thing is, if you don't mind me saying this, the thing is, you're not *too* good-looking, are you? Some of the fellas we get applying here are real lookers, you know, all pumped up and square-jawed and tall, dark and handsome and all that, and you know, the ladies really don't like that, they're actually much more interested in a normal, nice, average-looking fella with charm and good conversation, attentive, full of compliments – you know?'

I nod sagely.

'Now, here's our card.'

It's thick and glossy and gilt-edged like a wedding invitation. Down one side is an elegant line-drawing of a lissom Adonis. Handsome embossed lettering across the top says *Grosvenor – for Ladies*, followed by all the guff about races, operas and candlelit dinners for two. At the bottom – this is where I really have to gulp down the rising *hysterico passio* in my breast (down, thou climbing sorrow. You think I'll weep. No, I'll not weep) – I read the legend *Grosvenor – It's About Love*.

'We tried a number of suitable names,' says Caroline. ('Caroline' I've already labelled her. Real name, Dawn. Or maybe Sheryl.) 'We wanted to get it just right. Cavendish,

Wellington, Windsor, Beau Monde . . . but we thought Grosvenor sounded much the nicest.'

'Yes, much the nicest, I so agree.'

'And we don't go leaving these in any public telephone boxes neither!' she squawks. 'Now then, payment. What you get is quite simply a flat rate of £150 an evening, plus any travel expenses you incur, to be paid by the lady in advance. You don't pay us anything. The ladies pay a monthly fee to be members. So that £150 is all yours. And that means being available from 6 p.m. until midnight, when you will see the lady safely back to her hotel or apartment and kiss her goodnight.' A meaningful pause. 'I'm sure I don't need to add that that is absolutely *the end of the evening*. We are *not* an escort agency, we are simply in the business of offering companionship to single ladies for evenings out. Is that understood?'

'Of course. Of course.'

I wonder whether to touch her for a hundred now, just to be going on with, because I'm completely skint. But I don't quite have the nerve, even though I have less than a pound in my pocket. OOO have frozen my last month's payment and the voracious *vagina dentata* of the cashpoint machine has just gobbled up my card and spat back bespittled shreds of plastic in my face. So I have to walk home to the Bush.

On the way, I pop into Claridge's to cheer myself up and order a bottle of champagne. Sit at the bar with the newspapers, a leisurely cigarette. Towards the bottom of the bottle, I pluck my mobile from my jacket pocket and shout, 'Hello? Hello, I can't hear you, you're breaking up . . . I'm in Claridge's. *Claridge's*. Well, let's have lunch here. Fine. It went fine. Yep. 150K. Well, that's what they offered. I know, I can't believe it either, it's brilliant. That's why I'm sitting here at lunch time with a bottle of bubbly in front of me! Sorry, I missed that . . . You're breaking up again . . . Hang on, I'll have to pop outside . . .' At which point I shoot the barman a harassed smile, waggle my mobile at him and make indications that I'll just be a minute.

And once outside, I run so fast that I nearly sick up all that lovely champagne at the foot of the Roosevelt Memorial in Grosvenor Square. How appropriate that would have been.

I check out the Grosvenor website a couple of days later – and there I am, pixellated mugshot staring vacantly from the flickering screen: Thoby.

Thoby.

It seems I have been appropriated, rechristened, reinvented, rebranded by my new owner/occupiers, and am now to be relaunched on to the open market as Thoby™. What the fuck is wrong with Daniel? *Thoby*, for fuck's sake. I don't even know how to pronounce the name.

Still, I suppose it could have been worse. 'Bruno', for instance. Or 'Serge'.

I also note that I have grown a couple of inches and am 'a keen sportsman'. I smile grimly. Just wait till they see me with my clothes off. Just wait till the old biddies see my *knees*.

But I brace myself. I can work this game – *this business*, I quickly correct myself, I'm a *businessman* – for a while and then retire, withdraw from this unreal world and flee to some little cottage in the west of Ireland, beyond all reach of the madness. There I shall be poor and happy and daydream my days away to the sound of the Atlantic breakers falling on the lonely strand, the gulls wheeling in the blue air and perhaps some pretty colleen singing an ancient melody as she wanders barefoot through the heather, nibbling an oatcake.

I've seen too many adverts, scripted too many adverts, *made* too many adverts. You can tell. Unreality is ubiquitous. This new-born god, like a huge balloon growing monstrously fast, trawling low through the twilight skies, all-powerful, without malice, destroying our mother Memory, our history, culture, forests, justice, our games of life and practices of death . . . what is it? There is no escape, NO EXIT. It has us all in its net.

4

On the assorted sofas in Miles's Chelsea terraced house, G&Ts in hand: me, Miles, his girlfriend, Beth, and Emma (minus Clive, who is supposed to be on the way).

Miles Champney is an old friend from uni days, the only person whom I talked to in the first week and was still talking to at the end of the third year. Miles spends his days working out whether certain banks should invest in other banks, depending on whether or not those latter banks are underperforming. Although in fact, even if they are underperforming, other banks can still make money from these banks that are not making money, by putting money into them and then using the muscle that money gets you to make sure they do start making money. *Capisce?*

Miles has a short, stocky neck, a boxer's neck, almost as broad as his head, which it holds firmly in place as he shoulders his way through the crowds. I often picture his cannonball of a head buffeting its way through the crowds, to the bar or the ticket machines. He has swimming-pool-blue eyes and can talk about pretty well anything. And then there's the tight collars of his stripy Turnbull and Asser shirts, and his stubby neck, and his flashing eyes, and his big body on neat, lively feet, the whole ensemble quivering with a still-puppyish energy, which seems so egregiously and yet amiably at odds with the idea of a highly successful twenty-something City-something – investment analyst, I *think* – earning a comfortable six figures a year. Miles is also insanely competitive. When we play our ferocious games of squash and he loses – though it's pretty rare – his face goes puce. 'You really mind about winning, don't you?' I ask him later, when he's calmed down and looks less likely to break my neck. 'Stuff of life, dear boy,' he says. It's not just the Joneses he has to keep up with; it's the Goldsmiths, the Bransons and the Soroses too. I like him because he's so unlike me. I like his energy being so focused. He knows what he wants. I have energy too, and I piss it away talking till five in the morning about the meaning of life, or flirting with any available females.

Take the squash: we first played about five years ago, soon after coming to London from uni. I beat him hollow. After that, he avoided playing me again for about three months, always had some excuse why he couldn't make it. Then he rang me and fixed a date. We played and he completely wasted me. For the first few games I didn't win a single point. Funny, really. For those three months Miles had been taking lessons in secret, just so he could come back and trash me.

And now he has this fabulously exotic trophy girlfriend by the deceptively unexotic name of Beth. She's exotic, but I don't like her. She has that unmistakably glacial, bitchy edge, and I know Miles is going to get hurt by her. Still, it's been a while now and they're still going.

'So then, Beth –' this is the question I really want to ask her, but don't quite dare just yet – 'tell us, what was it that first attracted you to your millionaire boyfriend?'

I know the type.

Though it's rather annoying to learn later on in the evening that she went to Cambridge and isn't stupid at all. Don't you just hate having your preconceptions overturned?

At first I think she's just another Emma. I can't stand Emma either. This makes me sound like a misogynist, but it's just these two, really. A misogynist, *moi*? I wouldn't go so far as that. But you do have to maintain a certain wariness when dealing with the Enemy.

Emma is Clive's girlfriend. And Clive – the *Honourable* Clive Spooner – is someone whom I knew vaguely at school but who then turned up at Orme, Odstock and Oliphant. An

Hon. like him should never have been working in such a sleazy new industry as PR and advertising, of course. His father wanted him to be in the army, Guards regiment naturally, or else become an estate manager. Even work behind the counter at Berry Bros. But, almost by mistake, Clive fetched up at OOO. And after getting over the initial embarrassment of having known each other when we were both farting, wanking, pustular adolescents, we are now good friends. There are times when my admiration for the short but Honourable Clive Spooner knows no bounds. He is a much better person than I am.

Clive and Miles have got on reasonably well on the previous occasions when they have met through me – hence tonight's dinner invitation. Maybe Clive is slightly wary of him: big burly Miles with the wads of cash and the loud laugh. But appearances are very deceptive. Clive is supposed to be here now, but for some mysterious reason he has not yet turned up, which is why Emma is sulking.

On the rare occasions when she isn't sulking, Emma has a cut-glass laugh, and whether she is sulking or not, she is always tall and willowy. She dresses impeccably and has perfect, brittle manners. She strongly dislikes what she calls *silliness*. Of course, she loves Clive as he is (which is, admittedly, quite silly). She isn't with him just for his pots of money, as some girls would be, or for that charming little 'Hon.' that precedes his name on more formal social occasions. Of course she loves him, Emma *loves* Clive. But there are times when he can be a bit silly (a *bit*!), which for her is a bit embarrassing. There are times when her sibilant tone of voice, when she scolds him for such silliness, suggests that sometimes she finds him just a *teeny weeny* bit irritating. But of course she puts up with him as he is because she loves him dearly.

Admittedly he is especially difficult to cope with when he is with friends. Emma has been out for drinks and dinners with us lot before. And mixing with Clive's peculiar friends she finds particularly difficult. Miles and I have drunk too much for a start, and she's probably secretly glad that Clive *isn't* here, in a way, otherwise he'd get just as drunk as well and tomorrow morning he'd have one of his explosive sessions in the loo before dashing off to work, leaving *her* to go in there and throw all the windows open and spray that really rather naff but sometimes indispensable pine-scented air freshener all over the place and leave it for at least half an hour before she can even bear to go in there and brush her teeth.

Sometimes, men can be so revolting.

She's never liked me that much anyway. I swear too much for her liking, and she doesn't get my jokes, and she always looks like she's worried I'm going to say something lecherous to her. (*Yeah.*) Horrid, really. And I don't earn much money, and now I've no job at all, and yet I make jokes about the fact that I drive a car called the Rustbucket that Emma herself would be embarrassed to be seen in around London, quite frankly. What a loser.

OK, I did sort of make a drunken pass at her a while back, which she rejected out of hand. Not good behaviour, I know. But no reason for her to be quite so cold towards me. And she followed it up with a long lecture about loyalty to one's friends which left me utterly shamefaced. Cow.

At least Clive has plenty of money. Not that that's the only thing Emma sees in him, of course not, or even the main thing. But it is certainly a nice extra, an added bonus, on top of the fact that he is – well, an Hon., and that he isn't a lecher, for instance, and has a good job, and a nice car. Of course she loves Clive for what he is, but it is nice too that she only has to work part-time (Sotheby's) and that he lets her redecorate and design their flat as she likes, and that he pays off her Harvey Nicks account every so often, that is sweet of him, without even complaining, except maybe to make some silly remark about how much she's spent recently, which always irritates her slightly. She knows people who spend *far* more than she does on clothes and still don't look nearly so nice and elegant as she tries to, for Clive.

Oh yes, Emma does look elegant. Tall and willowy and healthy and elegant. Clive's love life is certainly sorted. Clive is certainly a very lucky chap.

Clive knows what I think of Emma, and seems to find it *amusing*. Once he even said to me, 'You know, I'm almost beginning to suspect you're *jealous* of me and Em.'

Jealous! What on earth can he mean?

Beth has these nicely depraved dark shadows under her eyes, but she is too skinny, and neurotic, and doesn't listen. Though she talks well enough, I have to admit. Pretty feisty, combative, which is better than Emma, who exudes nothing but deep-frozen silence. At one point we are having an argument about the fate of the Bulger boys, and suddenly she is leaning forward with her eyes blazing, gesticulating, with her cigarette clenched between her fingers, extraordinarily passionate and articulate and completely wiping the floor with us all. Clever bitch.

But she's still a mod – *ow*.

'Satisfying work, I imagine?'

She regards me through half-closed eyes, exhales in my face. 'About as satisfying as *advertising*, darling. But a *lot* better paid.'

Apart from the modelling she does, she's an up-and-coming actress, hoping to get a part in some lavish new TV version of *Pygmalion* some time soon. And there's talk of an American movie role . . .

Talk turns to my recent sacking, and indeed the whole JACKAL TV fiasco, in initially hushed and respectful tones – *de paene mortuis nihil nisi bonum* etc. But it doesn't last, and soon we are smirking guiltily at the thought of that balloon, its terrified occupants, lost and adrift . . . rather cruel, I know, but what else can you do? And anyway, they're not dead after all. Just *nearly* dead. So surely a ripe subject for mirth?

27

And then Beth goes off on a sustained fantasy riff about what might have become of the three much-loved telly people if they *hadn't* been rescued: icebergs, polar bears, Fox's Glacier Mints, seal-skin pashminas, Inuit initiation ceremonies . . . mad stuff. I always love people who can do these sustained fantasy riffs when the mood takes them. I can, and so can Kate's hippie little sister, Jess. And so, it seems, can Beth.

Everyone makes various unhelpful suggestions about my current unemployed state, including, inevitably, 'You could always try selling your arse at King's Cross.' This is Beth's offering, delivered absolutely straight-faced. But it is so close to the truth of what I *am* planning to do that it quite discombobulates me.

'How much do you think I'd get?'

She squints down at my posterior. 'You might get bought a cheeseburger, if you're lucky.'

Emma sits silently examining the furniture, the pictures, that rather poor-taste reproduction ginger jar stuffed, no, *overstuffed* with dried flowers. G&Ts come and go and soon come round again. Miles is on fine form as the host, expansive and ruddy-faced and getting into Emma's good books straight away by noticing that she's had a new haircut (even though it is only slightly different from her old haircut) and complimenting her on how well it suits her. Though why anyone would want to bother to get into Emma's good books is a mystery to me.

Before long, Miles and I are fondly recalling our retrospectively halcyon university days, deep in the muddy waters of senile reminiscence: mad Jeff the college porter, whatshisname arrested for dumping in the fountain, Bronwen the Welsh Mountain and her amazing string of seductions, or were they rapes? Homosexual Plumptre insisting on helping the choirboys to robe. Such reminiscences tend to be as fun for the participants as they are hellishly dull for the spectators. Emma turns to Beth and starts a rival conversation about families, which sounds a little like hard work, but I suppose they reckon the effort is worth it since at least it signals their conversational autonomy from the men.

We are draining G&Ts at an alarming rate, and scooping up handfuls of garlic mignons, and our laughter is oxygenating our blood and making us both rubicund and loud, and Miles actually starts to bounce up and down on the sofa chortling with glee, and then he starts to cough up little nuggets of garlic mignons that have mischievously found their way into his respiratory tract in a manner most unbecoming in a respected and usually well-behaved City-something.

Emma clears the plates and goes into the kitchen, martyrishly. Beth doesn't stir, looks very comfortable, leaning lazily back in her chair, stretching, laughing softly at Miles and me making complete fools of ourselves. Miles's face is flushed and happy, like a schoolboy who has just got back from a winter bike ride. Beth's thin wool cardigan stretches tightly over her small, neat breasts, and she twirls the cool stem of her wine glass between her fingers. I try not to stare.

Emma sighs loudly out in the kitchen.

After dinner, pasta something, Miles says, 'Time for a Bridlington?'

'A *what*?' asks Emma with inexplicable irritation.

'A small port,' I explain with a giggle.

I still love this joke, even though Miles and I have been making it for at least ten years now, ever since that first term at Oxford when we started drinking the stuff because we thought it was the appropriately Brideshead-ish thing to do. Only later did we come to appreciate that Sebastian Flyte's chosen tipple was probably not Sainsbury's Ruby at £4.99 a bottle. Now Miles will touch nothing but Taylor's vintage; but then he can afford to.

I lean over to Miles and whisper conspiratorially, 'I rather think a Plymouth, don't you?'

'Indeed,' says Miles, raising his eyebrows. 'Or even a Rotterdam?'

I'm in stitches. 'A fucking Yokohama!'

(Those long evenings when we sat and talked and drank and laughed and never minded the time because 10,000 days or more still stretched before us . . .)

'Gin, wine and port,' says Emma. 'Hm. Interesting.'

'Brandy for me,' says Beth. She likes her brandy, apparently. I notice she's drunk a lot, but it doesn't seem to show. I know her kind. She'll always be the one to want one more drink, one more cigarette, one more line. She'll always be on the edge and never seem to fall over. In a locked chest she has a selection of masks. In a hidden drawer she keeps a medley of spells and potions. Miles is blind.

'Never mix, never worry!' says Miles complacently, and pours two large ports and a brandy.

And so we're all fairly well lubricated when it happens.

Miles puts some music on the CD, some old jazz, and we mellow out. He lies prone in his vast armchair. Emma, me and Beth sit opposite in the squashy, scruffy leather sofa, stuffing bursting from its undersides making it look like some horribly disembowelled animal. Conversation is desultory, tending to the surreal. Emma falls asleep. In fact, she snores, which amuses us greatly. Then Miles nods off too.

Beth suddenly lifts her feet up and plants them in my lap. 'Do something useful,' she says. 'Tickle my toes.'

I do as instructed. She has nice toes.

'Mm,' she says after a while. 'You know how to give a nice foot massage, at least. Maybe you *would* make quite a good whore.'

I close my eyes smugly, squeezing her soles, parting the toes and running my fingers between them. Sometimes Beth giggles and twitches, sometimes she murmurs, 'Mm, that's nice.'

A few minutes later, she shifts again so that her head is snuggled up against my shoulder. 'Head,' she says softly.

It crosses my mind to riposte, 'Why, that's a very kind offer, yes please,' but I scold myself for being so crude. Instead I curl my right arm over her shoulder and begin to tickle and stroke her forehead very gently, very slowly.

There is silence. The atmosphere is simple and relaxed, that of friends together, smuggled up, warm and secure. The room is darkened, only a soft orange glow coming from the fire. Miles is in the shadows, further away. Time moves slowly. Beth reaches across and rests her hand on my stomach. I continue to stroke her head, while moving my other hand down so that it rests on the back of hers. I begin to stroke her here too. She turns her hand over and we tickle each other's palms. And it is at this precise point that the encounter becomes indubitably and irreversibly sexual.

My right hand moves gradually down the back of her head to her neck and shoulders. Beth is like a cat, stretching and purring. I suddenly have the thrilling, giddying feeling that with this girl anything goes. But if either of us stirs too much, Emma or Miles will wake up.

The fire glows, the music plays. 'Fever' by Peggy Lee. Beth has taken off her cardigan, her dress is loose. My hand moves around and over her collarbone and I stroke a middle finger down between her breasts. I can see the edges of a lacy black bra. Everything happens in extreme slow motion. Then I work my way down over her left breast, so slowly. My fingertips skim over the thin silk of her brassière and pause to stroke and circle and gently squeeze her nipple. Her head on my shoulder is turned towards me, she breathes heavily in my ear. She moves her hand by tiny degrees over my stomach, every movement a warm thrill. I feel as if my stomach has become a sexual organ, every inch of my skin is aroused. As if absent-mindedly, Beth's hand comes to rest in my lap. There she finds me stiff and begins to squeeze and massage me through my trousers. I bring my hand up to her mouth and run a fingertip ticklishly over her lips. Her lips part and she sucks my finger in, then I slip my hand back down inside her dress and inside her bra cup too, tracing over her bare flesh, wetting her nipple with the wetness of her own mouth. She loves this, stirs, arches her back, sighs, turns, nibbles my ear. I think she wants me to turn and kiss her but I don't dare, knowing I have to watch Miles in case he wakes up.

And then he wakes up. Stirs, yawns, rubs his eyes, looks across blearily at the three recumbent figures on the sofa. We've already withdrawn fingers and tongues from incriminating places and are looking convincingly sound asleep.

'Time for bed, I think,' says Miles.

We lurch to our feet. Emma kisses Miles goodbye. After a little hesitation, I give Beth a peck on the cheek. We say thank you for a lovely meal. See you soon. Miles offers to call a taxi but we say we'll find a black cab in King's Road. Goodbye again, go to the front door, step out into the street, wave farewell, the door closes, we're gone.

The cab drops Emma off in Fulham. I go on home, crawl into bed, don't sleep, think about Beth. My best friend's girlfriend. What a bitch. What a bastard. What a fucking cliché. *Jesus.*

5

It was just a drunken grope on the sofa. It changes nothing.
And yet I lie awake and think disconnectedly about it, about
everything.

> And along comes Eros imperious and goldskinned and
> seizes us by the hair when we lie sleeping and wakes us
> and leads us out into the dark streets. Eros commands and
> we obey. We can do no other. He is no rosycheeked dimple-
> buttocked boy on some serene Florentine ceiling. He is the
> silent hypnotic young god with the body of an athlete imperi-
> ous and goldskinned and cold eyed and all powerful and we
> are his slaves and we follow him down the dark city streets
> though longing for sleep and quiet we follow him slaves to
> his will not knowing if we wake or dream.

But happiness writes white. Happiness is dumb, zipper-
mouthed. Plays end with marriages and happiness is the
end of the story. Happiness is a long sleep, a lazy summer
afternoon, but not *life*; not life being lived. And when you
look back at last, over your one and only life, what more terrible and tragic and embittered thought could there be than
I never really lived?

I have the strangest feeling that I could fall in love with *any*
girl now. 'Beth fancies me! Gorgeous Beth! So other girls are
bound to fancy me! Even that haughty temp Amrita who
Clive is so mad about.'

But I'm no longer there, at Orme, Odstock and Oliphant.
There'll be no more Lisa on Reception to greet me in the mornings. I'm on my own now. Freelance. Gun for hire, floating on
the mercury surface of the global market. Who will buy?

*

What a sadness there is at the heart of sex. Because it is so intimately connected with mortality, the salmon's dying issue in the peat-brown silent pool. Sex is our attempt to cheat death, when only our genes can do that, can outlive us and achieve their own sort of immortality: those wretched, passionless, meaningless, purely aleatory strings of coded protein. Our bodies and minds wither away and passions fade. Ghosts are passions that outlive the person, in remote farmhouses or old country parsonages, in darkened corridors or on Jacobean staircases . . . but even they are not immortal and fade over centuries, with time or under the stern eye of the priest. And every time we make love we are confessing to ourselves – and to each other – our knowledge of our own mortality.

Make love to me, you whisper in your lover's ear. Make love to me, that I might cheat death.

And your lover hears you and is as helpless in your arms as you in hers.

Oh, let me sleep. Those long slim brown legs by firelight . . . leave me *alone*. Get out of my head. Let me get on with my work, my life. All this heartache is a waste of time.

But, ah no, all this heartache is . . . is *life*.

I decide that I need a talk with the Honourable Clive.

Apart from anything else, I want to know why he never turned up to Miles's on Saturday night. Was he playing away from home? But surely he wouldn't do a thing like that.

Clive isn't stupid, he just doesn't have the same kind of brain as me. He can at times come out with remarkably wise insights into life and love, like some kind of holy fool, while appearing quite unplagued by anxieties of any kind whatever, erotic or otherwise (and that's with a girlfriend like *Emma*). Gets on with everyone, everyone likes him, male as well as female, never known to lose his temper or even look particularly hassled, and apparently quite happy jogging along in his long-term thing with *Emma*. He can't have nearly as many notches in his bedpost as me, admittedly. But I mustn't be so crude. Grown-ups don't measure amatory success by the number of notches in the bedpost, they measure it in terms of depth of feeling, loyalty, stability, levels of communication – grown-up stuff like that.

On the other hand, while well balanced, contented and affable, it must be admitted that Clive is not immediately attractive to the opposite sex. The name, for a start. A sexy Clive is unimaginable. Then there is the ginger Brillopad hair and the Milky Way of freckles across his rather blank, pale face. And the smallish eyes, and the slack mouth, and the height: barely 5 feet 7. Oh, and the receding teeth. And the bald patch. And the unmentionable deformity further south. Although I suppose all these genetic misfortunes could be interpreted as evidence of solid aristocratic ancestry.

All things considered, although Clive isn't actually *ugly*, or grossly overweight, or distressingly smelly, you could say that in terms of looks, life has dealt him a fairly unkind hand. There is something about his general appearance that doesn't set girls' pulses racing. With his equable and unbrooding temperament and his incomprehension of the art of flirting, he is damned to the worst of all possible fates: he is regarded by his female friends as a *nice bloke*, a *laugh*, even as a bit of a *brother figure*. He would stand far more chance if he were regularly slagged off behind the doors of the women's loos as *arrogant, vain, a real lech* or even *a complete bastard*. But no, Clive is just *nice*.

I, on the other hand, during my glory days at Orme, Odstock and Oliphant, despite the prominent nose, the luxuriant eyebrows and a physique apparently devoid of musculature, was perceived differently, not least because it was common knowledge that only two Christmases ago, in the most lamentably clichéd of situations, Lisa on Reception and

I left the staff dinner party in the restaurant on the pretext of buying some cigarettes, sneaked back into the office and had sex on top of the photocopier in three different positions. (We fell off attempting a fourth.) And only two weeks before that – I was going through one of my uncontrollably concupiscent phases, I admit – I started and very quickly finished a sort of relationship with sweet, gentle Sarah, and broke the poor girl's heart (though it mended soon enough when she met *Adrian*). And all this was while I was supposed to be going out with Miranda, although we were admittedly in one of our 'off' periods at this point.

In contradistinction to the Honourable Clive, therefore, I manage to be reasonably successful with the opposite sex, despite being commonly perceived as: lecherous, untrustworthy, atrociously moody, sometimes downright sullen and extremely keen on prolonged bouts of self-pity. Because I can also be clever, tall, entertaining, complimentary and flirtatious. When is Clive going to learn about these things?

I phone him up.

'So where were you on Saturday night?'

Clive is mysteriously evasive. 'I, ah . . . emergency. Um . . . can't really tell you just now. Don't say anything to Em about it, OK? She thinks I was, ah – working. Urgent last-minute stuff. She's mad with me, but it's, ah . . . the necessary lie and all that.'

'Good, good,' I say, frowning, not listening properly.

'Well?' asks Clive.

'Well, actually, my weekend was, ah . . . complicated.'

'Oh? Come on then, spill the lentils.'

'It's – oh, I dunno. I mean, you're a man of the world, aren't you, Clive?'

'Absolutely.'

'You can keep a secret, can't you?'

'Scout's honour. Dib-dib.'

'Well, it's . . . it's difficult really, but . . .'

'Don't tell me,' says Clive. 'I can tell it all just from your pitiful, whining voice. You've been playing away from home.'

'Well, I haven't *got* a home, but . . . How did you know?'

'I can surmise these things. So. Are you going to tell me any more? The full Monty? The full match report?'

'Well,' I say defensively, 'there wasn't *that* much to it. I mean, OK, yes, I *was* playing away from home, in your vulgar phrase – or at least, on somebody else's home ground. But it wasn't exactly, y'know, the full ninety minutes.'

'Indeed?'

'No. No goals scored, if you like.'

'Or even shots at goal?'

'Not even that.'

'A bit of skilful dribbling in the goal mouth?'

'Clive, you're being obscene.'

'Sorry, sorry.'

'No, there was just a bit of friendly passing along the touchline, really. Just a bit of a warm-up.'

'Before the full match next week?'

'In my dreams.'

'And then what happened?'

'The ref intervened.'

'What?'

'Her other half woke up.'

'*She was . . . You were all sleeping together?*'

'Well, yes. Sort of. Not in *that* way – I mean, we're all in our twenties still, just about – and group sex and all that really hard stuff doesn't really kick in till your forties, does it? No, we were all just sprawled in front of the fire after dinner. OK, OK, I might as well tell you: it was at Miles's on Saturday night.'

'After Em had left?'

'Em was asleep too. Me and Beth sort of – got it together.'

'You *bastard*,' says Clive, with a potent mix of envy and disgust. 'You . . .'

37

'On the sofa,' I add. 'Kicking the ball around a bit.'

'Phewy,' he whistles. 'A close call, I should say. Still, you weren't caught actually at it, eh? Weren't shown the red card, banned for next season?'

'This football metaphor has gone on long enough. No, we weren't caught at it. Got clean away.'

'So what's the problem. Guilt?'

'Hardly. More like – I just can't stop thinking about her, that's all. Beth, I mean.'

'Hm. Tricky,' says Clive. 'She's a damn fine-looking woman, if I remember rightly.' He ponders for a while and finally pronounces. 'A serious case of sexual obsession, I'd say. Quite incurable, I'm afraid.'

'Thank you, Clive. You've been a great help.'

'No trouble at all,' he says.

'Bastard,' I mutter. 'You'll learn.' Louder, I say, 'Anyhow, where *were* you on Saturday night?'

He sighs. 'OK. Can't talk here. Let's meet for a drink. And I'll tell you a story all about the Princess and the Woodcutter's Son.'

'Ah. You mean Amrita.'

6

We have to go back a few weeks, to when I was still unhappily employed at Orme, Odstock and Oliphant. To the day when Amrita, the haughty Indian beauty, first started working at the office.

Clive is at the coffee machine, calling up number 12. After a ruminative, borborygmous pause for thought, the machine rumbles and belches out a white coffee (no sugar, but a piquant hint of plastic). Clive retrieves it and, turning to head back to his desk, almost bumps straight into a girl who has been waiting unseen beside him. She is tall, dark, slim and extraordinarily pretty.

'Blurrrhh . . .' says Clive, titubating to one side so as to avoid spilling hot coffee all over her. The girl looks at him with faint amusement – looks *down* at him with faint amusement, in fact, which doesn't help Clive's equipoise in the slightest. He struggles to regain his physical balance (his mental balance already quite beyond recall). She is the most beautiful girl Clive has ever seen – indeed, he thinks besottedly, the *only* beautiful girl he has ever seen. At once sultry and intelligent, sexy and composed.

She is wearing a plain white T-shirt and black jeans, which on anyone else would look far too casual, but on her bespeak an elegant, understated simplicity. She wears a gold necklace and several rings on her fingers. Her lustrous eyes are outlined with kohl. She has a delicate, abstract henna tattoo on her left shoulder, although Clive doesn't know this yet, of course.

'I'm sorry,' she says. 'Did I startle you?'

Her voice is soft and she enunciates very clearly. She holds out a hand. 'I'm Amrita.'

'Gosh,' says Clive, thinking to himself, *What a tit*, I haven't said *gosh* for about twenty years and now I have to go and say it to the MOST BEAUTIFUL GIRL IN THE WORLD, like some over-excited schoolboy. What a pillock.

He extends his coffee cup towards her and then recalls it and swaps it over to his left hand clumsily enough to spill coffee over both hands and then wipes his right hand down the side of his trousers and then finally reaches out and shakes – so slim! so brown! so beautiful! – her hand.

'And you are?'

'I'm, er, I'm Clive. Hi.'

'Hello, Clive. I'm new here, just started this morning.'

'Right, yes, so I see. You're . . .?'

'Only temporary.' She smiles.

'Oh, that's a shame. How, er, how long will you be here?'

'Just a month or two. I have to fly back to Delhi after Christmas for the wedding of the century.'

'That sounds great. A big do, then?'

'Ten thousand guests or something ridiculous. Three weeks of celebrations. Quite a big do. Are you all right?'

'So is that, ah, and who would that be, I mean, is that, like, yours, or . . .?'

'Mercifully not,' she says. 'My sister. I'm too young, I hope.'

'And, and, and, and, after that? What are your plans?'

'Well, after that, if I've saved up enough cash, a bit of travelling, and then I start my doctorate.'

'And, and, where would that be?'

'Here,' she says, jerking her thumb northwards towards Bloomsbury. 'UCL.'

'Oh, right,' says Clive. 'And what's your doctorate on?'

'Anthropology,' says Amrita. 'Palaeo-anthropology, to be precise.'

'But that's amazing!' exclaims Clive. 'Because that's exactly what my field is too!' (Thinking to himself all the while, *You're mad, you're barking, you are DOOMED*.)

Amrita arches an eyebrow. 'Really? What field exactly?'

'Er, well, teeth,' says Clive. 'Teeth and hair, that sort of thing' (babbling wildly now). 'And flints too, of course: hand-axes, skinscrapers, fleshcutters, clodhoppers, all that stuff.'

'How fascinating,' murmurs Amrita. 'You must tell me all about it some time.' Clive agrees he must. 'So how come you've ended up working here?'

'Ah, well, you see, I felt it had all been done, really. You know, the old anthropolology, it's a pretty well-ploughed field, a full furrow, I mean, it's just a question of plugging the gaps now really, isn't it, crossing the i's and dotting the t's? Listen, I must go, I've got stacks of work to do, perhaps we could go for a drink some time, um, yes, excellent, well, nice to meet you. Good.'

Amrita watches as Clive scurries away to his office down the corridor. Then she dials up her choice, 18, and stoops to retrieve a cup of mineral water, her slim body shaking with giggles.

Moments later Clive is back in front of my desk.

'Er . . . Daniel?'

'Hm?'

'Do you know anything about India?'

I look blank. 'Well, a bit, yes. I have particularly unhappy memories of a foolhardy mutton curry in Chandigarh. Why?'

'How about anthropolology?'

'Anthropology – and India. What, Indian anthropology?'

'No, no, I mean, anthropolology separately. Flints and things.'

I struggle to hide my amusement. 'Flints?'

'Yes, *flints*. And teeth.'

I'm hugely cheered by Clive's evident anxiety. The little red-headed chap is practically hopping from one foot to another in a violent fit of Indo-anthropological agitation.

'And why this sudden interest?' I ask. 'India, for instance?

Oh, by the way, have you met the new temp here, Amrita? *She's* Indian. Jolly attractive, too. You could ask her about it, surely?'

Clive looks agonized. 'Yes – yes, I've met her, I know I could. But I don't suppose –' he giggles nervously – 'I mean, it would be pretty far-fetched, wouldn't it, if she was an anthropolologist *as well*?'

I ignore him, stroke the back of my hand tenderly with a biro. 'She is *very* attractive, don't you think?'

'Is she? Yes, I suppose she's quite nice.'

'Nice? She's *beautiful*, I think. And so charming.'

'You've – you've spoken to her?'

'Briefly,' I say. 'Just to ask her how she's getting on so far. Charming girl. I said we must go for a drink some time.'

'*We?*' Clive almost screams.

'She and I, yes,' I say, aware that I am verging on outright cruelty now. Well, I think to myself, remembering Miranda . . . I don't see why I should be the only one to suffer.

'But, but . . .'

I sigh. 'I only said a *drink*, Clive, I didn't walk up to her and say, *Hey, babe, let's shag*.'

With the image of the lovely Amrita before his mind's eye, such a gross word to Clive's ear must be like the cold metallic otoscope of some particularly brutal doctor. He winces dramatically. I relent a little.

'In fact – when I asked her what she was hoping to do after temping, she said she was going to do a doctorate. In *anthropology*!' I chuckle. 'Now that, you must admit, is a coincidence!'

Clive stares at me. 'You bastard. You scheming . . . two-faced . . .'

'The pains and perils of love, dear boy. I'm only trying to get you accustomed to suffering.' My voice grows more stern. 'Because if you're going to go chasing top-class tottie like that, you're going to have to get used to more than a few sleepless nights, I can tell you.'

'Top-class tottie!' echoes Clive, outraged. 'She's . . . she's
. . .'

'She's probably got half the millionaire playboys in Delhi
after her. Get real.'

Clive stares at me for a long time. 'You just don't understand, do you?' he says at last. And leaves the room.

I sigh and spin round in my chair and stare out of the
window. 'Maybe not,' I murmur, 'maybe not.'

And that was the first I knew of Clive's hopeless love for
Amrita. Since then, it seems, he's been *seeing her*.

7

Meanwhile, my new career is blossoming. Well, what did I expect? I'm on call, available, up for hire. It could only be a matter of time.

I am summoned to an address in SW1 at 7.30 one chilly November night. Wear a dinner suit, 'Caroline' tells me.

Bloody *hell*.

In a daze I shower, shave, brush my hair, deodorize my armpits, shake talcum powder down my Y-fronts, worry about my Y-fronts, change them for cheeky alligator-pattern boxer shorts, change them again for sober navy-blue boxer shorts, put on my one and only dress shirt with the attractively yellowing collar, and then my (father's) pond-coloured, verdigris dinner suit that hangs in folds about my fleshless frame like the skin of a rhinoceros.

'A young girl's dream!' cries Kate, ascending the stairs as I descend.

I smile tightly. 'What about *an old woman's dream*?' I nearly blurt out.

I arrive at the appointed place at 7.26 p.m. The glossy black front door is opened by a tiny Filipina maid. She shoos me into a grandiose pseudo-library to the right. I check my image in the mirror: nothing there. Except, perhaps, a vague haze of terror.

'Good evening,' someone says.

I turn around.

About sixty, sixty-five. Heavily powdered. Fattish. Billowy. Heavy jaw. Black coat, white handbag. Metal eyes.

'Good evening.' I smile.

'Thoby, isn't it?'

She advances on me with surprising speed, offering a powdery cheek to be kissed. 'Call me Pamela,' she says.

'Pamela.' I kiss her.

'Good. Well then.' She considers her appearance in the mirror, holds her head at several different angles while her eyes remain fixed, compresses her lips tightly together, pats the back of her hair with an upward movement, smooths her coat with an open hand and is satisfied. She smiles at me, flicks open her handbag, checks the contents, plucks out a cheque and hands it to me, snaps her bag shut again.

The cheque is for £300. 'To cover travel expenses and so on,' she says. 'Shall we go?'

In the hallway I bump into a whippet-hipped youth wearing moleskin jeans and a silk shirt. He's got pretty, floppy hair and a dumb smile. Pamela steps in, pinching my elbow mischievously.

'My husband, Sir Derek, is *complaisant*,' she murmurs. 'And so am I.' Her metal eyes are fixed on me in a semblance of good humour. 'He has his Ruperts and I have my –' she pinches my elbow harder – 'Thobys. At our age one is inevitably more relaxed about these things.'

And she draws me towards the waiting taxi. I try to mumble some sort of 'nice meeting you' to Rupert, but I glimpse the lurking, ponderous shadow of Sir Derek down the hallway, approaching Rupert from behind, and the words rather freeze in my throat.

Pamela is not one for high culture. Wives of top industrialists are sometimes known to affect a taste for it, but not our Pam. Her choice of theatrical entertainment for the night is a bedroom farce in the finest West End tradition, *Your Wife is Wearing My Trousers!* or some such cack. I'm not able to give it my full attention, frankly, trapped as I am in a private box with Pamela's hand vice-like about my knee. Anyway, the plot is absurdly convoluted. People keep disappearing and reappearing at a tremendous rate, and you are supposed to find certain oft-repeated phrases achingly funny. 'But those are *my* trousers!' is one that I recall with particular antipathy. By the fifth or sixth time the line has been uttered, most of the audience down below are having to hold themselves into their seats for the sheer, uncontrollable mirth that grips them. And the more they have paid for their seats, the more they're gripped, unless they are in a corporate block, in which case they doze fitfully, waking only to worry about the FTSE and their irritable bowels.

After a glass of Chardonnay in the interval, things really hot up during the second half. The level of audience involvement down below is such that Pamela feels free to embark on a more forthright approach. Her hand is moving away from my knee and heading north. Heading unnervingly and with a steely will towards *the pole*. And, like Sir Ranulph Fiennes, Pamela will not easily be discouraged. I try twitching, and then shaking my leg, but to no avail. At last, disastrously, I try squeezing her hand painfully between my bony thighs, but this serves only to inflame her ardour the more. Ever northward moves her hand, while she smiles languorously at my right ear. And when she reaches the north pole, I think in wonder and terror . . . she will surely want to *pitch her tent*.

I could just get up and run away. I don't *have* to do this, surely? But then again – *il faut de l'argent*.

I feel her rough, bitter tongue at my earlobe. Her breath is hot and hungry. I shrink virginally before it. She grasps me tighter, savage with desire.

I turn to face her: metal eyes, false lashes, pendulous flews, powder thickly encrusted in the wrinkles of her shagreen skin. Maybe more like seventy, now I look closely. I close my eyes.

I give up. I give in. (Passive cynicism is the only answer.) 'Be gentle with me,' I murmur.

Afterwards, back at her place, between the silk sheets of her bed the size of a ballroom, gold light flickering off gilt in all directions – after *that*, she expects pillow-talk.

'The thing I like about you, Thoby,' she says, stroking my hair, 'is that you're not *too* good-looking.'

I approach my second appointment with altogether more resolution. I have been blooded now and can face the Enemy with greater determination.

And it is something of a breakthrough appointment, I must admit. A sour-faced Austrian diplomat's wife, forty-ish, ash blonde, immaculate, efficient, mercifully unfriendly. Almost sexy, in fact. I survive the ordeal with only a few outbreaks of violent trembling and feel able to look back on the experience with a kind of bitter pride.

Afterwards, she puts her dress on and turns her back to me without a word. A silent command. I zip it up for her. 'The tzing is,' she says, dropping her head forward so I can do up the hasp at the top, 'I'm not very, what you say in English, *looks-led*.' She turns and levels her gun-grey eyes on me. 'I feel comfortable with you, Tommy,' she says. 'You're not *too* good-looking.'

She calls me again a week later. We become quite a regular item, Margaretha and me.

When my third one starts in on a similar tack – 'The thing about you, Thoby, is . . . ' – I really have to interrupt. 'I know, I know, I'm not *too* good-looking.'

'Well, it's true, sweetmeat,' she says, taking my hand and laughing. 'We *maturer* ladies do often prefer men who don't look like male models. It makes us feel less self-conscious about our own shortcomings.'

'Excellent,' I say. 'Excellent.'

The next day, walking down Tottenham Court Road, I pass a stall selling T-shirts emblazoned with the legend *We Are All Prostitutes*. 'Five pound to you, my friend,' says the wizened huckster, stamping his feet for the cold.

I can't resist it. In fact, I buy two.

My working career involves a succession of women of various tastes and physiologies, mostly wealthy, and none of
them particularly unhappy or in search of something else.
This is the surprising thing. They just want a younger man
as a companion for the evening, and afterwards to take him
home and have passionate (or at least pseudo-passionate)
sex with him. It really is that simple. They say goodbye to
me the next morning with a glow of serenity, a halo about
them. So I must be doing something right.

The money is good. And the glamour factor is quite high.
Suddenly I'm getting to see operas at Covent Garden from
private boxes. I'm drinking champagne three nights a week,
often vintage. I have a bigger and bigger bank balance, and
nothing to spend it on anyway. There's a weekend in Paris, all
expenses paid, and then another in New York. I even get to
dine out in the sorts of top restaurant where the brilliant but
temperamental chef comes out and assaults you if you dare to
ask for pepper. I'm known at Le Gavroche, the Aubergine, the
Ivy, the Lanesborough, the Ritz, that new Philippe Starck
place, Blakes Hotel (followed by bed and breakfast).

I tell friends and family that I'm doing a bit of freelance at
home during the daytime. I get by. Kate especially doesn't
seem to believe me, eyes me like she thinks I'm dealing crack
to schoolchildren, or maybe having a secret affair with
someone famous.

'Sue Lawley,' she speculates. 'Gloria Hunniford. You've
been out three nights this week already. Who is she? Lisa
Tarbuck? An All Saint?'

'How do you know there's only the one? I might have
several.'

She laughs.

Hah!

*

Caroline at Grosvenor for Ladies presents me with a new dinner suit in recognition of my sterling service. And she nags me to quit smoking, and offers me her old exercise bike (I decline), and books me in for a vastly expensive haircut at a place called Fleur. Makes no difference whatsoever. Still firmly in the 'not *too* good-looking, sweetmeat' category.

I keep wondering if there will be any really strange encounters: beautiful Middle Eastern ladies requiring me to imitate a Nubian billy goat in a state of advanced arousal; lady coroners ordering me to lie in a bollock-freezing bath for ten minutes and then dust myself all over with talcum powder and lie down as if dead, so that they can 'examine' me; famous media feminists whose 'confessions' I have to listen to for several excruciating hours: every detail of their multitudinous personal hang-ups, ineradicable Catholic guilt complexes, their need for violent psycho-sexual exorcism . . . Perhaps a recently ordained woman priest, wanting me to wear a torn bedsheet and a 'crown of thorns' made out of hairpins? Or the odd celebrity, a minor Royal, the television-smut campaigner, the wife-of-someone-much-more-famous? So far, though, it's all been pretty average.

There is a county lady, Vanessa if memory serves, so pleased with me that she has me driven down to Hampshire one weekend when her husband is away and, after three bottles of champagne, requires me to service her in glutinous stableyard muck at 2 in the morning. And I can only shudder with horror when I recall the *thirty-six hours* spent in the company of blockbuster novelist Susan Spurtforth. But I suppose I can't complain.

Best of all, none of them recognizes *me*. I keep expecting one of them to start up in mid-thrust, in horrified remembrance, '*You're* the bloke who nearly killed those three people in a balloon – I saw your face on the news.'

But it never happens. I am truly favoured by the gods.

*

Caroline continues to regard me as her star employee, her 'sunshine boy', and showers me liberally with little gifts: aftershave, woven silk ties, cashmere jumpers.

And my bank balance is now looking obscenely healthy. Everything is paid for me: clothes, cabs, dinners, haircuts, even condoms . . . and I walk off with £200 a night, at least.

I begin to haunt auction rooms during the day, and buy the occasional oil or watercolour with the innate taste and discernment that new wealth invariably brings. I'm startled to find how romantic my tastes are getting in my dotage. I buy idealized nineteenth-century rural scenes, picturesquely tumbledown cottages, sheep haloed in gold by sunsets over distant fields, oyster girls on windswept shingle beaches, milkmaids and cows wending their way down twilight lanes and homeward. I buy a luminous watercolour of a solitary girl sitting by a river in the shade of an alder tree, a book in her hand, her eyes floating over it, reading nothing, daydreaming her days away.

Or else I simply lie on the sofa and daydream my own days away, picturing to myself that cottage to which I shall soon retire to write my epoch-making operas. Cornwall? Cumbria? Co. Galway? Seagulls, peat fires, heather, Atlantic breakers, clumps of thrift, tinkers, seals . . .

And a chick, of course. Must have a chick. Some wide-eyed local girl in an Aran sweater, hair tied back loosely with a ribbon. A name like Lizzie or Eliza. Some innocent. Some romantic and dreamer.

8

Home for Christmas.

But how does one go about breaking it to one's parents that one has become a prostitute?

At least I don't have to break it to my sister, I suppose: my world-wandering sister, currently somewhere between Kathmandu and Darwin, exact whereabouts unknown. What about my two half-siblings?

My mother might not mind. She doesn't mind anything I do. The sun shines out of my fundament, rain or shine. I am her baby and always will be.

My father probably *would* mind, on balance. My father was an accountant (now ret'd) for a firm that made bathroom accessories. Other people's fathers become florid and expansive at a certain age – pompous, even, and with a plump sheen of retirement and leisure and money. They fill up restaurants single-handedly and then everyone else has to squeeze in around them. But not my father, sitting there modestly in his Argyll sweater reading the *Telegraph*. On the other hand, how many other people's fathers won a medal in Korea?

After he'd won his medal, my father came home and married a demure young girl called Susan. They had two children, a boy and a girl, and then some time in the late sixties – this was before I was born, you understand – Susan suddenly shot off to Denmark to live in an all-female commune. Now I'm not saying my father would necessarily be the most exciting husband in the world. (I don't see him as red-hot between the sheets either, but then whose father is?) All the same, this seems a bit extreme of Susan. Especially as she took the children with her. After a long and vastly expensive custody battle, the children were returned to the normal male–female mixed society of suburban Surrey, and Susan and my father were officially divorced.

Then he astonished everyone in 1971 by marrying a gorgeous young slip of a gel called Jessamy Naesmyth: my mum. Why did she marry him? Something to do with the poignancy, maybe, the innate nobility of a single man (with a medal) bringing up two children on his own and never complaining. My father's dignity, his lack of bitterness or self-pity, and the seductive melancholy of the motherless household drew her in.

And a year later, I was born. Jessamy's only child and the apple of her eye. At least till my sister was born.

I'm pretty sure my mother must have had an affair since then, or even numerous affairs. But I can't be sure. Whatever. They're still madly in love, my parents, in their reticent, secretive English way. And even if my mother has had affairs, I still wouldn't call her promiscuous. Her generation, and even more my father's generation, were both less promiscuous and less romantic than mine.

The trouble with my lot is, we expect the fucking earth.

The luxury of the parental home always amazes me. One couple with four double bedrooms, a kitchen measured out in hectares, a double garage, immaculate lawns the size of cricket fields . . . I'm glad to say my parents *don't* have a tennis court or a swimming-pool, but they do have a small croquet lawn.

My old bedroom walls are still covered with reminders of my younger self: posters of defunct thrash bands, my student beer-mat collection, stinky old trainers under the bed that I'll never wear again but can't bear to part with. Even my desk drawer, filled with half-eaten pencils and rubbers and a Winnie-the-Pooh pencil sharpener that must have come in a Christmas stocking about twenty years ago, and some playing cards and a box of fridge-magnet poetry, and a school photograph and a pot of Humbrol modelling paint . . . they all fill me with a horrible, enervating nostalgia. So much so that I start hiccuping.

'So, darling – any young lady on the scene at the moment?'

My mother is sitting cross-legged beside me – and she has, I must admit it, fabulous legs. Her arm rests along the back of the sofa.

My mother always treats me in this slightly seductive way. I know it sounds weird but don't worry, this isn't going to turn into a mother–son incest story. It's just that there is something really . . . *flirtatious* between me and my mother that can quite freak people, but it is more like some elaborate, unspecified joke between us. She's flirting like mad with me now: the arched eyebrows, the quivering smile. The girlfriend question. 'Come on,' she says, 'don't be all arch. One can have no secrets from one's mother.'

'Maybe I've got several young ladies on the go.' (This is rapidly becoming the standard reply.)

'Oh, darling, I hope not. I wouldn't want to think of my son as a –' she leans close – 'a *Lothario*. A *lady-killer*.' She sits back again. 'Anyway, what *did* happen to the lovely Miranda? If you don't mind my asking.'

I hear myself sigh deeply and pitifully and she reaches out and takes my hand. 'She told me I was immature and insensitive and feckless. She said we weren't *going* anywhere.' My mother gives my hand a little squeeze. 'Oh, and idle,' I add. 'And oversexed. And aimless. Or did she say *unfocused*? No, OK, Miranda wouldn't use a word like that.' I shrug. 'She just . . . at first she thought I was really clever and cool and enigmatic. But it wore off, I guess. They said on the radio the other day that love only lasts two years maximum.'

'Oh, what do they know?' says my mother. 'That's absolute nonsense. I still love your father.' She says this without a trace of embarrassment or irony that is truly touching.

'OK then, not love, but *lurve*, you know. Passion and all that.'

'Oh, *passion*,' repeats my mother. 'Yeees . . .' She lets go of my hand.

I don't think I have any serious mother-complex, but I am a little hurt by this sudden abandonment. 'So what about you? Any boyfriends, toy boys, affairs with the bank manager?'

'*Darling*,' says my mother. And says no more. 'Now then – I think a G&T, don't you?'

I've just had a terrible thought. What if I was dispatched to a client in a hotel bedroom one day and it turned out to be *my mother*? Such a terrible twist that would be to my tale. It couldn't happen, surely? There's some film I seem to remember where a middle-aged guy calls up an escort and it turns out to be his daughter. So this would be an interesting gender reversal. A post-feminist metaphor for translated sexual roles: economically empowered, single, predatory women preying on impoverished, sexually subservient men.

Sometimes I already feel I'm stuck in some weird role-reversed version of *Pretty Woman*, except none of my clients has yet swept me off my feet and into a romantic dream. Nor would I look as good as Julia Roberts in a miniskirt and thigh-high boots.

My G&T arrives and I gulp it down. The iced glass chills my fingerpads. I press them to my forehead.

My mother squeezes in beside me, puts her arm around me, gives me a hug. I can smell her perfume. Givenchy, I think she uses. She evidently thinks I'm sitting here glooming over Miranda and my jobless state. Would now be the right time to break it to her that actually my main concern at the moment is my rapidly burgeoning career in prostitution? She runs her fingers through my hair.

The weird thing between me and my mother is empha-sized, no doubt, by the fact that she is actually closer to my age than to my father's, if only by a few weeks. There are twenty-one years between us, and twenty-one years three months between her and my father. Or something. This means that when we conspire against my father to tease him, as we do not infrequently, there is an almost brother–sister feel to it.

I'm just glad she's not my stepmother, or God knows what would have happened by now.

I think that the practical effect of being the sole object of adoration of my beautiful mother during my formative years has been . . . well, it could have turned me into a raving woopsie, of course, but that destiny seems to have eluded me. What it has done is a) make me love the company of women and b) assume, rightly or wrongly, that women are always going to love the company of me. Mainly women do like me, though. Not because of my dazzling charm and good looks, but because women, kind souls that they are, usually like men who like them. And most men, especially Englishmen, are still too stupid to appreciate women properly. It's laziness, perhaps: men's misogyny. It's much easier, much safer, to stick with the lads: they're just like you.

The next morning, absurdly warm and sunny for this time of year, the lads are having a couple of rounds of croquet. My father and I.

This morning my father is fetchingly attired in fraying Jesus sandals, Ribena-coloured socks, beige cavalry twill trousers and a National Trust sweatshirt. *Sweatshirt!* For God's sake, man, where's your dignity?

But of course my father's dignity goes a little deeper than his clothes. My father's dignity is all on the inside, where it counts.

We don't talk much. At one point I execute a rather neat manoeuvre through a central hoop, simultaneously clipping my father's ball on the windward side. I then go back, clip him again, and knock him several hundred yards away from his destined target. He strokes his moustache and murmurs, 'Rather cruel, Daniel,' before pottering off to start again.

This is what is called male bonding.

The great thing about my father is that he hates golf, in spite of having lived in Surrey. (Now it's Gloucestershire. Good God, that's almost real countryside.) But he does like a good few rounds of croquet.

Afterwards, when we are returning our balls and mallets to the coffin-shaped box in the shed, he murmurs again, 'Ah – any news on the job front, Daniel?'

My eyes fall on the dusty remains of my old train set, still laid out on a chipboard landscape in the far corner, and again I feel the physical wrench of my own childhood, myself busy for hours down here with my trains, in grey corduroy shorts, a stash of Curly-wurlies hidden behind the apple racks . . .

'No, not really,' I say. 'Just – just freelance.' I grin. 'Keeps things ticking over, though.'

I lie awake long after my parents are asleep. I've spent the evening with them, sitting through interminable and entirely unfunny BBC sitcoms that have them both rocking with laughter. I have a book cracked open on my lap but somehow it seems rude to read it.

Now I lie in bed and worry about a) the spiritual malaise of modern man, as so powerfully evinced by contemporary English society and mores, b) the fact that I seem to have lost touch with a younger, simpler, more innocent self and c) Kate.

I think of Kate because I'm thinking how amazingly small and cramped and occasionally squalid our pad in London is, compared to the space and luxury of the parental home: the bathrooms redecorated biennially, the warmth of the kitchen with its huge old beechwood table, the towels and carpets almost pornographically soft and fluffy. The sheer dimensions of the fridge, and the garden, not to mention the density and variety of the bedding plants.

And what is to be done about my landlady? Perhaps she should just get a cat.

9

New Year starts with a rash of amazing coincidences. (Not all of them *are* just coincidences, as it turns out.)

But first: Kate, the next exciting instalment.

Jess flings the front door open and, as soon as I step out of the car, shrieks from the top of the steps, 'Men! You're all bastards!'

I freeze on the pavement, staring up at her aghast, my throat petrified in mid-gulp. She can't . . . she *can't* . . .

Then Jess is laughing, clapping her hands together and doubling up. 'Crikey!' she cries out. 'Guilty conscience or what!'

I smile, resume and complete my gulp, tear my frozen feet off the pavement (leaving two little frosty outlines behind me), sling my jacket over my shoulder, saunter up the steps and give her a kiss.

'Hello, landlady's little sister. Now what's all this about? Bastard, *moi*?'

She hugs me and then leans back. 'It's official,' she nods. 'Kate says so. *All* of you, without exception.' She sighs. 'She's had another dreadful time with Tom.'

'I thought she'd dumped him?'

'This is another Tom.'

'Another time, another Tom? This is ridiculous.'

I follow her up to the flat.

Kate is at the kitchen table, smoking furiously.

'Well, well,' I say fatuously, sitting next to her and putting an arm round her (appalled to find myself vaguely turned on by this act of supposedly tender solicitude. For *heaven's sake*, man, I say to myself. What's the *matter* with you? Get a *grip*). 'You and your Toms,' I sigh.

Kate smiles sourly.

'But then, life's a bit of a lottery, isn't it?' I continue, contriving an amusing joke. 'A tom-bola, in fact.'

'Thank you, Daniel.'

'But you know, you shouldn't let men walk all over you and *tom*-inate you in this way.'

'Thank you, Daniel.'

'I hope you made him wear a con-tom.'

'Daniel, will you just shut the fuck up?'

I pull my arm away. 'I'm sorry. Just trying to cheer you up.'

'I'm fine,' says Kate. 'At least I was until you started. Sometimes your sense of humour is so . . . so *depressing*.' I must look hurt now, because Kate pats me on the back of the hand. 'Never mind,' she says. 'You can't help it. And Jess seems to appreciate it. Loon that she is.'

'I try,' says Jess. 'Coffee?'

'Wine,' says Kate.

Jess glances at the kitchen clock. 'Big sister,' she says, 'it is a *little* early. Anyway, you had enough wine last night.'

'And you should give up smoking too,' I lecture her.

'Hark at you! Charles Atlas, I think not.'

'And take up . . . cycling. Exercise can make you live ten years longer. So can marriage, apparently.'

'I'm lost,' she says. 'What about cycling *and* marriage?'

'Cycling can be very romantic,' I say. 'Surely.' (My cunning plan is beginning to work.)

'So,' says Jess, 'Kate tells me you're out overnight a lot these days. Who is she?'

I grin excessively. 'Maybe a different one each time.'

'Men are such incontinent, two-timing bastards.'

'Yeah,' says Kate, savagely stubbing out a cigarette and immediately reaching towards the pack for another. 'They're all bastards.'

'Surely not . . . every single one?' I query.

Jess smiles sweetly. 'All except you, honey,' and reaches out to squeeze my cheek.

'Anyway,' I say a little desperately, 'maybe some men are, you know, *promiscuous*, without actually meaning to be.'

'Oh, poor *lambs*, they just can't help themselves.'

'Or, or, you know,' I stammer, 'maybe they're male prostitutes or something.'

'What a bizarre idea.' Kate sucks on her cigarette.

'Anyway,' I say, 'this latest Tom.'

'You don't really want to know,' sighs Kate.

'Indeed I do.'

She exhales a vast nebula of smoke from her lungs. 'OK. Well, I thought he was really nice,' she begins. 'Oh, not *nice*. God, what a crap word. You know, considerate. Just *kind*, really. And grown up. And not bad-looking. A sense of humour, not irritating, not *always* joking like some blokes, just . . . there when you wanted it.'

'Where did you meet?'

She grins sheepishly. 'Casual pick-up.'

'Cool! Really?'

'Really. I was ranting to a friend about Tom – old Tom – in the cinema queue. With my friend Cattie – Catriona . . .'

'The one with the legs?'

'The one with the legs. And Cattie just puts her hand on my shoulder and says, "Face it, Kate. Tom is just a wanker." And this guy behind us in the queue gives this little cough, apologetically sort of thing, and says, "Oh, I don't think I'm *that* bad."'

I laugh.

'And so we both turn round and eye him up and down, with a look of total disgust I suppose, poor bloke, both of us thinking, Who is this creep butting in on our conversation? And Cattie says to him, the way she does, "Who the hell are you?" and he gives this funny little shrug, and . . .'

'And it was at that precise moment that you started to like him?'

'Why do you say that?'

I sit back and look infuriatingly know-all. 'Oh, just the way you called it a "funny little shrug". Not just "he gave a shrug", but "he gave this *funny little* shrug". You evidently found it a *likeable* shrug. It was a shrug that endeared the shrugger to you.'

'You, the shruggee,' puts in Jess helpfully.

Kate looks at us both. 'You really are on each other's wavelength, aren't you? *You* ought to get together.'

'I'm not disputing that,' I say, rather thrilled by the idea. 'But do you deny that it was the shrug that did it, that gave the first little pull at your heartstrings?'

'Look, do you want to hear the rest of the story or don't you? Right. Anyway, this guy gives this . . . *shrug* . . . and says, "Well, I'm Tom." Cattie is still pretty brusque with him. "A *different* Tom, possibly," she says. "There *may* be more than one Tom in London." That sort of shuts him up, and we two carry on bitching till we get to the ticket office. Next thing we know, we're sitting in the cinema and someone comes and sits right next to me, and you know how you never turn and look directly at someone who sits right next to you like that? So I didn't register at first, until he turns to me and says, "Excuse me, would you care for a Malteser?" And it was him again.'

'And you accepted said Malteser?'

'I did, yes.'

'Aha!'

'What?'

'Well, once some babe has accepted a sweetie off you, you're as good as there. Raise the harbour bar, you little minx, I'm a-coming in!'

'"You little minx",' repeats Kate, her voice dripping with disdain. '"I'm a-coming in."'

'Yeah,' I say, even more cheerfully. 'One Malteser and you're there. Sorted. Result. In like Flynn. Wham bam, thank you, mam.'

Kate and Jess exchange expressionless looks, and then,

deciding there is nothing they can do – I'm just an incorrigible dickhead – Kate resumes.

'We didn't say much more because the film started up, but afterwards he asks us if we want to go for a drink and Cattie says she has to get home, out of tact or something, I don't know, but either way I say yes, he can buy me a drink if it makes him happy. So we trot along to the nearest bar and he's really very, well, like I say, *kind*, really, and really enthusiastic about the film. You know how you go to see a film with someone, you immediately have to discuss it afterwards? And then you start comparing favourite films and getting all worked up and excited about the ones the other person hasn't seen and insisting that they must and it all gets quite impassioned, especially if there's disagreement. He thought *Paris*, *Texas* was boring, pretentious crap, for instance, and I thought the same about *Apocalypse Now*, and absolutely everything, ever, by Peter Greenaway. And then, one thing led to another and I suppose he asked me who this Tom was who was such a wanker, so I told him and poured my heart out to him a bit . . .'

'Aha, pouring your heart out. S'emotional self-exposure, innit?'

'Meaning?'

'Well, emotional self-exposure is an . . . *emblem*, if you like, of your willingness to go on to . . . you know . . . physical self-exposure.'

'What absolute balls,' says Kate.

'It is not! It's obvious!'

'It's crude and banal,' says Kate. 'So pouring your heart out to your male friends means you want to go to bed with them?'

'No.'

'Or your mother?'

'No, certainly not,' I say, rather too emphatically (suddenly remembering with alarming vividness my dream last night in which I got married to my mother). 'Of course not.'

62

'So really,' says Kate, 'your theory is quite compelling, apart from the fact that it is manifestly complete twaddle?'

'No no no!' I say, shuffling my feet furiously over the kitchen floor in a subconscious effort to regain my foothold. 'What I *mean* is, emotional self-exposure *can* indicate a willingness to progress to physical self-exposure, but obviously only if the person in question, the exposee, is a suitable partner in the first place.'

The two girls consider this for a while. 'Still twaddle,' says Kate.

'Mm, I dunno,' says Jess. 'Maybe there's a certain truth in it.'

'Anyway, where were you with Tom?'

'Oh yes, right. OK. So we got talking quite seriously, heart to heart and all that, and then he says he'll get a cab and take me home, and we decide we'd like to continue the conversation over coffee, so he came back to my place. And . . . well . . . you know . . .'

'No,' I say. 'What?'

Kate looks at me.

'Come on, what? What did you do?'

'You're such a perve.'

'Yes, stop it,' says Jess, pointing a finger at me. 'You old lech.'

'Just curious. OK. *Then* what?'

'Then the next morning,' says Kate, 'he gets out of bed and gets dressed and comes and sits back on the bed and says, "There's something I should tell you. I'm always very honest," he says. "I believe in honesty above all else in adult relationships," and all this bullshit. So I say, "Go on." He takes a deep breath, like he's being so fucking *manful* and *honest* with me, and he says, "I'm married."'

'Tuh!' I cry.

'What a bastard,' says Jess.

'Tuh!' I cry again.

'I just flip,' says Kate. 'I whack him with a pillow and bellow at him, "You call that being honest? You jump into bed with me and then AFTERWARDS you casually announce that you're already married, and you call that BEING HONEST? You don't even know the MEANING of the word!" He looks really hurt, like I'm being unreasonable. He starts to tell me that his wife is away at the moment, that he's been feeling lonely, that they're not getting on too well at the moment, that he's sorry not to have said anything earlier, and he really likes me and would love to see me again.'

'Tuh!' I say.

'I just kick him out,' says Kate. 'I haven't heard from him since, nor do I want to.'

There's a lull in the conversation while she lights another cigarette.

'Men,' says Jess.

'Tuh!' I say.

Kate looks at me. 'Will you stop saying "tuh" all the time? What does it mean anyway?'

'I'm sorry.' (What it *means*, I'm thinking, is 'Flipping heck, here am I, stuck with these two ferocious, bloodthirsty viragos all ready to turn on me at any moment and remove my private particles *dentally* . . .' I mean, what am I supposed to say?)

'I mean, what is it with men?'

I shrug. 'It's not *just* men. Women are quite capable of misbehaving too, I think.'

'But, OK, what is this constant struggle to *prove* yourselves, to see who can shag as many women as possible, who's got the most notches on their gun barrel?'

'We don't do it to *prove* ourselves,' I say.

'Well what then?'

Again I shrug. 'We do it because we enjoy it.' (I have the feeling this conversation is becoming quite fantastically ironic.)

'But it's so *boring* – one casual shag after another. Isn't it?'

'It is,' I say. 'And all some of us really want to do is to settle down with their one gal and have their babies.'

Beth. Beth.

'For a while,' says Kate. 'Before getting itchy feet after a few weeks and wanting to move on to the next one.' I study the table top. 'Wouldn't they?'

I look up at Kate. 'S'nature, innit?' Devil's advocate now. I don't mean a thing I say, like everyone nowadays. 'Lifelong monogamy is a pretty odd idea, isn't it?'

'I don't know that women are any keener on lifelong monogamy than men,' says Kate.

'Or any *less* keen on the idea of serial monogamy than men,' says Jess. 'Even the occasional orgy, just to liven things up a bit. A bit of variety and all that.'

'Well – OK,' I say. 'I mean, I'm sure that's true too.'

'But we're more *realistic* than you,' says Kate.

'Oh, I agree there,' I say, a little relieved to be off the *really* thin ice. 'Women are harsh realists in such matters. Men are the hopeless romantics and idealists. Women liking flowers and stuff, that's all a feint. It's men who are the daydreamers.' Jess starts to object violently but I insist. 'It's true! I don't know *any* bloke who could dump a girl the way evil Serena, the bitch from hell –' the daughter of Beelzebub and hand-maiden of Lucifer – 'dumped me.'

'Ah, you poor thing,' says Jess.

'Huh! You can sneer. You never knew her. The way she said it, "It's just over, there's nothing more to say. I'm going now." Just like that, total ruthlessness. And she walked out. I don't know *any* bloke who'd do that. That *calmly*, like she was just keeping an appointment in her Filofax.'

'No,' says Kate, 'a bloke would just keep hanging on instead, lying through his teeth and all the time messing around with other women.'

I take refuge in general observation.

'Look,' I say, just like Mr Blair, 'there *is* a huge difference between men and women, even if I happily accept that your modern, *Cosmo*-reading girl-about-town might fancy the occasional casual shag now and again, no strings, just pure sex with some bloke she's met in a bar. Just any old Tom, Dick or Harry. Or even another Tom . . .'

Kate's scowl is pure vinegar.

'But the point is that blokes would like that *every* evening, if they could get it. For life.'

What am I *saying*?

'Which just goes to show how shallow they are,' says Kate.

'Not at all. It's *nature*, it's *biology*. We didn't choose it that way. Look, give a woman fifty husbands and she can't have any more babies than she could with one husband: one a year or whatever it is. So there's no benefit in it. But give a man fifty wives and immediately he increases his ability to father children *fifty times over*. Now that is a slight difference, you must agree.'

'But it's not just to do with babies,' says Kate. 'So all that guff about nature is irrelevant. Because, as you've just said yourself, you're perfectly happy to ignore all those primitive, chest-beating "I want to fuck every woman I see" urges and to settle down with the one gal you love.'

'Though one is always *aware* of those primitive urges. They never go away.'

'And they make you unhappy?'

'Not exactly unhappy. But I mean, we're as much victims of these primitive urges as you are.'

'Poor li'l you.'

'We didn't choose to feel them, we're *tormented* by them. Life would be so much more peaceful, and indeed driving so much more safe, if I *didn't* have to turn round and look at every pretty girl who passes me in the street.'

'And you do that, do you?'

'Well, yes, *occasionally*. I mean, all blokes do it, it's only . . .'

'*Natural*,' they chorus.

I smile. 'But it's not as if I go round with permanent neck ache, straining my eyes in all directions at once so as to cover the maximum possible acreage of female butt visible at any one moment. It's just . . .' I shrug.

66

'It's just, *you can't help it*. You're a *bloke*.'

'Like I say,' I insist, 'we don't choose it that way. And no, I'm *not* a "New Lad", or whatever the rebarbative phrase is.'

'A New Fogey, maybe,' says Kate.

I ignore her. 'Anyway, you look at blokes' bottoms too, all girls do.'

Kate and Jess giggle. 'Not all the time,' says Kate.

'Very restrained, I'm sure.'

We sip our coffees and eye each other warily. So far, I think, in this small but perhaps significant skirmish in the eternal battle of the sexes, so good. I may have sustained one or two hits, but mere flesh wounds, mere grazes, nothing serious. And more importantly, I believe that the honour of the Regiment of Chaps has been upheld. I think we are evenly matched. I'm holding my ground. They are indeed becoming a little perturbed by the strength of my defensive position, they are inspecting my bristling gun emplacements, my solid revetments and entrenchments, with their powerful, standard-issue 'Spot the Sexist Bastard' binoculars, and wondering hesitantly whether to launch an all-out frontal assault.

While they thus hesitate, I decide to go for a classic diversionary tactic to distract their attention from the main target – myself. This takes the form of a brief Sortie in the Direction of an Abstruse Fact: always a tried and tested male ploy when pinned down in a foxhole under heavy machine-gun fire from the fearsome Women's *Eierzerbrecher* Battalion of the Monstrous Regiment.

'Look at those worms,' I say.

Kate replaces her coffee mug heavily on the table, looks around the kitchen and back at me. '*What* worms?' she says, her voice slow, heavily freighted with sarcasm.

'*Those* worms,' I clarify, 'in the paper. They had these worms they'd studied . . .'

'And don't tell me, the little boy worms were all much happier when they had as many little girl worms to shag as possible, whereas the little girl worms were happiest when they had lots and lots of little baby worms, snuggled up all cuggly-wuggly in their nice bright cosy bedrooms with Mummy while Daddy was out on the town drinking worm lager with his pals and chasing more little girl worms. And don't tell me, the scientist who conducted this experiment was a *man*. Forty-something, pot-bellied, worried about his impotence, blaming it on his wife, who's really let herself go recently, not surprising he can't get it up any more, contemplating making a pass at the new young assistant with the big hair, what's her name, Cindy or Carmel or something, and then he discovers by an AMAZING COINCIDENCE that, in his situation, making a pass at Cindy or Carmel is *exactly what the worms he's studying would do*! S'natural, innit? But of course, all scientific research is strictly objective.'

I am open-mouthed. 'Wow. You're *so* cynical.'

'But Kate knows all about scientists,' Jess reminds me, patting her big sister on the shoulder. 'Used to go out with a particle physicist.'

'Hm. Sounds grim. But no, as I was saying, these worms.' Kate and Jess groan. 'No, really though, it's interesting, and it's not what you think. They were this special kind of worm, nemesis worms or something, and basically what they found was that the little boy worms, as you put it, were much happier, and *lived longer*, that was the thing, when there were no little girl worms around and they didn't have to think about sex all the time. Y'see? Proves my point. It'd be much *easier* for us not to be tormented by the sights and sounds and smells of pretty girls all the time. It's exhausting. It *ages* us.'

'Why don't you become a monk then?' asks Kate.

'Well, of course – I mean, I'm not saying it's *all* torment and nothing else. You know.'

'You're so kind. And what about the little girl worms? Were they happier in single-sex . . . wormeries or whatever?'

I frown. 'I can't remember now.'

'Typical,' says Kate. 'It all sounds a bit feeble to me.'

'So,' says Jess. 'We're just like worms.'
'Marvellous,' says Kate.

Later the two girls go off shopping and leave me brooding and solitary. I wonder whether to go for a walk in the park, but the weather, grey and with a chilly, gravelly north-east wind, is distinctly uninviting. Or I could potter down to Mr Indajit Singh and buy a *Private Eye* and then install myself in the caff and toy with a small, bitter espresso and chuckle inwardly to myself at the follies and vanities of mankind. Ideally I would find myself a corner seat, from where I could see and not be seen: that position of ultimate omnipotence and omniscience in café society. There I could read of pseuds and poseurs, fraudsters and politicians, publicists, pimps, soap stars, media trash, petty princelings, usurers, bubble-brain celebs, lechers, whores, thieves, shysters, bull-shitters, liars, cheats, thugs, pundits, boffins, hacks, litera-teurs, art dealers, car dealers, arms dealers, lawyers and all the gorgeously coloured, chattering, jabbering, drooling, simian parade of notables, baboons in designer suits, a tri-umphal progress down the gold-paved boulevard in a cloud of flashlights and dahlings, all of them unaware that at the end of the boulevard is a sudden drop and then nothing . . . a blind void with nothing but the faint whiff of baboon excrement rising from the pit.

No. I decide I do not want anything to do with my fellow human beings for the moment. Nor do I really feel that I need the exercise of a walk. I could just sit and think about Beth . . .

Ah – fatal thought. Beth's eyes . . . her smile . . . the feel of her hair falling about my face . . . the dark mysteries she hint-ed at, the decadent, degenerate past, the subtle intimations, the sense of a life thrillingly on the edge and teetering out of control . . .

No. That way madness lies. I shall be debonair, charming, something of a playboy, a dilettante of love . . . aloof, unmoved. The pursuit of pleasure. Dandyish. I don't know exactly what I mean, but . . . *I refuse to suffer over her*.

To that end I start to run a hot bath with woodspice bubble-bath. I hang up my suit in the wardrobe and chuck everything else in the laundry basket. Then I choose my clean clothes with care and discernment: silk boxer shorts, check socks, black jeans, no, green corduroys, *no*, black jeans, no, OK then, settle for black moleskins. Then the shirt: freshly ironed, cream, double cuff, silk-knot cufflinks. Cravat? No, don't be affected. I don't want to look like a *poove*, do I? I want to feel elegant, debonair, dandyish . . . *uninvolved*. While the bath continues to fill I do twenty press-ups and fifty sit-ups and then scrutinize myself naked in the full-length mirror. Not bad, I think. Not *bad*. Except for the knees, of course. The knees could be better. The knees are, admittedly, *unfortunate*. Cold white pebbles fringed with spindly black hairs. Not attractive, it has to be said. The shins, too, would not look out of place attached to the under-carriage of certain large birds. But nobody is perfect. On the whole, not bad. Not actually *bad*.

I lie in the bath and close my eyes and wonder if I ought not to be sipping a G&T. But instead I lie and ponder abstruser questions of ethics and aesthetics in what I hope is a dandyish fashion. After bathing and washing my hair, I wet-shave with great care until my face feels as smooth as an egg. I briefly contemplate plucking my eyebrows, my famously luxuriant eyebrows; but no, that would just be too ridiculous. A dandy is not the same as a mere fusspot, nor, come to that, a vain, preening, primping narcissistic cocoa-shunter. Eyebrow plucking indeed! Come come. (Nosehair clipping, on the other hand, becoming a sad necessity.) I then apply aftershave balm 'with baobab bark extract', deodorant, talcum powder and a suggestion of aftershave. And finally, dressed in my appointed vestments, and walking in a languid yet authoritative (and possibly hieratic?)

manner (although if Kate saw me at this moment she would probably think that I must have a particularly painful blister on my foot: she just doesn't *understand*), I process into the sitting-room. I pause briefly at the bookcase to take down the dictionary and look up the word 'hieratic', before raising my forefinger to my lips and gazing intensely and aesthetically out of the window and musing to myself, 'Hieratic: ye-es . . .' I then replace the dictionary, take down a coffee-table book called *La Belle Epoque*, zap on the CD – Chopin – and stretch myself upon the sofa. A dandy, you see. Not a restless, heartsick, melancholy, faithless, twenty-something male whore, but an aesthete, with my mind on higher things.

Serene.

Contented.

Uninvolved.

10

And *then* there are all these amazing coincidences.

The least remarkable of these is my meeting Miles for a drink in the crap new pseudo-Oirish bar that nobody ever goes in. Except, it would seem . . . Clive and Amrita, she freshly returned from the wedding of the century in Delhi!

'Well, *hello*!' I cry, walking straight across to them. I glance back over my shoulder. 'This is my old chum, Miles. Miles, this is Amrita, who joined Orme, Odstock and Oliphant just before my own tragic demise. And you know Clive. You don't mind if we join you, do you?'

Clive looks at me with something approaching hatred. He has taken a big risk coming down here alone with Amrita, I suppose, knowing that at any moment his absolute ignorance of palaeo-anthropology, teeth and clodhoppers might be cruelly exposed. But now that the evil and scheming Daniel Swallow is here, he's *bound* to expose his ignorance for him. Just for a laugh. That bastard.

'So,' I say, swinging a stool backwards between my legs and sitting down directly opposite Amrita and fixing her with my moody, dark, humorous, irresistible eyes. 'How's the anthropology going?'

'Oh yeah, here we go,' murmurs Clive.

Amrita smiles and nods, sipping delicately from her glass of vodka and tonic. She has already got me sized up, I fear, the way she looks at me.

'I suppose you've discovered that you and Clive have a common interest,' I say.

'We have,' says Clive, absolutely expressionless. 'Our fields are a little different, though.'

'Really? I thought you were palaeo-anthropology too?'

'It's a large field, Daniel,' says Clive, in the most patronizing voice he can muster. 'Amrita's work has focused primarily on the transitional stages of hominid development around the time of the first appearance of *Homo sapiens*, whereas my work was at a much more *primitive* level.' Amrita modestly objects, but Clive insists. 'No, really, it was. I was just a dogsbody, really, classifying changes in flint-knapping techniques between late *Homo habilis* and early *erectus*.'

For only the second time in my life (the other occasion being a traumatic Victoria sponge-cake incident in early childhood), I'm rendered speechless. The toerag, I think. He must have actually gone to the library and done some bloody homework. I don't believe it. I gawp at Clive. I would never have thought the little tick had it in him. Clive looks directly at me and raises one triumphant eyebrow.

'Don't worry,' says Amrita, in what she intends to be a soothing voice but which in fact only makes me feel smaller than ever. 'Not *everyone* is supposed to know about this stuff, you know.'

'I . . . I . . .'

'I know bugger all about it,' says Miles cheerfully, 'but I'm pretty clued up about foreign currency deals right now, which is jolly interesting, don't you think?'

Amrita laughs. 'Fascinating.' She claps her hands together and her bangles jangle and slide down her slim arms, gleaming against her coffee skin. Clive's jealous instincts immediately switch from me to Miles. I, meanwhile, have subsided into the easy cynicism of the fox who couldn't reach the grapes. *Look* at us, I muse. Three grown men, two of us attached, in one way or another, sitting around this one girl – OK, this intimidatingly, challengingly brain-the-size-of-Norfolk, admittedly rather beautiful and exotic and vaguely mysterious Indian babe – but still, with our tongues practically hanging out. If we worked this hard nine to five we'd be millionaires by now. I mean, it's pathetic, is what it is.

Have we no willpower, no sense of shame and decency?

Nope, none whatsoever.

When we get up to go for a meal, Amrita says she has to leave. 'Work to do.'

'Sorting your flints?' I say.

'Exactly. Sorting them, labelling them, washing little bits of mud off – takes hours.'

In the street outside I grin and lean towards her and put my arm around her waist. 'I won't hear of it,' I say. 'The flints can wait. You're coming with us.'

'Ooh Daniel, you're *so* assertive,' says Miles.

'This is ridiculous,' says Clive.

'OK, look,' says Amrita, detaching herself politely from my hold. 'Tell me where you'll be and I might join you later.'

We tell her.

'Right. See you then,' she says, walking away, turning back in mid-stride, extending her hand and waggling her fingers towards us. And vanishes into the passage-tomb of the underground.

'She is gorgeous,' says Miles. 'Clever, too.'

'She is,' says Clive, staring after her.

'Come on,' I say. 'Let's go and get pissed and talk about girls.'

She doesn't join us later.

11

The next coincidence is much more extraordinary.

I haven't really thought about Beth since the dinner party weeks ago – I mean, not *really*, not apart from the occasional manstuprative fantasy, lying across the rank stew of my enseaméd bed of a Sunday morning, slack-jawed and vacant-eyed.

Beth, compared to my last girlfriend, Miranda: Beth, taller, darker, half-closed eyes (mad green eyes), dangerous, 'go-on-dare-me' laugh and rare, long coils of auburn hair for trapping spellbound men. And Miranda, always smiling, preposterously happy, 'sunny Miranda', with her blonde curls and rosy cheeks and healthy outdoor skin, her cheerful contempt for the fashions and pretensions of metropolitan life, her continual amazement and amusement at their more extreme and puerile manifestations. Her inability to lie. Her absolute honesty. (Honesty enough for both of us. Ouch.) And Beth I can picture anywhere, background doesn't matter. But with Miranda it is always out of doors, Miranda and me, somewhere beautiful and windy under a wide sky, tramping across Exmoor or the Black Mountains, or on the coastal paths of Cornwall, or doing the Ridgeway.

Ah, happy memories.

And that's the whole point, maybe. The longer you're with someone, the more memories you have of being together. You may get irritated with each other as time goes by, more used to the other, less charmed by their idiosyncratic little way of opening the milk carton, for instance. But whatever happens, good or bad, the memories accumulate, with interest. A steady couple is an island in an ever-growing sea of memories. And for one lover to leave the other, they have to cross that sea of memories first before they make landfall. And the longer they are together, the more many miles of lonely sea they have to cross ... *alone* ...

Which is why husbands, whatever promises they may make to their gorgeous and adoring younger girlfriends or mistresses, in the end very rarely leave their wives. Much less often than you would expect. They're too frightened of crossing that lonely sea of memories.

But crossing that lonely lovelorn sea I am.

And then one evening I am summoned to a hotel bedroom in Mayfair and my life veers off course for ever.

I report to the leather-padded marble reception desk in a vestibule the dimensions of a cathedral. I tell the verrucose flunkey which room is expecting me, and he phones through and nods expressionlessly and tells me that I'm to go on up. I take the lift to the fourth floor and step out into the corridor and tread down the crimson carpets to the door numbered 404. Knock.

Long wait. They always keep you waiting. Last dab of perfume, quick check of the hair, the lipstick, and then probably a long scrutiny of the prospective fuck through the security eyehole. At last the door opens.

A long and peculiar silence, during which she fixes me staidly with her cool green eyes and my own orbs flutter around like gassed moths. At last she says, in her most sarcastic drawl, 'Well, well. So I see you took my advice after all.' I stare dumbly. 'Career-wise,' she explains. 'Selling your arse.'

I click. 'Well, sort of. Not at King's Cross, though. Give me some credit.'

We stand there awkwardly for a while longer. I really have no idea, no *instinct*, what to do next. Laugh? Cry? Run away? Pretend all is normal and proceed on the appointed course?

She comes to the rescue and decides for me. 'Come on then,' she says, and turns into the room.

More of a suite.

'Fuck me,' I say.

She turns and smiles and I know she's thinking of the obvious, bad joke, but instead she announces that she's the new Amañuna girl. (NB: Amañuna – a revolting new concoction currently on the market, made of mango juice, industrial spirit and lots of sugar. The kind of 'liqueur' that is so popular among the lower middle classes at Christmastime.) For a run of cinema ads, anyway. The suite of rooms is for the week while they're shooting some colossally expensive and unlikely underwater sequences at Shepperton, in which she, as the plucky heroine of the filmlet, saves an entire Twenty Thousand Leagues Under the Sea city on the ocean floor by plugging a hole with an upended bottle of said beverage.

'It's total shite,' she adds, rather redundantly. 'But loadsa money.'

She's not *allowed* to live at home. She *has* to be in a hotel. She also gets a chauffeur to drive her to the studios every day and her own personal stylist. 'In fact,' she says, glancing at the monstrous gilt repro-Louis Quatorze clock on the wall, 'Fatima will be here for me in an hour or so. So . . .'

And she begins to undress.

'Um, look, wait a mo . . . you're joking, right?'

She freezes and stares at me, utterly blank-faced. Cold green eyes, horribly penetrating and blank, giving nothing away. She says nothing. Gives absolutely nothing.

'I . . . I hardly know you.'

As fatuous comments go, I admit that a prostitute objecting to sleeping with a client because of an insufficient level of personal acquaintance must rank pretty fucking high up the Great Fatuous Comments of All Time league. But I know what I mean, even if she doesn't. Or at least chooses not to.

She slips out of her dress. She is wearing nothing underneath. Lies back as naked as a corpse across the unmade bed. Small breasts. Neat little triangle. Pale skin, no tan lines. Her eyes fixed on the ceiling, glazed with *taedium vitae*. 'Look,' she says, '*darling*. You're a prostitute. But that's OK.' A little smile hovers over her lips, a little joke purely between her and the ceiling. 'We are *all* prostitutes. Even my friend Alex, when he's short of modelling, he does just what you do – works as a male prostitute. Mind you, he is a *lot* better-looking than you and probably earns ten times more than you do. Or works only a tenth as hard.' She sighs, bored even with her own conversation. 'Whatever. Now do shut up and fuck me.'

I start to undress and then something in me rebels, at the sheer . . . I dunno, is it arrogance? Unfriendliness? It must be more than that, to get to me like this, but I don't have time to analyse it.

'Why me, anyhow?'

She props herself up on one elbow, gaze flicking up and down over me. 'Because I'm hardly likely to *fall* for you, am I? A penniless whore with a body like ET.'

I kick off my boxers and stand naked in front of her. Smile sweetly. 'And just what kind of whore would you describe *yourself* as, my dear?'

Silence. Injured silence, I hope.

'Oh, and by the way – I'll take the money upfront, if you don't mind. You really can't trust some people.'

She lies motionless for a few seconds. Then she snaps up and swivels round and, sitting on the edge of the bed, pulls open the bedside drawer and takes out a chequebook and writes me a cheque with a gold ballpoint. Hands it over.

It's drawn on Hoare's – inevitably. And it's for double the amount. I look at her.

'Just a little extra, to keep the wolf from the door,' she says. 'I can afford it. After all, I *am* the new Amañuna girl.' And she smiles an entirely mirthless, distant smile and lies back down again.

And I am a prostitute, and I am about to fuck one of my best friends' girlfriend, who is, I have just found out, a Class A, A1, gilt-edged Bitch.

But hey, life's like that. This kind of thing happens all the time.

So I finish undressing and get on top of her and fuck her. She keeps her eyes tight shut.

Afterwards:

'Oh, don't sit there in a post-coital gloom,' she says, lighting up a cigarette and flicking another into my lap.

'It's not gloom. Pity.'

'Oh, *please* don't pity me, I couldn't bear it.'

'Not you, you self-obsessed cow! *Miles!*'

She turns on me furiously. 'You leave Miles out of this.'

'Just like you have, huh?'

'Exactly.'

I light my cigarette. We subside into glowering silence. How I do love a little tender pillow-talk after sex.

I ask her about her lines in the Amañuna ads, but she says she doesn't have any lines. 'I don't have anything to *say*,' she explains. 'I just have to be there. I'm paid for my body.' She reaches out and flicks me on the nose, quite hard. 'Just like you, darling.'

What I really want to ask her is, what the hell is she *doing*? I mean, what am *I* doing here? If she's that bored with poor, steady, dependable Miles, why can't she just go into a bar and pick up any man of her choice, any night of the week? But I suppose the answer is obvious. She's not paying for the sex, she's paying for me to go away afterwards. She's paying for the *absence* of certain things. Commitment, emotion, seriousness, intimacy.

But still, what about Miles?

We skirt around it instead. An uncomfortable, unromantic, unreal *pas de deux* around unspoken questions. And another thing, she has needle tracks on her arms. It's my one, mean-minded consolation: she's a lot more fucked up than I am.

But I take the money and run. It's got nothing to do with me. Sounds callous, maybe, but actually I know I have no choice. This is not the sort of girl who is suddenly going to start opening up about her *prahblems*. Beth the Ice Maiden, so sexually available, so generous with her favours. But in everything else so impenetrable, so emotionally shuttered and closed off.

I don't even kiss her goodbye. That would be ridiculous.

12

And then along comes yet *another* unlikely coincidence. (This is getting like a Thomas Hardy novel.)

Perhaps it's inevitable, though, given the number of women I see who are approximately from the same social circles as I am, that the Beth thing should happen again: that rather awkward initial greeting at the door, 'Oh, *Daniel*, well, *hello*, so *you're* the prostitute that I've just phoned up for, what an *extraordinary* coincidence, well, *do* come on in . . .' But it is slightly unnerving when much the same thing happens again *less than a week later*.

Eleven p.m., to a quiet side street in Pimlico. Eleven p.m. signals that the client is looking for a fuck and nothing else. No night at the opera, no candlelit dinner for two, fingertips touching over the lobster bisque in some quiet, romantic corner golden with dim lamps and lovers' smiles.

Eleven p.m. = straight fuck.

It's Olivia. Lady Craigmuir. Clive's mum.

She's wearing a black silk kimono embroidered with gold and crimson birds of paradise, she is beautifully made up and is smoking a black cigarette. Being Olivia, of course, she carries it off with tremendous panache and no embarrassment whatsoever. She laughs: a genuine, uproarious laugh. Her laugh was always uproarious.

In her untidy but stylish sitting-room she pours me a glass of champagne and reclines in an armchair, her arm thrown across the back, smiling over the rim of her glass at my discomfort. I perch on the edge of the sofa, trying not to look quite so stricken and hare-like and twitchy.

'Well well,' she murmurs. 'I heard from Clive that you'd

got the heave-ho from that dreadful place, what was it called? But, *darling* . . .' She leans forward and touches me on the knee. 'I had no idea you'd become a *rent boy*.' She tilts her head to one side, smiles quizzically. 'Or do you prefer *gigolo*?'

'Er – well, "escort" is the favoured term, I believe.'

She laughs and turns to tap her cigarette ash into the bowl beside her. 'Well, I must say, Daniel, I think it is very *brave* of you. Really.' She raises her glass. 'Bravo!'

I raise my glass too. I can't tell if Olivia is cruelly taking the mickey or if she really is off-the-wall enough to think that prostitution is a tremendously exciting and imaginative new career move.

'Does Clive know?'

'No. None of my friends do. Well, except one . . .' I say no more. It would be just too complicated to try to explain the Beth thing. Anyway, I'm not even sure how it happened myself.

'Well,' she says again, and begins to stand. I jerk upright and leap to my feet, primed and ready to drop my trousers where I stand, rubbing my sweaty palms down my thighs as I do so. It's not that Olivia isn't attractive – she is, extremely. It's just that – there is something unidentifiable about this situation which is making me nervous. Perhaps it's the memory of the way Beth handled a similar situation less than a week ago. In a trice, Olivia will be spread-eagled across the Persian, saying, 'Now get on with it and fuck me.' And I'm awash with the strangest mixture of embarrassment, gaucherie, trepidation and, I have to admit it, wretched uncontrollable lust.

Perched on the edge of the armchair still, Olivia looks up at me over her half-moons, surprised. 'Are you . . .?'

'Well, I . . .'

'You want . . .?'

'Well, I just thought . . .'

'You're not . . .'

'You're not . . .?'

'Oh, *darling*,' she says, lying back in her armchair again, eyeing me with amusement and reproachfulness. 'You're not *really* expecting us to jump into bed together *now*, are you?'

'Well . . . what, you mean . . .?'

'Nor indeed at any time in the future.' She giggles. 'But never you mind, I'll write you a cheque or something, but I *really* don't . . . I know you won't be offended, I've always thought you were very sweet, but I really don't want to start having sex with you, or indeed with any of my son's friends. It would just be too – too *oedipal*.'

'Ah yes, quite,' I say, smiling politely and sitting back down and crossing my legs in the sort of languid, spacious, diagonal formation that men favour when trying to conceal an appalling hard-on. 'I just wasn't sure.'

She looks at me again, definitely flirtatious, her big blue eyes peeping over the rim of her champagne glass. '*Very* flattering though, darling.' She pauses. '*Especially* that enormous bulge in the front of your trousers. Looks like you were positively *looking forward* to it.'

And we both laugh.

Oh, how we laugh.

But it is nothing, I insist, to do with my having a deep-rooted older-woman complex. And I certainly don't have a mother fixation, as I think I have said before. It is simply that Olivia is, as I say, a very attractive woman. For her age.

And so we pass the next couple of hours in pleasant gossip and schmooze. Olivia pours me another glass of champagne or two, plies me with cigarettes, and we end up talking about Clive.

'Oh, God, that *dreadful* girl,' she says (meaning Emma). 'I find her *quite* appalling. She's latched on to him like some revolting . . . *sea creature*, with those great rubbery suckers, and she just will not let him go. Poor *lamb*.' Olivia inhales deeply. 'Mind you, I don't think he is in *love* with her in the slightest, or even pretends to be. Last time we spoke he kept veering off on to this Indian girl he'd met. At work, I think.'

'Oh – you mean Amrita?'

'Is that her name? How beautiful. Is she?'

'Yes, she is actually. Really tall and slim and kind of . . . *haughty*. Not like Emma-haughty though. More just – genuinely proud and self-possessed. It's really attractive. And she's very clever. She's a palaeo-anthropologist.'

'Hm. Amrita,' she muses. 'Intelligence is always attractive certainly.' And then her eyes glitter wickedly. 'The best thing of all would be breaking the news to His Lordship, though, eh?'

'?'

'My *husband*,' she explains. 'You know he's a pig of a man anyway, I'm sure Clive has told you.'

I start to protest but she silences me with a single wave of her black cigarette. 'No really, darling, quite dreadful. Really ghastly. You know he's the Grand Master of the League of the Defenders of Albion?'

'I . . . it doesn't mean much to me, I'm afraid.'

'Well, what do you *think* it might mean, darling?'

'Well, at a wild guess – I suppose it might mean that a group which adopts such a name might *occasionally* display . . . a certain, ah, *insensitivity* to, ah, ethnic minorities?'

'Darling,' she cries, 'you might as well accuse *Hitler* of insensitivity towards ethnic minorities! Oh, I can't wait,' she resumes, when the laughter has subsided. 'When can I meet the lovely Amrita?'

'Well, they're not an item as such, just yet. Far from it.'

'Nonsense,' declares Olivia. 'I am quite sure she would be perfect for my darling Clive. Poor *lamb*.'

Some time after one she says it has been a delightful evening and gives me a peck on each cheek and ruffles my hair and sees me off into the night in a cloud of cigarette smoke and *au revoirs*.

She never does give me that cheque.

13

Men and women want totally different things. They don't even speak the same language. The gulf is unbridgeable.

On top of which, my memory is playing bad tricks on me these days. Either it keeps reminding me of how permanently paradisial things were between me and Miranda. Or else it does a complete change of cast and I dream of doing things with Beth that I really did with Miranda.

Lying half awake in the mornings, I remember so vividly Miranda's eyes shining. Kissing her, my nose getting tickled by her golden curls, the smell of her usual shampoo, the smell and touch together as familiar and as comforting as re-reading an old and favourite storybook, or revisiting a place where you holidayed years ago and finding it still unchanged and as you remember it.

There is no chronology to the memories, they flood in like wrack on the tide, time-torn, storm-disordered, unsorted, meaningless in their way. Except that they are all happy memories. *The heart's memory eliminates the bad and magnifies the good.* That is one of its sovereign duties, in order to persuade us that life is essentially OK and worth persisting with. The heart's memory is fastidious about what it lets in. Sunny days: yes. Holidays: yes. Schooldays . . . rather grudgingly and not very vividly. Schooldays are admitted to the archival vaults only in black and white, with a crackly soundtrack, smelling of chalk dust and grey socks and anxious changing-rooms; so we don't linger too long over them but pass quickly on to holidays: Padstow and Rock, Exmoor, Suffolk, Skye, Brittany, Crete, Tuscany, the Dordogne, all brought back to you in dazzling colour and full surround sound, with smells of sea air and French bread and cloudberries high in the heather.

So these memories of early days with Miranda that I keep getting are of gardens of jasmine and sunshine perpetual, hedgerows of honeysuckle, fields of meadowsweet . . . while all memories are ruthlessly suppressed that are of thistles and thorns and slow days grey as rain.

What a fickle and untrustworthy organ, the human heart! What a terrible unpredictability it possesses, and what a troubled and uncertain relationship with Objective Truth!

And yet, for all that, the heart's memory is well meaning. Like the meddling maiden aunt at Christmas who always tries to bring the family together and only ends up making things worse, the heart means well. But unfortunately the effect of its filtering out bad memories and emphasizing the good is to make what's gone appear a golden, unsullied Eden, and the present, the as yet unfiltered present, in comparison disappointing, a compromise with imperfection, a fallen realm. A decline from the gold standard of the past. It takes reason and the cold mind to tell us that the past is in truth no different from the present and it is only that we have forgotten, or edited it. For every day running free on the moors of Devon, in those sunny early days, there was always a fortnight of commuting to work crook-necked on the tube, or in bed, too tired or too hungover, or in the supermarket bickering over baked beans.

We're in the kitchen at my place: Kate, Miles, Clive and me. Saturday morning, after a party. Black coffee all round.

'And what's her name again?' says Kate.

'Amrita,' I say.

'Indian,' says Miles. 'Stonker. Down, boy!'

'Stonker?' repeats Kate, making the two curt syllables last for a surprisingly long time.

'Well, you know . . . I mean . . . attractive and that.'

'Really?'

'Yep,' I say.

'Beautiful,' says Clive.

'Babe,' says Miles.

'Fox,' I say.

'Top-hole tottie,' says Miles.

'You don't . . . I mean, you haven't even *heard* of feminism, have you, you two?' says Kate.

'Isn't it something to do with tampons?' asks Miles brightly.

'I'm going,' says Kate.

'No, don't, *please*,' we chorus. I hold her arm. 'We wouldn't have anyone to show off to then.'

'Well, stop being so laddish.'

'We can't help it,' says Miles. 'We're lads.'

'Don't talk rubbish. You're too old, too middle class, and you both know better.' She sits down again. 'So,' she says, 'tell me about this – Amrita.'

'Well,' I begin, 'she is *very* attractive. Tall, slim, jet-black hair. High cheekbones.'

'Beautiful eyes,' says Clive.

'These big olive eyes,' I agree.

'Sloe eyes,' says Miles.

'Are they? What the fuck are sloe eyes?'

Miles shrugs. 'What the fuck are olive eyes, for that matter?'

'Eyes like olives? OK, then. Dark eyes. Big, almond-shaped dark eyes.'

'There you go again,' says Miles. 'Almonds.' He turns to Kate and flicks his hands and says with irritation, 'The man's *obsessed* with fruit'n'nuts.'

Kate giggles.

I persist. 'No make-up.'

'Yes, she does,' objects Miles. 'Eyeliner.'

'OK. Eyeliner. But very subtly applied.'

'I need the loo,' says Clive, getting up.

'But this is just her appearance,' says Kate. 'What is she like as a *person*?'

87

Miles and I look at each other, minds blank. At last I say, 'Well, she seems quite nice.'

Miles thinks about it for a while. 'Yeah,' he agrees eventually. 'Quite nice.'

Kate sighs in despair. 'Anything more perceptive?'

'Um,' I say. 'Well . . . kind of *haughty*.'

'Yeah,' says Miles. 'Nice – but *haughty*.'

'And Clive?'

'Oh, *he's* interested all right. Not a hope though.'

'And why not?'

Miles shakes his head in agreement. 'No chance there. Too short.'

'And too *ginger*,' I say.

'You are horrible,' says Kate. 'Clive's sweet.'

'Sweet he may be,' I say. 'But, sister, in the naked and ferocious jungle of the mating game, *sweet* don't count for diddly.'

'How do you know? Clive might be just the sort Amrita is looking for. He might . . . make her feel safe.'

'Yeah,' I say. 'Safe from what? Attack by a vole?'

'And anyway, not all girls are quite so obsessed with SIZE as you seem to be. Or physical appearance generally, for that matter.'

Clive returns from the loo.

'Men fall in love through their eyes, women through their ears,' says Miles sagely.

'But what about that symmetry thing?' chips in Clive. 'You know. It's been demonstrated that the more symmetrical you are, especially facially, the more shags you get.'

I, with my lopsided grin and non-matching ears, fall strangely silent at this point.

'Oh, rubbish,' says Kate.

'No, it's true,' says Miles. 'I read it too. Men as well as women. We all judge on physical appearance. It's just that women don't admit it.'

'Yes!' I say, re-entering the fray. 'You call us sexist, but in

88

fact you're just as sexist. We're no more sexist than you, we're more *honest*.'

'Hm,' says Kate. 'But there is a point at which honesty merges into stupidity.' And leaving us feeling not a little rattled by this gnomic observation, Kate raises her coffee mug and murmurs, 'Santé! And how's Beth?'

'Mm,' says Miles, swallowing a mouthful of coffee fast. 'In Amsterdam. Very well, I think. Phones me every night to say so, anyway.'

'How sweet,' I say.

'And she still enjoys doing all that stuff?' asks Kate. 'The catwalks and all that?'

'Not really, but it pays,' says Miles. 'No, actually she hates it. She can't wait to get into acting more. She just did these ads for Amañuna, you know.'

'You don't say?' I murmur.

Somehow we get on to babies and marriage and all that. I'm fuming inwardly with Beth the Bitch from Hell, and myself, I suppose. My anger takes the form of reactionary conservatism.

'Yes, of course you stay together. If there are children involved, then they take priority. I can't stand all this bollocks about *you have to live your life, go for it*, all this New Selfishness. You fucking well stay together for the sake of the children. It's called self-sacrifice, instead of . . .'

'Sweetpea, you're shouting.'

But I don't really register because I'm shouting: '. . . this fucking me-me philosophy where you get these repulsive egomaniac dried-up old forty-something wives sitting in their fucking Hampstead wine bars sighing over their espressos and confiding to their best friend Vanessa, *I just refuse to accept that at forty-something my life is over, darling, you know, Gerry just isn't interested in me physically any more, and though naturally I love the boys, Toby and Paddy, I just have to get away, I have to find my own space again, to paint again,*

darling, sometimes one just has to put oneself first. Of course, dar-
ling, says her equally egocentric repulsive dried-up hag of a
friend Vanessa soothingly, *of course, darling, which is exactly*
what I have done leaving George, even though I love the girls,
Alicia and Tabitha, so much, I just had to get away . . . '

Both Miles and Kate are giggling at this extended rant,
although I think I'm being deadly serious.

'So,' says Kate, 'it's all women's fault.'

'No, of course not, but all this bollocks about *finding oneself*
does seem to be mostly menopausal women.'

'Whereas men just leave their wives and children for some
bit of fluff twenty years younger.'

'Well, yes, no, *no*, not at all . . . I just mean, women seem to
want to *justify* it to themselves. Men just say *fuck it* and walk
out.'

Later Kate goes off to town to meet a girlfriend and shop till
they drop. Miles and Clive go home.

Kate and her friend, she tells me later, spend six orgiastic
hours in Kensington High Street amassing bags full of
clothes and shoes and jewellery and make-up and pausing
only for the necessary victualling: coffee and prawn sandwiches. Kate has found that, remarkably, despite the dozens
of bananas and the two family-size boxes of Belgian choco-
lates that her metabolism has assimilated since Tom left her,
she has actually *lost weight* and now hovers tantalizingly
between a size 12 and size 10.

'Size 10! That'll show the bastard.'

'What bastard?'

'*The* bastard. I dunno. *All* of them.'

I, meanwhile, have spent most of Saturday congratulating
myself on how many objectionable household chores I managed to get done before one p.m., and also on how few lust-
ful thoughts I have had about Beth.

I have taken a linen suit to the dry-cleaners, watered all

the houseplants (cursing both the coarse exuberance of the spiderplant and the panting valetudinarian delicacy of the maidenhair fern), polished two pairs of shoes, ironed four shirts, done sixty sit-ups and twenty press-ups while listening to my new CD, *Bangin': 40 of the Best Dance Trax Around Right Now* and hating every minute of it, returned my library books and got out four more (including *The Story of Early Man* – just in case – and *The Origin of Consciousness in the Breakdown of the Bicameral Mind* – will look good on the tube, I can't help thinking), enjoyed an opulent wet-shave with many an exotic unguent applied both before and after. And oiled my bicycle.

So that after an early lunch I face the luxury of an empty Saturday afternoon before me. Furthermore, having been out and about all morning, and reminded myself just how ugly and objectionable the great majority of the human race appears when doing its push'n'shove Saturday shopping, and with the weather distinctly January-ish, in the least attractive way – too early yet for bright yellow spring but plenty of wind and rain and grey skies – I feel no obligation to go out again. Instead I am free to toot along on my clarinet for a while, in accompaniment to a recording of Poulenc's Sonata for Two Clarinets, with its deliciously melancholy middle section, and then to settle back on the sofa with a coffee, Gorecki's Third on the CD, and to brood over the exquisite unattainability of my beloved, and the fate of East European Jewry.

My idea of what constitutes a pleasant, relaxing Saturday afternoon is not, perhaps, the usual one.

In the evening Kate returns, and Jess comes round, and we watch *Monty Python and the Holy Grail* on video and the girls smoke a few joints, though I stick to wine, and we spend the rest of the evening saying 'ni!' to each other, in between long and impassioned discussions (only dope can do this) about genetic engineering (a Bad Thing), decriminalization of dope (a Good Thing) and the phenomenon of Ann Widdecombe (impossible to judge, but certainly a Very Strange Thing).

Around midnight, I suggest a game of strip poker, but the girls think this is also a Bad Thing, so we find a spare duvet for Jess and she promptly falls asleep on the sofa. Kate and I retire to bed. Separately, of course.

Oh, OK, OK, we go to bed together. But we often sleep together and it's entirely asexual. Well, almost. Sometimes we have a goodnight snog. But it's just a friends thing. Honest. Kate actually hates sleeping on her own, and I'm not too keen on it myself.

'*The Story of Early Man*,' says Kate in amused tones, picking up the book by my bedside. 'Er . . . *why?*'

I shrug. 'It's interesting.'

She leafs through it. '"The men would go out on hunting expeditions while the women stayed nearer to home, foraging for plant foods. And although the popular image of Stone Age people is of big meat-eaters, in fact it is reckoned that over 80 per cent of their diet was plant food, provided by the labour of women."' She snaps the book shut. 'So there you are!'

'Hmph.'

Lights out.

Goodnight kiss.

Sleep.

14

I'm meeting Clive for lunch, in a cheap and cheerful Italian on the fringes of Covent Garden. I want to know if he's getting anywhere with his Indian babe, and whether Emma has contracted some horrible disease yet, Ebola or something. Also, I'm really determined this time to tell Clive about my new career, after a steadying bottle or two of Chianti. I have to tell someone, and I think Clive might take it reasonably well. But somehow, I never get round to it. Clive has dramatic news of his own.

'A lady doctor!' says Clive, bustling over to the table where I'm sitting.

I lay my cigarette down in the ashtray and regard him quizzically.

'Lady doctor!' repeats Clive with great enthusiasm. 'White coat, specs, severe hairstyle – the works!'

I lean back in my chair. 'Clive, what the *fuck* are you talking about? Is this another one of your weird priapic dreams?'

'Company medicals,' says Clive. 'All day today. You must be missing that sort of thing, in your lonely freelance lifestyle.'

That seems a good moment for me to broach the delicate subject of my new career. 'Clive –'

'I bet you'd have forgotten even if you were still working there. You always did. And the lady doctor, she'd, she'd . . .' Clive is jiggling up and down in his seat now with sheer excitement. 'She'd, I mean, you'd have to go in and see the Lady Doctor, and she'd look at you severely over the top of her thick black specs and say, "Oh *dear*, Mr Swallow, this is rather remiss of you," and then she'd delve in her drawers . . .'

'Clive –'

' . . . and bring out a little glass phial about the size of an egg-timer and ask you, *command* you, *severely*, to go behind the curtain and pee into it . . .'

'Clive –'

' . . . and you'd be so nervous you wouldn't be able to pee at all and you'd be standing there shaking like a leaf with your todger the size of a matchstick in your hand and you'd look up and she'd be standing there, the Lady Doctor, looking down at your efforts with a smile of disdain and cruel lechery . . .'

'Clive, will you *please* shut up.'

'Aha! Too near the bone, eh? Too near the boner? Eh? Eh?' Clive chortles. 'Anyway, there's a list of times up outside. I'm due back at 2.15.'

'It's like being at fucking school again,' I say. 'What's it got to do with the company how your health is? It's already no smoking, no drinking, no wanking, no shagging, no picking your nose everywhere you go, what do they want a fucking *sample* for now? I think I'd know if I had diabetes or cancer or whatever.'

'Rumour has it that it's a new policy to do random drugs tests on us.'

· 'You're kidding. Does Oliphant get tested too? The man's a walking pharmacy.'

'Dunno,' says Clive. 'Company policy.' Suddenly he sits up, his face pale and shiny. 'Oh, fuck.'

'What? What? You been snorting coke in the washrooms too? I thought you knew better.'

'We had a joint on Saturday night.'

'What, you and *Emma*? Surely not.'

'No, no, me and . . . It doesn't matter now anyhow.' Clive pauses, bites his lip.

'Oh, by the way, have you managed to cop off with the Indian babe yet?'

'I beg your pardon?'

'Amrita? I assume you've taken her home and given her a good seeing-to.'

'Swallow, you disgust me sometimes. I *walked* her home and kissed her goodnight and said it had been a wonderful evening and I looked forward to seeing her again. You know, the *romantic* stuff.'

'Hm,' I say vaguely. 'OK. It's a start. Now about this dope. How long does it stay in your bloodstream?'

'Ages. Three weeks or something.' Clive shakes his head. 'But they're not asking for my blood, are they?'

'Not yet,' I spit. 'No doubt that'll be next. *All employees must provide a litre of blood daily to the company, all alcohol Verboten, any smokers vill be shot on sight, anyone laughing in the office vill be sent for psychiatric help to Dr Heinz Kiosk, anyone so much as LOOKING at a member of the opposite sex vill have their eyelids stapled shut, Oliphant's anus must be felched by all employees thrice daily, and remember, at all times, that ARBEIT MACHT FREI!*'

'Daniel, you're shouting.'

'Well, for fuck's sake.' I stub out my cigarette with great violence. 'What are you supposed to do? Are you sure it's three weeks?'

'In the blood, yeah. I dunno about your pee. That might not show up.'

'*Might* not. Oh, great. A confident basis for a medical *that* is, that it *might* not fuck up your entire career. Such as it is.'

'Thanks. Well – it is technically illegal, after all. Dope.'

'Yeah.' My brow furrows and then miraculously clears. 'You can have my pee!' I say.

'You're so generous.'

'No, I mean it. I mean I could go and do a sample in the bog and you can take it in as yours. I don't think I've had a smoke for three weeks.'

Clive stares at me. 'Swallow, that's actually quite a cunning plan.'

'Indeed it is,' I say proudly. 'As cunning as the whiskers on a weasel's cheek.'

'And you're sure you haven't drunk too much coffee this morning? Caffeine level in excess of company health guidelines?'

I laugh. 'I'll order a bottle of mineral water.'

That evening, I get a call from Clive.

'Well? How did it go?'

'My life is in ruins.'

'Ah. Not so good then. Have you been fired? Want to join me in a career as a male prostitute?'

'Be serious. I've utterly ballsed up.'

I sigh. 'Tell me all.'

As Clive was ascending in the lift to his floor, after our lunch, he suddenly realized to his horror that the bottle in his inside jacket pocket was leaking. Plastic bottles. ('Fucking cheap Italians you take me to,' he snarls as an aside.) Another man's urine was dribbling down his shirt. Some chaps might find this sort of thing attractive. There are those kind of clubs, in Earls Court etc. . . . But not Clive.

In a blind panic, he rushed out of the lift and into the staff kitchen. He hunted through the fridge and the only suitable alternative receptacle he could find was one of those poncy spring water/fruit juice drinks. He glanced at his watch in desperation. 2.10. He was due for the Lady Doctor in five minutes. It would have to do.

He grabbed the spring water/fruit juice bottle and emptied it into the sink and refilled it with my pee from the plastic bottle and then binned that bottle and sighed deeply. Saved.

He tried to pocket it but it wouldn't fit, so he held it half concealed beneath his jacket. At that moment, Amrita, the Most Beautiful Girl in the World, swept into the kitchen. 'Hi, Clive,' she said, smiling radiantly. She opened the fridge door and then looked up.

'Oh, *you've* pinched it,' she said, really quite crossly. 'That's *my* drink, Clive.'

Everything occurred in terrible slow motion. He stood pressing himself back against the kitchen cupboards, frozen, clutching the guilty bottle in his right hand.

'No, it isn't,' he said woodenly.

'Well, *that's* funny,' said Amrita, with heavy sarcasm. 'It looks strikingly *similar* to my bottle, which has just vanished from the fridge.'

Clive looked down at the bottle. He thought he might burst into tears. By evil chance, the hue of his pee was indeed almost identical to the hue of the spring water + peach juice concoction that it had just replaced.

'Can I have it back please?' She reached out her hand – so slim! so brown! so beautiful! – and looked very determined.

'No,' he said, even more woodenly. A performance of hewn mahogany.

'What do you mean, *NO*?'

'I . . . I'll buy it off you.'

'It's not for sale. Don't be ridiculous, Clive, just give me back my drink. I'll give you a swig if you like.'

'I . . . I don't want a swig, honestly.'

It was a waking nightmare. He considered just telling her. Perhaps even offering her some. After all, maybe she'd smoked dope on Saturday night too. She might be fired, deported, bundled back to India on a P&O steam packet. And it would all be his fault.

Clive felt he was losing it, badly. But no, he couldn't tell her, really. It would just sound too odd: 'I haven't *stolen* your drink, as such, Amrita, I've just poured it down the sink, and replaced it with the urine of Daniel Swallow – you know, the guy who nearly killed those three minor but much-loved television personalities recently, in that bizarre hot-air ballooning accident.' What girl is going to fall for a tale like that?

And how did Amrita stand on the dope thing anyway? There was no knowing. Anything that might have developed between them was finished. Finished! There was only one thing for it.

Clive turned round and, feeling the outraged, liquid brown eyes of Amrita staring down the corridor after him, he ran away.

What a *weirdo*.

'You *ran away*,' I repeat, trying not to sound as aghast as I feel.

'Yes,' says Clive. After a long silence he asks, 'What do you think?'

'Well, your job's safe anyhow. For the time being.'

'Not the job, you fool. *Amrita*.'

I sigh. 'Amrita. Ah . . .'

'I've fluffed it, haven't I?'

'I'd say – well, I'd say that the course of true love never did . . .'

'Oh, balls.'

15

OK – so Clive's love life is a mess. But what about *mine*?

I am reclining peacefully on the sofa one Sunday evening, bottle of beer on the floor beside me, *The Man Without Qualities* perched on my knee (he may be just a hollow shell of a man but he weighs a fucking ton, let me tell you), when the doorbell goes. My beloved landlady must be back early, too drunk to use her own key, or even to locate it, in the space-time vortex that is her handbag. *Damn.* I love her dearly, but I was looking forward to a whole evening of brooding, pensive solitude. Hence, vain, deluding joys . . .

I'm halfway to the front door when the bell goes again, with a needy, irritating urgency. O God, let me guess: another Tom has dumped her. Her life is a mess too. She needs my shoulder to cry on.

I pick up the entryphone. 'Hello?'

It's not Kate, it's Beth.

'Hi, er . . . well, come on in. Or do you want to go for a drink?'

'Come in,' she slurs.

God. *She's* drunk too. Why are all young women so *drunk* these days?

She's not drunk. Or not very. The reason she's slurring so badly is because her mouth is so messed up. Her top lip is deeply cut and her bottom lip is plum-coloured and fatly swollen, like a raw venison sausage. Blood has trickled down into the corner of her mouth and then over her chin, where she has wiped it into a red smear across her cheek. More blood has dripped down on to her white cotton sweater, a scarlet exclamation mark. Her nostrils are crust-ed with little droplets of dried blood too, and her left eye is almost closed under a bulging bruise. Her hair is tangled and torn, she is walking with a slight limp, and she has broken a fingernail or two. All in all, she's not looking her best.

'Jesus, what happened to *you*?'

'Someone hit me,' she slurs, the sibilant bite of sarcasm sounding even through her swollen lips. 'Didn't see who it was.'

She's trembling. There are a hundred and one questions I want to ask, and there's someone out there I very much want to kill. But I have to rein all that in for now. It won't help her. Though underneath the cool crust, the worldly, wisecracking mantle, I'm furious magma, I'll keep myself cool and clinical for her sake.

I say no more, put my arm around her shivering shoulders, guide her towards the bathroom. It looks far worse under the harsh glare of the striplight. She stares at herself in the mirror as if without recognition. I reach up and snap the striplight off, switch on the gentler overhead light instead, half turn her so that she is facing me. Whistle. 'Quite impressive. It wasn't Lennox Lewis, was it?'

I run a basin full of warm water, find a clean flannel in the bathroom cupboard, return, touch my fingers under her chin. 'Tilt your head back. Now, this is going to hurt.' I soak the flannel in warm water and wring it out loosely, then lay one hand on her shoulder and with the other I begin to dab away the blood from her nose and mouth. She winces but doesn't pull back. I lather up a little soap and wash her chin and cheek clean of dried blood. Then tears start to her eyes.

'Does that hurt?' I ask, stopping.

She shakes her head, buries her face in my shoulder. I cup my hand around the back of her head, rest my cheek on the top of her head, breathe in the perfume of her hair: Chanel, cigarettes, sadness. Then she pulls away again. 'It's OK,' she says. 'I'm sorry. Carry on.'

I dab away the tear-streaks from her face and she winces when I touch her left eye. I place both my hands on her shoulders. 'Look up at me.' She does so. The left eye hardly opens. 'OK – don't move.' Very slowly I place my forefinger over her eyebrow and my thumb under her swollen lower eyelid and open it a little. Her mouth twitches but she doesn't move. Her eye is tearful but clear. 'You can see all right?' She nods. 'And you weren't knocked unconscious at any time? You don't feel sick or dizzy?' She shakes her head, laughs, a sad, anxious little laugh. 'OK.' I put my arm around her again. 'You'll live.'

She smiles. 'Such an impressive bedside manner. How come you got so good at treating cuts and bruises?'

'Rugby,' I say manfully. 'Just be thankful they didn't kick you in the balls.'

(*Rugby* indeed! What do I know about rugby? The truth is, I don't really have a clue what I'm doing, but Beth thinks I do: that's the point. I'm fulfilling the role of a kind of human placebo here.)

I drop the flannel back in the basin. 'I think you'd better take your sweater off too. I'll wash it for you.' A look of panic crosses her face, which I clumsily misinterpret. 'You can have one of my shirts.'

She raises her arms to pull her jumper off over her head and gasps and fails. 'It's my shoulder,' she says. 'My arm doesn't want to move that way.'

I try to help her and we get nowhere fast. She can't lift her left arm up without real pain, sucking in air, her face creased and clenched.

'OK. Right arm first.' She leans a little and I ease her arm out of its cotton sleeve. Then off over her head and down over her limp left arm. When I see her bare left shoulder, I tut.

'Those are quite some colours you've got there.'

She twists and squints down. 'Bloody hell,' she says. 'No little off-the-shoulder numbers for me for a while. I look like Elmer the Elephant.'

There's no point bathing it. There are no cuts, just one giant, livid bruise.

'They must have hit you with a fucking baseball bat or something.'

'I think they kicked me when I was down,' she says flatly. And then again tears start to her eyes, again she buries her face in my shoulder.

I kiss the top of her head again and cradle her and whisper, 'It's all right now, you're safe now.'

After a while she pulls away and turns side on, undoes the zip at the side of her skirt and drops it to her feet and steps out of it. She winces again. She bends and picks up the skirt. I take it from her and retrieve her sweater, then go into the kitchen, examine the labels for washing instructions, throw them into the machine and put a warm wash on.

When I turn back she's there in her underwear, leaning against the door jamb with her good shoulder, head to one side, smiling, as much as her messed up mouth permits. 'You're quite sweet really,' she says.

I squeeze past her out of the door. 'I'm the original golden-hearted whore,' I say.

She laughs sharply and then sucks in air and cradles her stomach all in one abrupt movement, and begs me not to make her laugh.

In my bedroom I find an ancient brushed-cotton shirt in a drawer and when I stand up and turn round she's there in the doorway again. Following me round like a puppy. Doesn't want to be left alone: cool, distant, independent Beth. Not for one second. Then she walks over to me and loops her arms around my waist and again buries her head in my shoulder. This time there is something different about it. Something more urgent. She is holding me so tightly, nuzzling me very slightly with her wounded mouth.

It's not every day that you have a beautiful young actress-model in your bedroom clad only in her underwear, pressing herself against you. And I'm ashamed to say (although actually, when I think about it, not *that* ashamed to say) that my generative parts respond accordingly. Instead of recoiling in girlish horror, Beth is quite clearly pressing herself harder against me as she feels me hardening against her. Indeed, she is almost grinding into me now, one leg thrown around the back of mine, her face still hidden away from sight.

But I know it's not sex she's after. Sex is the last thing on her confused mind. With a huge effort of will, I take her elbows in my hands and pull her away from me. She looks up, expectant. I bend down and kiss her very gently, barely touching, on her lips. We stare at each other unblinking for a moment. At last she says, 'No?'

I shake my head. 'Don't be daft.'

She drops her head, repeats, 'No.' Then she looks up at me again and we stare at each other again, gazing somewhat foolishly into each other's eyes, and then we both smile at the same moment. She steps back further and retrieves the shirt from the bed. Examines the label.

'Millets,' she reads. She looks up. 'Hm. I don't think I've ever worn anything by Millets before.'

'*From* Millets, surely?' I query. 'It may be *by* Kenzo, *by* Versace. But it's definitely *from* Millets.'

She pulls it carefully on and buttons it up and flicks her hair free from the collar. It comes down to mid-thigh and she looks absurdly good in it. I have to swallow.

'What do you think?' she asks. Demanding to be admired.

'You're quite sweet really,' I quote back at her. 'Now go in there and choose a mindless video. And what do you want to drink? Whisky? Water? Orange juice?'

'Hot chocolate.'

I nod. 'I can do hot chocolate.'

'I'll need a straw,' she says, touching her bottom lip in explanation. 'Or else I might dribble all over your priceless shirt *from* Millets.'

'Hot chocolate with straw coming up.'

'I have to say, though,' she adds, 'it's nice to see you doing something for a lady for *nothing* for once. Instead of charging by the hour, I mean.'

'Don't worry, you'll be getting the bill. I'm not *that* much of a golden-hearted whore.'

She grimaces. 'Oh, and Dan . . . I don't suppose there's any, like, Vallies around the place, are there?'

'Valleys?'

'Valium. Sleepers or something.'

'Oh, right. Um – I think Kate takes the odd . . . I'll see what I can find.'

Halfway through making the hot chocolate, I poke my head round the door again.

'Do you want me to phone the police?'

She doesn't look up, sounds deeply miserable. 'I knew you'd be on at me about that sooner or later.'

'OK – so you don't *want* to talk to the police. But don't you think you should?'

Since my sister got jumped in Finsbury Park, I've been a real bore about this. Though being my sister, she came off far better than her attacker in the end. But she still gave me a lengthy lecture about the importance of reporting all such attacks to the police, which quite impressed me at the time.

'The bastard or bastards are still out there until you do,' I go on. 'Looking for someone else just like . . .'

'OK, *OK*,' she snaps, looking up. And again I see a look of unmistakable panic on her face. 'I know all the arguments, and yes, it's very selfish not to report it to the police in case there's a next time, and what about the sisterhood of woman and all that . . .' She sighs, fiddles furiously with the tattered corner of the sofa. At last she says, 'No, it's no good. I can't do it.'

I don't push it. She may change her mind.

She's curled up on the sofa when I enter with a tray bearing goodies. The video she's chosen: *The Secret Garden*. One of Kate's favourites.

I set down the tray and hand her the hot chocolate with a straw. We drink. After a while, I just start in on the story of my sister being jumped in Finsbury Park, and how much better she felt after reporting it. Beth looks at me almost with hatred.

'OK, ring them. I haven't got much to tell them anyhow.'

I go and phone.

'Vallies?' she says when I come back.

'To come. Some WPC is on her way first.'

'Stop being so fucking bossy,' she hisses. 'There's a difference between being *bossy* and being adult, and you don't seem to have spotted it yet.'

I stare at the TV.

'Now *if* I may have my *drugs . . . Please?*'

I go and get her the pills.

We sit watching the screen, tensed up and waiting. We're well into the film when the doorbell goes.

The WPC is called Lynne. Lynne Bunn. She says it's OK for me to stay if Beth doesn't mind. Beth doesn't mind.

'Are you her boyfriend?'

'No, just a friend.'

'Right.' Lynne doesn't bother to write this down. She asks Beth if she can tell her what happened.

'I suppose it was an attempted rape,' says Beth very quietly. 'They didn't steal anything. But they didn't rape me either. Got scared, I suppose, and ran off.'

'Right,' says Lynne. 'What more can you tell me?' She's good, calm, doesn't do any sympathy act, doesn't ask any leading questions. ('Are you *quite sure* none of them was black?' for instance.)

There is a long pause, and then Beth gives a description of one of them. There might have been three, she thinks, she can't even be sure of that. They must have jumped her from behind. She saw very little. But one was definitely white, and he had *A.L.I.E.N.* tattooed on one arm, and on the other he had *Britney Spears*. Beth laughs. The WPC doesn't.

I'm already picturing to myself getting on the bus one day and seeing the guy, sleeves rolled up, *Britney* and *A.L.I.E.N.* on either arm, and walking over to him and grabbing that skinny adolescent arm, one hand clamped around his wrist and one around his elbow, raising it and bringing it down hard and snapping it clean in half over the back of the seat in front.

'Do you know how old he was?'

'Quite young, obviously,' says Beth. 'Teenagers, I guess. Not very serious about it.'

Lynne makes no comment, writes away. Asks again where it happened, and what time. Beth is vague, soft-voiced, looks down. But at least she's going through with it.

'About – just after ten? And just outside.'

'What, right outside? In this street?'

'No, just off Goldhawk Road. I – don't even know which street. Sorry.'

'That's OK. Would it help you to look at an *A–Z*?'

I fetch one and Beth stares at it for a while. 'I'm sorry,' she says again, 'I really can't tell.'

'OK. What did they sound like?'

'Just – London, you know? Actually, now I think about it – the tattooed guy had a *lisp*.' Beth laughs again. 'Really weird. Yeah, he had a lisp, and short, cropped blond hair. He wasn't very big, but – wiry. It's funny how it comes back to you after a while.'

'But you don't remember the others?'

She shakes her head. 'One had on silver trainers. Um . . . no, I really can't.'

Lynne asks a few more formal questions: what Beth does for a living, home address and phone number. She thanks her for reporting the attack, says they'll be putting out a description tomorrow and maybe doing a street search tonight. Tells her to get in touch again if she needs to, or if she remembers any more details. Anything, no matter how trivial it seems. Beth says she doesn't think she will, but thanks her anyway. Then Lynne goes.

So she did it. I give her a hug, very gently, say 'Good effort,' thinking what a patronizing git I sound. But she's mellowed out now. Vallied. I go and make another drink and come back. Start up the video again.

She sips her drink delicately through the straw. I can feel her watching me as I roll a joint.

'So,' I say, not looking at her, concentrating on the task in hand. 'Why didn't you go to Miles? Or – I mean, I'm very flattered and all that, but – why didn't you go to a friend's?'

'Miles is away. Just for tonight. Isn't that typical? The very night I get mugged. Or raped, or whatever it was. And you were the nearest.'

'I'm surprised you knew my address.'

Again she says nothing. She's good at silences.

I light the joint, take a sharp drag and pass it to her. She puts it to her lips and flinches. 'I can't . . .' she says.

Her lips look more swollen than ever. I take the joint back, take a big mouthful of smoke and then lean towards her. She smiles and winces, stops smiling. Her lips are just apart. I touch my lips to hers, very gently, and breathe out. She inhales deeply. I sit back. She has her eyes closed, is holding her breath. Then she exhales. She slowly opens her eyes and smiles.

'Mm, she says. 'You give a good blowback.'

We smoke the rest of the joint, and then another, without exchanging a word, sweet smoke passing from my mouth to her mouth and vanishing in air. Meanwhile Mary and Dickon have started rescuing the secret garden from its lost and forgotten state.

Beth looks like she is nodding off already. I move to the other end of the sofa, lift her up very gently, avoid touching her bruised shoulder and squeeze in beside her. She murmurs wordlessly and rests her head down again in my lap. I stroke her head and she falls asleep. She dribbles a little, unable to close her wounded mouth. I graze the back of my forefinger over her chin as I would with a baby, wipe it away. She nestles down further. I watch the rest of the film. But mostly I watch over her.

My legs are numb by the time it's finished. I raise her head and slip out from under her and turn the TV off. I go out to the hall and prop my bedroom door open with a shoe and turn back the duvet. I come back and kneel before her and scoop my arms underneath her, one beneath her knees and one around under her shoulders, and shift her gently towards me so that her head turns and rests against my shoulder, and then I lift her and get to my feet. I walk with her into my bedroom and lay her down and pull the duvet back over her. I stroke her hair, bend down and kiss her cheek. I am turning to go when she stirs and murmurs. Says something. I wait. She murmurs again. 'Stay here. Stay with me.' One arm lies across the duvet towards me, palm upturned. Her eyes are closed.

I watch over her for a while and then go and wash and come back and undress and slide in beside her. She half turns and nuzzles against me. I lean over and kiss her bruised shoulder. I lie back again. She murmurs something. And then she is asleep, breathing slow and deep against me.

The whole interview thing was wrong, I have already decided. Now is not the time for an inquisition, but there was a lot of acting going on, a lot of not-Beth on display. A lot of supererogatory facts that came straight from Beth's imagination, not her experience. (*Britney Spears*, indeed. How many teenage muggers do *you* know with *Britney Spears* tattooed on their arm?) WPC Lynne Bunn didn't know her well enough to tell that, but I do. My dark suspicion is that Beth knew her attackers all too well. Who were they? Her dealers? Her suppliers? Some bastards like that.

What I do know is that if I ever bump into the scrawny little runts, with or without lisps and *Britney Spears* tattoos, their lives aren't going to be worth living.

*

And that is how I sleep with my best friend's girlfriend for the second time, in rather different circumstances from the first. Though I don't sleep much. I lie awake beside her, listening to the sound of her sleeping. It's a sweet sound. I don't sleep. I lie awake and think about hot chocolate and dreams of flying and blood and secret gardens and my best friend, Miles. And the girl sleeping beside me, about whom I know absolutely nothing.

16

I get up to go for a pee and it is dawn already. The fluorescent London night is giving way to grey. Odd, the way London nights are more colourful than the days. Nature reversed. The traffic is starting up again, the air thickening with engines and fumes and drills and diggers and that jittery buzz that tells you anything can happen.

When I come back I don't get into bed but stand beside her, lost in thought, my mind surging with mad impulses. I have always believed that there is only one thing to be done with mad impulses: give in to them.

And some of us round here need a holiday.

I dress swiftly and stride around the flat chucking stuff into a hold-all: toothbrush, toothpaste, shampoo, clothes, cigs, dope, half a bottle of gin . . . I knock on Kate's door and there's no answer, so I go on in and she's not back from last night. Some girls would throw a prolonged and wearisome wobbly if you snaffled their underwear without asking, but not my beloved landlady. Not if she knew the circumstances. I bundle up some bras and knickers and stuff them in with the dope and gin and toothpaste, and find a pair of Kate's oldest, most threadbare jeans. From my cupboard I grab two old shirts and a couple of jumpers and head down to the car and bundle everything in the boot.

I leave a note on the hall table.

Kate –

Gone away for a few days and stolen yr. knickers, – felt need to explore my feminine side etc., explain later

I'll phone you, lotsolove,
Dan

She's comatose, which makes it easier. Though I do wonder if I should really have put the whole half-dozen sleeping pills in her hot chocolate. But she looked like she needed it at the time.

I try to pull the duvet off her to lift her up, but she only clings to it all the more protectively, like it's a life-jacket. So in the end I roll her over and over in the duvet a few times – it's a bit like rolling an enormous joint – and then scoop up the whole bundle.

In the hall, the sight of her feet dangling nakedly from the end of the duvet roll reminds me that she also needs boots. I lay her down on the sofa and go back and borrow a pair of Kate's boots and thick socks. I also have to take a road atlas, and there is no way I can carry it all at once. So I stuff the socks under my belt and clench my teeth on the road atlas and then, with a chuckle, I unlace the boots and put them on her bare feet. She wriggles and murmurs at the touch of cold leather but still doesn't wake. Then I pick her up again and walk out of the flat, looping my foot around the front door and flicking it closed behind me.

I lay her in the passenger seat, pushed right back on its runners and reclined, and hop in beside her. She sleeps on. In her bra and knickers and the duvet wrapped around her and her shoulders peeking out bare and her sockless feet clad in scuffed old brown leather walking boots and her head back against the headrest, her eyes closed, her cut lip, her left eye still swollen, her hair tousled and tangled and frankly all over the place . . .

She looks quite beautiful.

I kiss her on the cheek and she murmurs and burrows down deeper into the duvet. I start the car and we drive off.

I stop at the end of the street and nip into Indajit's for some chocolate. Indajit is mercifully less ebullient than usual. In fact, he is positively downcast. The India vs. Pakistan test match is not going at all as he had hoped. 'These bloody bastard cheating Pakis,' he mutters, morosely working his way through a Hot'n'Spicy pot noodle.

But Indajit perks up when I spend nearly ten pounds on chocolate, and then perks up even more when he recalls a story in today's paper. 'It is really very funny,' he says, 'all these televisions made out of sponge.'

What the fuck is he talking about?

He whisks a copy of today's *Daily Mail* off the top of the pile. (Indajit is a great *Daily Mail* reader. 'They understand the importance of the family,' he says. 'They show respect. And they do not like the ladyboys either, and nor do I. I do not like the ladyboys at all. They are far too many.') Tucked away on page nine is a bizarre story, one of those short, foreign 'funnies', reporting that a huge number of small, foam-rubber televisions, each one stamped with an image of a cute, spaniel-like jackal, have started washing up in Gdansk Bay, thickly clotting the shoreline all the way to Kaliningrad. And the fucking Russians especially – inevitably – have started collecting them with a furious, materialistic zeal, desperate to get their fur-clad mitts on the very latest Western-style digital tellies. And *it's all my fault*. 'The original idea for the stunt came from a young PR whiz-kid at Orme, Odstock and Oliphant, called Daniel Swallow, who has since left the company.' Bastards. I don't know which is worse: being held solely responsible for the whole sorry fiasco or being labelled a 'PR whiz-kid' in a national newspaper. Perhaps I should write a strongly worded letter pointing out that I am now working as a prostitute.

'And again, you see,' puts in Indajit helpfully, leaning across the counter and pointing, 'a man with your name is involved! Daniel Swallow. Is that not extraordinary?'

'It is, Indajit, it really is.'

'And it says he has had to leave his job too. Are you not working today, my fren'? A Monday morning?'

I smile at him. '*In*-dajit. You're not suggesting . . .'

Indajit roars with laughter. 'Of course I am not suggesting, Daniel Swallow, my fren'.' He is suddenly serious again, brow furrowed. 'Now this "foam rubber". My daughter tells me that this is sponge, is this right?'

'Dead right.'

He beams with great pride. 'Oh, she is a clever one, my daughter. She is the very top of her class already, you know.' He leans close, conspiratorially. 'You know that the great Mrs Tatcher, the fren' of the small businessman like myself, *her* father ran a corner shop too?' He moves back. 'And you know, things change. Of course, my daughter will marry a good Sikh boy, no question. But who is to say that one day she will not also be *prime minister* of this great country?'

'I don't doubt it, Indajit. I don't doubt it at all.'

We drive down Goldhawk Road, sneak down Chiswick Lane and on to the Great West Road and head west and hit the flyover with that sudden surge of liberation as the car touches 60 m.p.h. and London thins out behind us. Beth sleeps on.

After a while on the motorway I pull into a service station for petrol. It's going to be a long drive. I also buy two cups of coffee.

When I start the car again, Beth finally stirs and wakes, peering blearily around her and out of the window. I can see she's trying to formulate a question but she's still too doped to get it out.

'We're on the M4,' I explain cheerfully. 'We're off to Cornwall. Oh, and up to 10,000 little foam-rubber televisions have started to wash up on the shores of Gdansk Bay.'

Initially, this is too much for her. I don't blame her. It's too much for anybody. She leans her head back against the headrest and then raises it again and asks, her voice thick and blurred, 'Why are we going to Cornwall?'

'You need a break. So do I, come to that.'

113

'But, but . . .' Suddenly she is really awake, wide awake.

'Have a coffee,' I say, gesturing at the styrofoam cups on the dashboard.

'But, but . . . I've got appointments, I've got . . . What day is it today?'

'Monday.'

'Shit. I've got a show tonight, and what about the result of my movie audition? My agent was really buzzy about it, there's no way I can . . . I mean, for fuck's sake.'

'There's no way you could anyway, darling.' My voice surprises me with a bitter edge. 'You really think a little touch of foundation is going to cover up *that*?'

She flips down the passenger sunshield and stares at the mirror. After a long while she flips it up again. Says nothing.

I lean down and retrieve my mobile from the door pocket and hand it to her. She takes it and starts to dial.

'Though I still don't see why we have to go to Cornwall. What's in Cornwall?'

'Tin mines,' I say. 'Pasties. Herrings. Stone circles. Piskies.'

She gets a connection and starts explaining to her booker or agent, Heidi or Trixie or whoever, that she was beaten up last night and there's no way she's in a fit state to work this week. She's in a taxi on her way to the hospital now for a quick check-up to make sure no bones are broken – hence the noise of traffic. (Smart girl. Good liar.) Heidi or Trixie clucks sympathetically and wishes her well and Beth stabs Call End.

'Sorted,' she says. 'What about you?'

I shake my head. 'One of the pleasures of the freelance lifestyle. Impulsive flights to Cornwall.' I ruminate for a while and then I say, 'I don't believe you, by the way.'

'Hunh?'

'All this "I didn't see very much" stuff. "They must have jumped me from behind." You're not that good a liar.' I give her a while to light a cigarette. The silence is stretched taut between us. Then I say, 'What really happened?'

'I told you. I don't know.'

Another pause. I stare at her. The interrogator's silent stare, radiating disbelief. Then the interrogator's other trick, the abrupt change of direction. 'Where do you get your drugs from? What were you *doing* in unfashionable Shepherd's Bush last night anyway?'

I think she breathes in sharply, but it's very quiet, almost inaudible. 'I don't know,' she stammers. 'I don't even remember . . .' Her stammering stops. Her head falls forward and for an instant she raises her arm as if to shield her eyes in the crook of her elbow. Then she drops her arm, sits up again, strokes back her hair. Her shoulders relax. She takes an extra long draw on her cigarette, turning slightly towards me and then away again. She sighs. 'OK. It was my dealer who did it. Stan. OK?'

'Why? Because you couldn't afford to pay him? Bollocks. I mean, *darling*, you're the new Amañuna girl.'

She says nothing, meets my sarcasm with her own scorn.

I don't feel any triumph, vindication, relief. I only feel that it is all getting far more complicated than I ever dreamed. We don't speak again for another hour.

Eventually she says, 'I need the loo.'

'I'll stop at the next service station.'

'No, I mean, like . . . now.'

She's demanding, this one. She's high maintenance, high insurance group, low reliability. And needs a new clutch every 3,000 miles.

I indicate at the next exit and turn off left and loop back over the motorway towards Malmesbury, then strike off down a tiny lane westward. After a while I pull in under some trees. I get out and open the boot and find her Kate's jeans and one of my shirts and jumpers. When I slam the boot down again I find her standing there, shivering in her underwear and Kate's walking boots. I hand her the clothes. She puts on the shirt and pulls the jumper over her head and, carrying the jeans over her arm, turns away and walks into the wood. The shirt and jumper come down just over her thighs. She looks grungy, sort of unkempt, gypsyish, unbearably sexy. She walks with grace, high-stepping over bracken and brambles like a fawn. She disappears among the trees.

When she comes back she has pulled on the jeans. They are too short for her, leaving a wide rib of ankle between hem and boot, making her look even more ragamuffin than ever. Ravished urchin. The jeans are also too baggy. She's holding them up on one side, the other hand holding her hair back over her forehead. She's shivering. Tousled orphan in her loop'd and window'd raggedness, begging for shelter at shelter's door.

She gets in and pulls the duvet over herself again. 'Freezing,' she mutters.

'We need to eat.'

'What, round here? What are we going to eat, haycorns?'

'There are such things as country pubs.'

'How do you know where they are?'

'I don't.' Suddenly I find this weirdly funny, the whole trip is weirdly funny. 'We don't know where we're going or what we're doing. We're completely fucking lost.'

And she laughs too. Laughing uncomfortably, feeling like escaped laboratory mice, we skid off down the lane in search of the Perfect Country Pub.

We find it, of course. It's that sort of day.

Wooden beams, flagstones, huge log fire and a malodorous, rheumatic, dribbling, 'I-love-everybody' retriever called Oscar with an insatiable appetite for barbecue-flavour crisps. There's a menu on the blackboard that takes five minutes to read, instead of your standard 'Cod & Chips OR Omelette & Chips'. There's Wadsworth's 6X. And there's a beaming old granny behind the bar, instead of your usual wall-eyed, lank-haired, rum-sodden East Ender temporarily hiding out in the country on account of a small unpaid debt he has with the boys back in Canning Town . . .

It's a pint of 6X and a venison pie for me. Beth has a glass of Chardonnay and lobster bisque: traditional West Country fare. After that we each have another drink and a ciggie. She settles her head back in the armchair.

'What are we doing here?' she drawls, her eyes closing.

'Having a break.'

'Break from what?'

'From . . . everything.'

She thinks about this for a while and then nods almost imperceptibly. She raises her head and opens her eyes and smiles at me. 'You're very sweet really,' she says. 'Rescuing me.'

'We both need fucking rescuing,' I growl. 'So – how often does he beat you up?'

She is unfazed, sets her wine glass down, doesn't miss a beat. 'Stan?' she smiles. 'Never, normally. It was my fault, I really . . .' She shakes her head. 'It wasn't even over money. I was beastly to him.' She sighs. 'You know nothing about it, OK? How can you know what goes on between us?'

She's a good liar. I know that already. But maybe it was Stan, after all.

She drains her wine. 'Come on, let's just enjoy it while we can. This mad break you've abducted me on.'

She insists on paying because I've paid for the petrol. We get back in the car and head west. After we've been going for a while, she says to me, 'Cornwall, yeah?'

'Yeah.'

'Have you ever seen *Straw Dogs*?'

'No, why?'

Long pause. Then she mutters, 'Just as well.'

We drive on.

A song comes on the radio, one of those sad, dreamy, restless songs, Everything But the Girl, *And I miss you . . . like the deserts miss the rain* . . . , and halfway through I realize she is crying. I reach out and take her hand and we drive like that for a while. Finally I say, 'Why are you crying?'

She doesn't answer straight away, and when she does it isn't an answer. She says, 'Sometimes I think I deserve it.'

'Don't be so monstrously fucking stupid,' I say gently.

Later the sun comes out, as we cross Bodmin Moor of all unlikely places. The clouds break apart and the sunlight falls on the road ahead of us and the everyday A30 is a silver river across the moor. We pass Dozmary Pool, granite outcrops, and further on the china clay pits and the odd deserted chimney stack of a deserted tin mine. Beth is fascinated by the strangeness of it all. She has never been to Cornwall before. The Maldives, Cuba, Vietnam, yes. But not Cornwall. 'It's like the moon,' she says.

And still the sun shines down on us, happy for us. Pathetic fallacy, I know, but as pathetic fallacies go it's a good one.

We stop in Marazion.

'Where are we going to stay?' she asks.

'I have plans. Trust me.'

This is a barefaced lie, obviously. I have no plans whatsoever. I never do. But as I saunter back towards the high street to inquire at the local hotel, I see a postcard in a newsagent's window.

Fisherman's cottage, simply furnished, sea views, sleeps two, available for holiday lets. Tel: . . .

I sprint back to the car, desperately trying to hold the number in my short-term memory, grab my mobile and phone.

All goes smoothly. A soft-spoken middle-aged Cornishwoman answers the phone. Margaret. Yes, the cottage is available, free for the next three weeks. One week is fine. It's £80 a week. No, no central heating, but there's an open fire in the sitting-room, and electric fire in the bedroom, and anyway the rooms are so small that once it heats up we'll be 'as warm as toast'. She gives me directions and I say we'll be there in an hour.

I pocket the phone, go round and open the passenger door. 'Come on then.'

'Where are we going?'

'Shopping.'

First stop, the chemist, where she buys assorted cover-up creams and lotions and puts them on back in the car. They work surprisingly well. We avoid the tatty supermarket: it's all tinned meatballs and three-month-old bananas. Instead we get stuff from individual shops, romantic shopping: crusty bread and cakes from the baker's, chicken, minced beef, bacon, sausages, milk and eggs from the butcher's, onions, carrots, sprouts, satsumas, kiwis, apples from the greengrocer's. In the off-licence we buy whisky and red wine: those seventies-style bottles of Chianti you don't see any more, swag-bellied, straw-corseted. And in the deli we get rolls, cheese, chocolate, teabags, olives and pasties.

'*Six* pasties?' queries Beth.

I narrow my eyes at her. 'Elizabeth Cassington, you're not one of these perpetually dieting models, are you? I mean, you're not going to devour one of these delicious sheep's-entrails-and-turnip pasties and then sick it all up again, are you?'

Beth cunningly evades the question. 'I'm not a *model*, I'm an *actor* who models part-time to pay my fucking bills.'

'Hm. OK.'

'All the same, I can't help noticing just how enormously FAT some of the women are around here.'

'Nonsense,' I say, circumspecting. 'I haven't seen any.'

'Oh, you're *blind*. In the deli, that woman in front of us had an arse the size of the Albert Hall.'

'Absolute twaddle. The Cornish are renowned for their

slim, elfin figures. I haven't seen a *really* fat person in all the time I've been here.'

'You will,' says Beth. 'You will.'

From the top road we turn right down a lane bordered by high hedges, the blackthorn in blossom, winding and narrow and getting steeper all the time. Finally we emerge almost at sea level and Beth gives a little gasp. It is truly beautiful. The sea glints silver in the pure spring sun. Under the cliffs and shadowed from the sun it is blue-black and deep. Backed into the towering cliffs, the village is compacted into tiny-windowed cottages and narrow lanes that can't take cars. There is a single-lane road between the sea-front cottages and the sea wall, and then there is a narrow strip of shingle beach and a cobbled slipway black and serpentine with weed and water. The smell is thick enough to eat. The small harbour has a man-made sea-break, a sturdy wall stretching out into the waves some fifty yards against the south-west. In the shelter of the wall are a handful of fishing boats, some with cabins, some open. The top of the wall, as wide as a house, is strewn with chains, ropes, plastic crates and lobster pots.

We drive through the village and on the other side we park in the small car park by the sea wall and walk back and find Captain's Cottage. And there is Margaret. And Margaret is quite enormously fat. Beth looks at me but I avoid her eye.

In fact, Margaret is so fat that she can't get up the stairs. She physically will not fit. This is not due only to Margaret's gargantuan dimensions. The stairs wind up spirally from the sitting-room. The sitting-room is about 10 by 8, straight in from the street. There is an open fire and an exhausted sofa. Through the back is the tiny kitchen. Upstairs is a bedroom under sloping eaves, with paint peeling off the window frames and a superb view of the harbour. Next door is a loo and a shower and basin crammed into a broom cupboard.

I go back downstairs, leaving Beth hunched at the bedroom window, staring out at the sea. I ask Margaret if she'll take a cheque and she nods. 'It's perfect,' I say.

She hands me the key, nods again. 'It *is* haunted,' she says. 'But not badly. It's just a child that sits on the stairs and sings sometimes.' And she waddles off.

I go back to the car and unload stuff. It takes two trips. When I'm in the kitchen unpacking, I yell up, 'Don't you worry, I'll do all the work!' There's no reply. When I take her up a cup of tea she's in bed, fully clothed, fast asleep. I bend down and kiss her on the cheek, and she mumbles something and turns over. I leave the tea by the bedside.

I've unpacked everything and laid the fire and lit it and brought in a whole stack of logs from outside the kitchen door and stacked them neatly beside the fireplace and poured myself a large whisky, and I'm just lying back on the sofa feeling triumphantly palaeolithic and hunter-gathererish, having sorted out my cave and made it comfortable and inviting for my woman, and I'm just staring cat-like into the fire watching the bridges falling, the castles rearing into flames and dissolving, the tigers burning bright . . .

The door at the bottom of the stairs creaks open and there she is, half asleep, smiling sheepishly.

We pass the whole evening lying together on the sofa, drinking whisky, hardly talking, doing nothing, staring into the fire, lulled into a trance by the heat and the unexpectedness of it all. Later she goes into the kitchen and makes us both bacon sandwiches.

It must be eleven when she stirs and sits up and mutters that it's time to go to bed. She perches on the edge of the sofa and then suddenly turns to me and says very seriously, 'You were right.' She tilts towards me and gives me a big hug.

I give her time upstairs before I follow, but after a while I hear her struggling downstairs again. I watch and wait, the corners of my mouth twitching unaccountably. There's a lot of scuffling and inventive cursing. I've never heard a duvet being so roundly abused before. At last the door creaks open and she reappears. It has taken her so long because she's pulled all the bedding off the bed, brought all four pillows down too.

'Damp up there,' she says. 'Sleep here.'

She's changed into a long T-shirt, and her face looks pink and scrubbed and flushed. If I kissed her now she would taste childishly of toothpaste. I watch her with amusement. She doesn't see me, she's half asleep already. She drops the blankets down on the carpet in front of the fire, then the pillows, wraps the duvet around herself and topples down.

'And anyway,' she adds, just before drifting off, 'this place is haunted. There's a child on the stairs.'

Oh, so she's psychic now, is she, as well as psychotic and fucked up? Well, thanks a fucking lot. What am *I* supposed to do about it?

I can tell you one thing, I'm not going back upstairs on my own. I watch over her for a while, drain my whisky and then go nervously over to the corner near the stairs door. Make sure the door is firmly shut. Turn the light out. The fire jumps and dances in the dark, like a pretty girl at a party, delighted to be the sole source of light and heat. I undress in the orange shadows and crawl under the duvet beside her. She's right, it is warm down here. Beautifully warm. She backs into me, making spoons, murmuring. I reach out my arm and put it round her, lean over her and kiss her goodnight, settle down again and withdraw my arm. She wriggles into me, murmurs again, says, '*Arm*.' So I put my arm back round her. 'Mm,' she says.

There's no fireguard. I wonder whether to damp down the fire. But it is so beautiful in the orange light, everything. What the hell. If we burn, we burn.

Fall asleep dreaming of a great house on fire and a ghostly child sitting on the stairs in the heart of the inferno, singing softly to itself, forgotten.

17

On Tuesday the sun goes in and it clouds over. The sea changes from blue to turquoise to green to grey. Beth is fascinated, kneeling on the narrow window-seat in the sitting-room giving me regular colour-match reports. During the turquoise stages she says, 'Now that would be just the right colour for a dress, don't you think?'

I come and lean over her and regard the sea. 'What, for you?'

'Of course for me. Me me me, always me.'

I examine the colour of her eyes, look back at the sea. 'Mm. Yes, you're right. Girl with the wild green eyes. *I will make you a dress of all the colours of the sea, green, as green as your eyes . . .*'

'What's that from?'

I shrug. 'Dunno. Just made it up. Perhaps I imbibed too much W. B.Yeats as a youth.'

'You sound like a real poove sometimes.'

'Thank you. You know, occasionally I think you might be really quite likeable, if you weren't such a vicious-tempered, sour-tongued bitch.'

'Sorry,' she says vaguely, not registering, not meaning it. She turns back to the window and then, one of her odd tangents: 'Do you think if we stayed here long enough, we'd forget all about London?'

I laugh. 'Maybe.' I add, 'London would certainly forget all about us.'

After a long while she says, 'That might be good.'

There's no rain yet but there's a buffeting wind blowing up, and the sea sprays white foam under it and bellies and then by afternoon is beginning to swell heavily. We're both kneeling side by side now on the narrow window-seat. Our knees are cold and numb but we're riveted, our chins cupped in our hands. We've started this running joke about how we are runaway children, runaway orphans, and it's making us ever more childlike. The adults are out looking for us, with their flaming torches and their fierce black dogs. But they'll never find us. Not here.

Round the headland comes a small red boat and a little later a blue one with a white cabin. 'Must expect a storm,' I say knowledgeably. (I'm completely wrong, as it turns out.) 'Where's the radio? We might be just in time for the shipping forecast. I *love* the shipping forecast.'

'Everyone does,' she says. 'That idea of being safe indoors, wind and rain, a force 7 rising force 8, severe gale force 9 in whatever it is, those evocative names, Lundy, Fastnet, Rockall, Finisterre . . . Although I always found Channel Light Vessel Automatic somewhat discordant.'

'You sound like a real poove sometimes,' I say.

After a few minutes we get it. There isn't that much wind, it says, but visibility is poor and worsening, and everything seems to be backing north-easterly. Meanwhile the fishermen are down there in the thickening gloom, tying up by the powerful arc lights on the boat roofs, in the shelter of the harbour wall. I decide to run down and ask if they can sell us a lobster.

'Do you know how to cook it?'

'Boil its balls off or something. They'll tell us.'

'Hang on, wait for me.'

It's cold outside, the wind is cruel, north-easterly indeed, and we've brought no coats. By the time we're out on the harbour wall we're both sniffling, concave-chested, arms coiled around our abdomens. The fisherman standing on the wall in his orange oilskin dungarees doesn't look up.

'Any chance of buying a lobster?'

He doesn't move, continues unknotting a tangle of rope.

Surprisingly deft, considering his fingers are so stubby and dry and cracked, like ancient clothes-pegs left out in the sun. 'Not in this weather,' he says softly.

'Really? What, you mean . . .'

'Not in a ground sea, and with a nor'easter.'

'What, the lobsters actually . . . *go away*? Or just don't eat?'

'Nothin' there,' he says. 'Too cold for 'em.'

'Wow, I never realized . . .'

'You might get sommin' in town. Or over at Newlyn, the fishmarket.'

'Right.'

Beth and I continue to sniffle and stare watery-eyed for a while and then Beth, with chattering teeth, stammers, 'We'll have to go into town anyhow.'

'Oh, why?'

'To buy some more fucking clothes.'

The fisherman glances sidelong and grins at this. 'Aye,' he says. 'It's a cold one.'

We drive into town, car heater blaring out hot air full blast.

We park in the high street and Beth takes my hand and leads me back over the road to a charity shop.

'You're kidding me.'

'I'm bloody not,' she says. 'If I'm here for a week I at least want to escape without frostbite.'

'Yes, but *here*. I mean, I go to charity shops all the time, but that's in London. Here it'll be all Terylene slacks and nylon shirts.'

'Don't care. "Better Terylene slacks than no trousers at all," as my old granny used to say to me.'

'Did she really?'

'And did you know that there's no such word as "gullible" in the dictionary?' Beth laughs at me. I mean, really guffaws. 'God, you're stupid sometimes,' she says.

'Quite often, actually.'

*

125

We try on half the shop.

Beth does a voice-over as we twirl around in front of the mirror. 'This season's fashionably dressed Cornish oyster-girl,' she simpers, 'is wearing woolly socks, combat trousers, two knackered acrylic jumpers, a cotton shirt and a tartan donkey jacket. Her fella sports shapeless corduroys, a kind of sea-captain's navy-blue wool felt cap, a chunky off-white, tea-stained polo neck and navy-blue donkey jacket.'

I check my image in the mirror. It certainly feels warm.

'You look quite good actually,' says Beth. 'Almost *rugged*. Almost *manly*.'

'*Almost*?'

'Like whatshisname in *The Guns of Navarone*. Or *In Which We Serve*.'

'John Mills? Kenneth More? *Cool*.'

The old dear behind the counter, who has been watching us suspiciously at first, then exasperatedly, is at last pinkly pleased and beaming when we finally shell out a massive £18, for which we get four whole bags of stuff.

And then we find a second-hand bookshop and buy things like *Frenchman's Creek* and *The Little Princess* and *The Princess and Curdie* and *The Once and Future King*.

That evening I concoct a kind of chicken casserole that is rather good though I say so myself, and we get through two bottles of red wine and do a lot of lying supine in front of the log fire with the radio on quietly so we don't actually have to listen to it. She reads me *The Princess and Curdie*. I check her injuries, make her lift her arm up and it seems OK. Then I push up the sleeve of her jumper and turn her arm over. She doesn't react. I look closer then look up. Her eyes are blank in the firelight.

After a pause I say, 'These needle marks. Some of them are quite fresh, aren't they? These red ones.'

She says nothing, pulls her arm away from me. 'Leave me

alone.' She scoops her hair back over her ears and looks at me. 'I cope. I work. I'm reliable.' Reaches for another cigarette.

Yeah, right.

'These bad things that you do, which you sometimes feel you *deserve* to be beaten up for . . .' I pause, momentarily unable to go on. *That fucking bastard. 'Stan'. I'll kill him, I truly will. Break his fucking nose, see how he likes it. How can he? I can picture him already, lank-haired, weasel-faced, impacted eyes and receding teeth . . .*

Take a deep breath. I can feel her looking at me slightly curiously as I sit there, mouth cramped against my bunched fist. Another breath, then I say, 'These things. How bad?'

She tells me. She and her friends, her acquaintances . . . OK, so she has a wild past. I might have guessed that anyway, you can tell just from the look in her eyes. And quite a wild present, too, by the sound of it.

'I'm a fuck sight better than I was,' she says. 'And no, they're not fresh marks; not *that* fresh. I'm a good girl now, compared to how I was.'

'What's it like? Doing hard drugs, I mean. Injecting.'

A lot of people take drugs not because they like to take drugs but because they like boasting to their friends the next day, 'Hey, guess what *I* did last night?' It's supposed to be some sign of having been initiated into higher mysteries than ordinary mortals can dream of; like those worshippers of Mithras who wore the sign of the raven on their foreheads. But I don't think that's Beth's way.

She accuses me, mildly enough, of being prurient. I shrug. 'I suppose so. Curious, prurient, whatever. The fascination of the abomination.'

She smiles her odd smile and tells me. She talks like she's dreaming, or like Patti Smith in performance, free form, stream of unconsciousness.

'The man comes to your door, his rusting white Ford Granada parked up slewed outside your house, a lone Ford in a street of Porsches and Mercs and 4x4s, his hair lank and unwashed, grin-

crumpled but all very civilized, home delivery service, you buzz
him in on the intercom, you shut the door behind him, you hand
him the cash, one hundred and twenty in twenties, he counts them
out, licking his fingertips, twenty, forty, sixty . . . he hands you the
bag, a little plastic bag, a bank-bag for 50p coins, but now light, so
light, as light as a bird, as a bird's feather, pure white, good stuff he
says, he hasn't cut it he says, 50 per cent he says, 60, and with his
crumpled grin he goes, and trying not to hum, trying to but ah
humming, you go into the kitchen and push up your sleeve and
with a dressing-gown belt you tie up and knot off and you're lighting a candle, it'll be something to look at, you'll look at it for hours
quite happily, and shaking a little into a teaspoon of water, a tiny
crystal waterfall falling a crystalfall and dissolving quite away and
far away in the warming water and cooking up nicely and giving
the teaspoon a little shake, a little thrill across the surface of the
water, humming all the time, and the powder is gone far gone and
you're far gone foregone forsworn and you're flexing your fingers
and groping for the needle there by the sink where you left it after
cleaning it carefully because you're so health conscious, you smile
with cold water-bleach-cold water and then you're taking it up into
the chamber and you're sitting back in the kitchen chair you meant
to go into the sitting-room and get comfortable on the sofa but now
you just can't wait just can't be bothered and you find a nice
plump vein and pop the needle gently in you never did like injec-
tions and watch the blood cloud the chamber and you think that's
good now that's really rather good so my blood's still under pres-
sure my heart's still pumping I'm still alive well I suppose that's a
good sign and then down goes the plunger and easy does it and in
seconds you're there you're not there any more or ever again
you're nowhere you're up and away amid the snowy mountains
and there's nothing under your feet or over your head but fluffy
white clouds and you feel like nothing on earth you remember
nothing not the schooldays nor the bad days nor any bad days
before or since nor any bad days of your life oh those empty
Sunday afternoons and anything really anything anywhere anywhere but ah here because that's all very far away now and in

128

another country and all that happened then happened to another
girl not you not you because now your head falls and you slump in
that kitchen chair and your head falls hard on the table and yes it
is good stuff pure stuff and happiness flows in your veins as happy
as nothing your blood is the colour of happiness fluffy and white
and you see a slow smile somewhere and this hit will last and last
and you wonder whether to take another but no need no need at all
now nothing at all this is fine for now this is lovely everything is
fine for now and far away now everything is just perfect . . .'

She stirs, smiles, comes back to earth – as much as she ever does. After a long pause, the reverential pause after the revelation of some profound religious truth or the enactment of some sacred ceremony, she drawls, 'Satisfied now?'

'Not sure,' I say. 'What else?'

'We were into some pretty weird things.' She smiles. 'Sex, drugs and rock'n'roll – you name it.'

Lots of sex, too, it seems. And I thought group sex was just something middle-aged marrieds got up to, out of sheer boredom.

She used to go to these clubs: nightclubs, of a kind. A year or two ago, but not any more. It was her Bad Patch. After spending the daylight hours smacked out of her mind, Beth would actually feel like going out. In her bedroom she'd dress in black. Beth likes black. Black lacy underwear, black suede boots and a long black dress that clings and shimmies in the candlelight. Finally she'd fix a black velvet choker around her neck, sit at her dresser and smile at her reflection in the spellbound mirror. She'd smile at her reflection. The reflection would not smile back. 'I remember it so well,' she says. 'Instead it would close its eyes, expressionless, like a meditating Buddha.'

She'd take a line or two of coke – I picture her lowering her head delicately, like a horse drinking from a stream. She looks up again, sniffs, checks her nose. Smiles again.

She'd go to fetish night. Not hard, not actually *hardcore*, that's for pot-bellied middle-aged accountants in leather posing pouches. No, this was young beautiful people playing at games. She liked that idea. Sometimes she'd go with Lesbo Livvie, sometimes a male friend, sometimes alone. She wouldn't be wearing as much leather and rubber as some people there, but I can't imagine that mattered too much since Beth would look right for a fetish night even if she were dressed like a schoolteacher. She used to head straight for the washrooms and once she found the top of the cistern had been treated, studded with marbles, just to stop people like her, but nothing stops people like her, so she thought *fuck it* and brazenly chopped out a line beside the washbasins and sniffed it up.

And later she remembers once being back in the washrooms, the ladies' or maybe the men's, she can't remember, with two guys, or was it a guy and a girl? – she can't even remember that – and she was pressed up against the wall of the cubicle with her face crushed and her eyes closed and her dress half torn off and the two behind her are snuffling and grunting like animals and yet she'd enjoy it she'd enjoy it *so much* and she didn't care either way really, abused like this and worthless as she was, because she wasn't there she was many miles and years away falling or flying through the star-spangled night sky with the cool wind in her face so pure and the starlight glittering so many years away in her hair and far below her is the storybook world in the blue moonlight of little woods and fields and mazy country lanes and plump cottages and among the cottages and in their gardens are happy families of husbands and wives and playing children running about and laughing playing in the blue moonlight . . .

But all this was a long time ago when Beth was a lot younger and going through her Bad Patch. She doesn't do stuff like that any more. She's better now. Beth's all grown up now. No, indeed. She stays in at night quite happily by herself when Miles is away, and watches television, a nice old film, and makes herself a cup of hot chocolate and has an early night. Gets to bed by eleven.

Of course she does.

'Oh, and the occult. Mind you, with *my* parents . . .'

On top of it all, she has occultist parents. There are darker hints, but I don't think she means anything ordinary, anything *suburban*, like her father raping her on the carpet in the front room while wearing a Batman cape. It was weirder, more bohemian, more intellectual, than that, her upbringing. An unstable legacy. A big, decrepit country house, lots of brothers and sisters, parents' lovers coming and going all the time amid clouds of hash and Tantric sex. Oh, and she's psychic. Hence her seeing the ghost child sitting on the stairs. But maybe she had just caught a glimpse of herself in the mirror. That's how I think of her already. A ghost child sitting on the darkened stairs, alone, haunting us. Haunting both of us.

She is a proper actress too, though. I hadn't quite realized. She's been the Duchess of Malfi in Dublin and Cecily Cardew at the Manchester Exchange. But of course there have been long gaps in between, when she's modelled.

'And are you in love with Miles?'

She looks taken aback. 'I . . . yes, of course I am.'

'So when are you and him getting shackled, then?'

'Oh, one day, I expect. Not yet, though.' She remains serene, immune. 'You're just a hopeless romantic,' she says.

'Guess so.' I lean forward, oddly urgent. 'Romantic love's no more dead than Jesus Christ,' I tell her. 'It's all a matter of what you believe.'

She just smiles. 'For me, I reckon it's time to get pragmatic. Things would be OK if I behaved myself and didn't keep fucking other people.'

So it's as simple as that, is it? I wonder. 'And that time – I hope you don't mind me asking this, but I think I have the right – that time you summoned me to that hotel bedroom, in my capacity as *prostitute* – was that . . . I mean, what was that?'

131

'A moment of madness.' She giggles. Actually *giggles*. 'I am completely mad, you know that. Not to be trusted at all. But it wasn't an amazing coincidence, of course. I was looking for an escort anyway on my laptop, not necessarily a fuck, either, honestly, just an escort for the night, I wanted to go dancing and Miles was busy, and suddenly I came across *you*: your funny little face staring out at me from my screen. I thought it was so hilarious, I couldn't resist it.' She studies my expression and then reaches out and takes my hand. 'I'm sorry. But you must admit it was quite a good joke.'

Brilliant.

But it doesn't sound right. She's not *that* good a liar.

And another thing I have to worry about: I am in a very serious pickle indeed, for not only am I an incorrigible slut myself, but *so is the woman I think I love.*

'And, you know,' she resumes, slightly hesitant, 'not all love is the romantic kind.'

'The kind you're supposed to grow out of,' I say sarcastically. 'The kind that doesn't last.' (The kind that dies young, as passionate Veronese lovers do. The kind that burns up like a flame without fuel, the kind that hates old age and quietness and contentment, the kind that makes you feel alive like nothing else, that makes you long for the whole world and to live for ever but lasts no longer than a day, the kind that destroys young lovers in a kiss of fire, though sometimes making them immortal, that leaves you restlessly aching with hunger for things you cannot name. The poets' and lovers' philosophy that can wonder though never understand and love though never possess. That kind. Yeah, I know it.)

18

On Wednesday we go for a long walk along the headland, our whole bodies oxygenated and high on Atlantic air, teetering giggling on the brink of beetling cliffs to watch the white surge bellowing below, clutching each other's arms, red-cheeked.

I buy some fresh mackerel straight off the beach from a kid who can't be more than nine. Evidently they start work young in these remoter parts. We also buy some postcards, to keep, not to send, and we find a phone box tucked away round the side of the pub. (Neither of our mobiles works down here.) We both phone home to pick up answerphone messages. I've got nothing important, but I leave a message in turn for Kate, saying I'm having an impromptu week in Cornwall with an old friend, and I ring my parents and get my mother and tell her the same thing. But when Beth comes back from the phone box, to find me sitting on the sea wall, she's got big news. She's trying unsuccessfully to stifle a smile.

'Well?'

'Got it.'

'Got what?'

'My first big movie role. I mean, the movie's big, not my role. Still, it's a start.'

I feel a sick heave inside me. It's not jealousy, or not only that. It's – it's her, out in LA: the limos, the swimming-pools, her a collagen movie star who once played the Duchess of Malfi to rave reviews (*Cover her face. Mine eyes dazzle. She died young*), now fucking around, losing herself, a fat coil of coke spilling from her handbag, what's that line in *Story of my Life*? 'Some kind of white stuff in every orifice.' And inside, still the same little ghost-girl singing softly to herself on the darkened stairs.

'Well, don't look too pleased.'

'I'm not . . . Is it in the States?'

'No, filming in London. Starts soon, too. Next month.' She ruffles my hair. 'Oh, *darling*, I do believe that you're jealous.'

False smile. 'Hardly. And *don't* call me "darling". You're not some fucking movie star, not yet.'

She freezes, stares at me, then yells, 'Well, fuck you!' and stalks off down to the beach.

Fuck.

I light a cigarette, badly. Exhale at the seagulls. Get up, follow her.

We walk side by side, saying nothing, crunching over bladderwrack and tidewrack and seaspawn and all that Stephen Dedalus stuff. Finally I try to break the silence, and impress her, by quoting it. 'Like Stephen Dedalus on Sandymount Strand,' I say, '"seaspawn and seawrack, the nearing tide, that rusty boot". Then he starts off about Thomas Aquinas and I lose him completely.'

'Aristotle.'

'Hunh?'

'He goes on about Aristotle at that point, not Aquinas. What you can see and all that.'

'You see!' I turn and grab her shoulders and spin her round to face me, triumphantly vindicated. 'You see!'

'See *what*?' she says, laughing despite herself at my sudden vehemence.

'You can correct me about what's going in *Ulysses*, for God's sake. What are you doing in some shlocky movie?'

'Oh, don't start again.' She turns away. 'Anyway, how do you know it's shlocky?'

'Well, isn't it?'

'Swallow,' she says, flicking back her hair from her face, glaring at me straight between the eyes. 'You're such a fucking . . . *hypocritical* . . . *ignorant* . . . *pseudo-intellectual* . . . *snob*.'

Wednesday evening, we've hardly said a word to each other since, the atmosphere simmering gently. An excellent holiday. She cooks. I drink. She brings in two steaming platefuls of shepherd's pie, we eat with plates perched on our laps.

After only a couple of mouthfuls, she says, 'OK. Here's the plot: a multi-millionaire playboy, idle, good-for-nothing son of a Premier League business tycoon, gets married to his childhood sweetheart in a lavish winter Wedding of the Century – the idea's to film in the rose garden in Regent's Park, with fake snow and stuff. Only during the wedding there's an attempted kidnap by a gang of vicious Latin American mobsters, but they bungle it and in the ensuing bloodbath the beautiful young bride of only a few minutes –' she flattens her palm against her chest – '*moi*, is gunned down in a hail of bullets. I mean, totally *wasted. Peckinpahed.* And in a trice, the idle, good-for-nothing multi-millionaire playboy is transformed into a remorseless killing machine, hellbent on vengeance. The rest of the movie consists of him tracking down the *bandidos* one by one and dispatching them straight to spic hell, with many a merry quip on his lips and in increasingly outlandish ways, until the very last, the mustachioed, black-silk-shirted head honcho himself, is spectacularly and messily dismembered, chained between two eighteen-wheelers driving in opposite directions. Slowly.' She pauses for breath, takes another mouthful of shepherd's pie, ruminates, swallows, lays her fork down, hooks her long hair back behind her right ear and looks at me in perfect innocence, head quizzically tilted. 'Now tell me, what on earth is so "shlocky" about that?'

God, I love her.

Falling asleep in each other's arms that night, she says, apropos of nothing, 'Miles has porn on his laptop.'

I almost laugh out loud. I don't know whether she's really telling me this Great Secret or talking in her sleep.

'Beth,' I say – it's odd using her name, oddly thrilling – '*all* blokes have porn on their laptop. Even Cliff Richard has porn on his laptop.'

'Not that sort,' she says.

'What sort?'

'Not that sort.'

There is silence while I let this sink in, bemused, amused. And then we're both asleep.

On Thursday there's a foul north-east wind blowing again and we stay in a lot. She reads me more of *The Princess and Curdie*, and I start on *The Once and Future King* as well. We eat a lot of chocolate biscuits and drink a lot of tea and do a lot of staring out of the window at the gun-grey sea. It looks really mean today.

We go for a drive in the afternoon and in the evening she cooks chili con carne and we drink Chilean Merlot. We sleep in front of the fire again, and when I kiss her goodnight I add, 'I do love you.' Slips out quite easily, unembarrassed. Even weirder, she looks back at me, straight in the eye, and says, 'I love you too.'

It shouldn't be that easy, surely.

On Friday the weather has changed completely: typical Cornwall. That dry, flesh-freezing, carnivorous north-easter has wheeled round to the normal south-west again, and it's mild and damp and drizzly. Just the weather for a day on the moor.

We tramp for miles along black peaty paths and over rough, ankle-twisting moorland grass and sedge. See a pair of buzzards overhead, and a little further on a dead lamb in a ditch, half eaten. Rest for a while leaning against a dry-stone wall under a crabbed old hawthorn, scuffing at the lichen with outstretched palms, and then resume. Finally find the Longstone I'd been looking for.

'It's Bronze Age,' I explain to a distinctly underwhelmed Beth. 'Around 3,000 years old.'

'Sort of thing my parents would insist on dancing round,' she says, gazing at it.

'What, naked, by moonlight, anticlockwise?'

She regards me scornfully. Then she takes my arm and begins to lead me round, clockwise. '*With* the sun,' she says. 'They're not Satanists. Not quite.'

We circle the Longstone three times and then she tells me to make a wish. It isn't difficult to know what to wish for.

'And you?' I ask.

'Yes,' she nods. Looks hard at me. 'It's no good making a wish for something that's totally impossible, though. You know?'

'What's impossible?'

She shakes her head. 'You useless romantics.'

In the evening we go down to the pub and drink pints and presumably look so scruffy and unLondon that the locals actually talk to us. Want to know what on earth we are doing down here at this time of year. Before I have time to answer, Beth has blurted out, 'We're on honeymoon.' She slips her left hand behind my back to hide her naked ring-finger. Simpers, 'Married just last week.'

They all think that's nice, even buy us a drink. We clink glasses and I lean forward and kiss her on the lips. She can't exactly pull away, so I make it a long one. Sit back. 'My darling wifey,' I murmur, gazing sottishly into her eyes.

'Don't push your fucking luck,' she murmurs back, smiling sweetly. 'And don't ever, *ever*, call me *wifey*. Or *honeybun*, or *my little cuddly bunny rabbit*. Not if you don't want me to vomit on you.'

'OK,' I say. 'My wife. Missis. My beloved.'

'Beloved.' She nods. 'That's all right.'

*

We return home arm in arm, zigzagging up the main street, not from drunkenness but from the buffeting wind that is lashing spray off the surface of the sea and flinging it over the harbour wall against our stung cheeks.

We get inside and slam the door shut behind us and grope for the light switch and both our hands find it simultaneously. Look at each other, look away, embarrassed.

The fire is still smouldering, so I pile it up with more logs and kneel in front of it and blow it back to life again. When I stand up Beth is immediately behind me. Eye contact again. We both lean towards each other: a mutual kiss. Only this time neither of us pulls away. She reaches out and puts her arms around my waist as I put my hands round her neck and pull her closer, and then slide my hands down underneath her coat and drag it down off her shoulders. At some indiscernible moment there is an electrical surge and we both feel it and know it and then we are tearing each other's clothes off while still held together in an unbreakable kiss. It is almost like child's play, rough-house, tumbling, breathless. Except that we don't laugh. We know it is deadly serious.

Afterwards we open a bottle of wine and smoke a cigarette – share one, for some reason – and lie under the duvet on the sofa with our hot limbs pleached and plaited and we say very little. We don't even smile that much at each other. It has all gone far too far too fast. And when we make love again, I lean back and look at her and she clasps her fingers through my hair with her eyes tight shut and she says, 'This isn't sex.'

And she's right. It's a lot more than sex, a lot better. And a lot worse.

After that, the last two days, everything is different. We talk a lot, but it's not the same, and in between talking we do a lot of staring at each other, inarticulate, almost shy. I think we

138

both know that there just aren't the words for it. But in the evening again she strokes my hair and looks at me, so sadly, saying, 'What are we going to do?'

On Sunday we drive back to London and it feels more like the end than the beginning. She stays with me that night.

On Monday I get up late, sleepy and dazed and knowing that something is wrong, and I find a note on the kitchen table.

She's gone back – lazily – to Miles.

She's sorry but she can't live without him, she says. She's gone back to him, and with a lot of explaining to do. She doesn't know what the future holds, she really doesn't. Nothing is clear. She says thank you for the week away, she needed it. But it was only meant to last a week. And she needs Miles in a way she can't articulate. He makes her feel safe. That's what her note says: he makes her feel safe. 'I don't expect you to understand,' she says, and no, she's too fucking right, I do not understand.

She signs off: *I love you, Daniel Swallow.*

I love you too, Elizabeth Cassington.

You mad bitch.

You coward.

19

How can I live without her?

I cannot live without her.

I try to ring Beth. She sounds distant, quiet, says we need a cooling-off period. I shouldn't ring her for a while. Yes, she's OK, and Miles is delighted to have her back. No, he doesn't know that she was away with me, he thinks she was just away working and the work took longer than she expected. In Edinburgh, for some reason. And anyway her filming for the movie starts soon, and she's really looking forward to it all, and she's just going to concentrate on that for the time being and try to forget about everything else.

'I'm sorry,' she says. 'But it was never going to work.'

I phone Caroline at Grosvenor and go back to work. I might as well.

Over the next two weeks I escort six ladies for evenings out and fuck three of them. It's a reasonable ratio.

And the work is easy now. I'm so listless and numb, my smiles and compliments mean nothing to me, I go through the motions, I'm efficient and polite and praised more than ever for my soulless prowess in the sack. Don't they know they're sleeping with a zombie? Mummified from the inside out. Perhaps they prefer me like that, the way some men prefer inflatable dolls.

You think such grief might ennoble you and you're so wrong. All it does is cut you off from others and make you a bore at parties, brings out your spots, leaves you sighing and sleepless and hating yourself almost as much as the person you've loved and lost. You hate them most of all – which is only fair. But you're not exactly enamoured of your own reflection in the mirror either, pasty and harrowed and stoop-shouldered and reeking of failure and failed hope. Does this add up to wisdom? Wisdom is just hope abandoned.

When I'm not servicing businesswomen in hotel bedrooms, I try to be sociable. It's a useful veneer that works sometimes. And Kate is good to talk to, as well. I tell her everything, and she listens, doesn't judge, doesn't sympathize *too* much, and offers sound and practical advice at the end of it all. The only trouble is, her advice consists of – oh, the exquisite irony of it all! – 'You should just go out and get laid as soon as possible. Even someone you don't particularly like.'

Now would I do such a shallow and heartless thing?

Men aren't very in touch with their own emotions, are they? We know that already (don't we, boys?) because superior, smug-voiced, mothering, smothering *women* are always reminding us of the fact.

OK, so I haven't a clue how I really feel. But I do know that all is not quite right. For instance, in the supermarket the other day I was unable to buy anything. Physically unable. The laden shelves hovered and hummed around me, and people pushed past me or rammed their trolleys into my ankles, and I stood there in mid-aisle, holding my breath, seeing stars, a shopping list in my jacket pocket, furiously fingering it into soft warm shreds.

And I do know that the other day, about to cross Cromwell Road, I looked up and registered an oncoming bus that would certainly mow me down if I stepped out just at that moment. And then I stepped out just at that moment. (I only avoided being mown down because a guy behind me grabbed me and pulled me back.) This wasn't a suicide attempt, believe me. It was only extreme absent-mindedness.

My mind wasn't on the job of practical strategy and survival, it was elsewhere. And I know where.

And I do know that my most recent nightmare – a typical example from my current back catalogue – involved Beth holding my hand, tenderly, gazing into my eyes, saying, 'Now this is going to hurt,' while pushing a kitchen knife slowly, slowly, into my passive crimson palm.

It's time to call in a favour from Clive. I don't want Miles to find out about Beth and me. Well, I do and I don't. But if she really wants to stay with him, then I suppose I should make sure he doesn't find out about us.

God, I must be a saint.

So Beth has been in Edinburgh. And I've just been around town.

'Hello?' says an icy voice.

'Ah, hello, hi, Emma. Um . . . is Clive there?'

'Hello, Daniel. How are you?'

'Oh, fine thanks, fine. Um, and you?'

'Very well, thank you.'

'Good, good. Excellent. Um . . . is Clive there?'

A horrible pause, the kind of pause only ever heard during a conversation with Emma, or else in the Antarctic between one blizzard and the next. Then she says, 'Just a moment.' From the sound of clean white plastic on polished oak hall table, I can tell just how *neatly*, how *primly* and *proprietorially* Emma has set down the receiver.

There is a long wait.

I strain to hear the exchange, and occasionally think I catch the icy whispers of Emma's voice, like a cat scratching at a frozen windowpane. Then Clive comes to the phone.

'How was your weekend?'

'Oh, fine, quiet and stuff. Em and I went out for a meal in town on Saturday.'

'She paid, I presume?'

'What?'

'Just my little joke.'

'Well, yes, she did actually.'

I'm a bit aghast at this. That horrible moment when your fixed image of someone is rudely shoved aside, and the real person steps up from behind to tell you what a deluded, prejudiced and *lazy* person you are. 'So – Saturday night, you and Emma were out?'

'Er – ye-es.'

'Clive. You wouldn't do me a favour, would you?'

'What?'

I wish Clive wouldn't say *what?* in quite that wary tone of voice, it'll only alert Emma's acute sensitivity to conversational dramatic tension. I can see her now, in the sitting-room beyond the hall, leafing through the latest copy of *Harpers* that lies open on her lap, her legs elegantly crossed, wondering if her cream tights are *quite* right with this skirt. And her ears will perk up and take on a life of their own, growing as long and luxuriantly pliant as slivers of Parma ham. And they'll snake their way down the back of the sofa and across the polished oak floor and insinuate themselves around the door into the corner of the hall, the better to hear what Clive is saying to that idiot friend of his Daniel. Not that Emma is in any way given to spying on Clive. Of course not. She is entirely happy that he should remain as independent of her as she is of him: two responsible adults in a mutually supportive, trusting relationship. Intrusiveness into the other's most private thoughts would be intolerable: a *policing* and *control* of the other's individuality. Oh no, Emma has no desire to do anything like that. But at the same time – well, it is more her concern for Clive, her love for him, that leads her to feel concerned for him, and her ears to extend in this egregious fashion when he is on the phone. Clive is so easily led, so naïve, yes, that's it, so *naïve*, he needs looking after, she almost feels that that is what she is doing, looking after him, protecting him, because of people like

Daniel, with whom Clive is so inexplicably still friends. OK, so they go back a long way, she knows that. They are old schoolfriends, but that doesn't explain to her for one moment what Clive sees in him. And he, Daniel, encourages Clive to be so *silly*, and if there is one thing that Emma can't bear it is *silliness*. Daniel is always pulling some silly face or making some silly joke, as if everything in life is ridiculous and doesn't really matter. Well, what *does* matter then? He encourages Clive to be silly, and, she strongly suspects, to waste his money, drinking and putting pound coins into those silly fruit machines that everyone knows only take your money and never give it back. What is the *point*? It is just *silly*.

But I have to get on and ask Clive for a wee favour.

'What sort of favour?' asks Clive.

'A very small one, *tiny*. A favourette. In fact, it's quite possible that you won't have to do anything at all. It's just – in case.'

'Just in case of what?'

'In case – you should happen to see Miles, and he should happen to ask what I've been up to lately.'

'What have you been up to lately?'

Emma's ears will really be sensing elements of high drama, and even male duplicity and desperation, in the developing conversation now, positively *wriggling* with moral indignation, slapping softly against the wainscoting by the sitting-room door.

'Ssssh,' I say. 'Keep your voice down.'

'What?' hisses Clive. 'What then?'

'Just in case Miles asks, can you just kind of make a joke of it and say we've been out a couple of times this week, and got rather pissed and you can't really remember?'

'Oh, God,' says Clive. 'And what if he asks Emma?'

'He won't,' I say, with more confidence than I feel. 'Don't worry.'

'And what *have* you been doing?'

'I've been with Beth. All week. In Cornwall.'

'Cornwall? Shagging?'

'Once or twice. It wasn't really that, though. I'm in love.'

'You arsehole. OK, I'll give you cover.'

'What about you and the Indian babe?'

'Don't ask.'

The Honourable Clive Spooner.

And then he has to face Emma. Something like this, I imagine:

'What did he want?' she asks, her ears retracting to their original dimensions only in the nick of time.

'Just a chat,' says Clive.

'Oh. I thought he sounded like he wanted something more.'

'What sort of thing?'

'I don't know, you're the one who talked to him. I thought I heard you say something about doing a favour.'

'Oh, that,' says Clive.

'Well?'

'Well, yes, a little favour he did ask for.' (Funny, thinks Clive, how one's syntax goes completely to pot under interrogation from Emma.)

'Which was?'

'Oh, nothing really. Just a helping hand, you know.'

'And why were you being so abusive?'

'*Abusive?*'

'Calling him rude names. I'm not repeating them.'

'Oh, that. Well we always call each other "arsehole" and . . .'

'Clive.'

'Well, you know. "Rude names".'

'Sounded serious to me.'

'Not really.'

'Not *really*?'

'Well, you know.'

'Sounded to me like he'd done something really stupid and was asking you to cover up for him.'

Clive stands helplessly by the fireplace, his arms hanging by his sides. She is unstoppable. She is wasted in her present job. She should be working for MI5, or the CID at least.

'Has he done something really stupid?'

'Um. Sort of.'

'And he wants you to tell lies to cover up, is that it? Is that the favour he is asking for?'

'Um. Sort of.'

'Well, Clive, I think it's outrageous.' She lays the copy of *Harpers* down by her side and folds her hands. 'It's absolutely outrageous that he should expect *you* to lie . . .'

'He doesn't *expect* it, he just asked.'

'*If* you will let me finish . . . that he should expect you to lie, just because he is a *two-faced, untrustworthy, feckless* . . . whatsit who as soon as he is left alone for *one day* is off chasing other women.'

'Only one other woman, actually. He says he's in love.'

'Don't be facetious, you know perfectly well what I mean. Well, Clive, it's up to you, but if you really think you can live with yourself lying to other people about his behaviour . . . that's your affair. Isn't it?'

'Yes,' he says miserably.

'I never have liked him. He's a two-faced so-and-so.'

'He's not really,' says Clive. 'He's . . . honest.'

'*Honest!* How can you *say* that?'

'OK, he's a wanker. But he's honest about being a wanker.'

'Just because you admit to your faults, doesn't make them any less, does it? And Clive, *please* don't use language like that. It's horrid.'

'OK. Sorry. He's an idiot then.'

'You can say that again.'

'He's an idiot then.'

'What? Oh, I suppose you think that this is a good time to make pathetic jokes, do you?'

'No,' he says, even more miserably.

'When one of your closest, or at least *oldest*, friends is playing around? And as long as you lie it will all be OK?'

'I probably won't have to lie.'

'And if you do?'

He shrugs, stares at his fingernails, at the miniature ginger jar he has unconsciously picked up and is twirling between his fingers, its cool china blue and white somehow evoking a world far more peaceful than this one, of jasmine gardens and pavilions, and Taoist sages sitting tranquilly under Bo trees, untroubled by the nagging voices of . . .

'Because you're not involving me in this, you know. If I am asked, I shall say I know no more about that Daniel Swallow than I wish to know, and that is very little. But he certainly hasn't been with *us*.' Emma closes her eyes in disgust. 'Probably with some *slut* from a council estate.'

Clive nearly laughs. 'Why should she be from a council estate?'

'Oh, I don't know,' sighs Emma, opening her eyes again. 'There's just something so . . . *grubby* about it all. I want nothing whatever to do with it. And if you had any sense at all, Clive, then neither would you.'

And with that, Emma picks up her copy of *Harpers* and begins to read again. The latest thing, apparently, now that pashminas are *so-o-o* nineties and *éculé*, is a shawl made from the chin hair of Punjabi dwarf mountain goats. Jemima Khan has several, and Tara and Tamara, and Liz Hurley, and even Diana wore one on occasions. They cost thousands in this country, but if you go round the really poor bits of India and Pakistan you might pick one up for only a few hundred. Emma sinks into a lovely Indian travel reverie, seeing herself driving a Land Rover through a dusty Indian village, or no, *being* driven, by a handsome, dark-eyed aid worker called . . . Craig? Vincent? Yes, Vincent . . . a rangy New Zealander with a broad, manly smile and strong, suntanned hands on the steering wheel, while a crowd of little laughing children run along in their wake. She imagines her hair tied

147

back with a simple white silk ribbon. And no make-up. Perhaps just a little moisturizer? All that dust is terribly drying on the skin. That must be why they all look so prematurely old out there.

Clive, meanwhile, has sloped away, feeling as if he is suffering from acute internal bruising to whatever organ of the body it is that houses the ego.

There is something about Emma when she is in this mood . . . when she is on the trail, a bloodhound on the traces of someone else's misdeeds – some *male's* misdeeds, preferably, although female misdeeds will do. Male misdeeds that deeply offend her sense of propriety include financial ineptitude and/or inadequate salary; boorishness (especially burping – quite unforgivable); beery breath (so often a prelude to burping, quite apart from being horrid in itself); excessive body hair; men who say that their underwear doesn't matter because nobody ever sees it; men who complain that she has too many clothes; men who are forever itching their feet. Of all these offences, she finds it difficult to say which is actually the horridest: either inadequate salary or burping, she can't decide which. Female misdeeds include girls who wear too much make-up; girls who boast they *never* wear make-up; girls who dress like they are off some council estate – saggy old leggings, sweatshirts, trainers, indeed gymwear of any sort worn other than when actually at the gym; girls going jogging and getting all hot and sweaty. She has seen them doing it, round Kensington Gardens on the hottest days. How *can* they? She remembers sitting outside the White Horse, Parsons Green, last summer and a really quite pretty girl who had been jogging came up and collapsed in a chair with a group of boys she obviously knew very well, and *wiped her perspiring face with the bottom of her T-shirt*, and then said, *God, I'm dying for a pint.* At first Emma had thought she must be an Australian, but it turned out she was actually *English*.

148

Oh, and girls who laugh at boys when they are being silly, or even boorish. It is dreadful to see a boy getting drunker and drunker and sillier and sillier and only being egged on by the girl he is with, laughing at him as if she finds him genuinely funny.

Oh, and dumpy girls.

Oh, and girls who talk about 'going Dutch'. What does it *mean*, anyway?

Oh, and girls who think it is funny to joke about periods and things. Talk about being 'on the rag'. Just *horrid*.

Clive goes into the kitchen and makes himself an Ovaltine. While the milk is boiling, he goes back and asks Emma if she'd like anything.

'No, thank you,' she says, not looking up.

'No, thank you,' he mouths in the doorway behind her, waggling his head prissily. 'No, thank you.'

'And don't stand behind me mouthing either,' says Emma, calmly turning a page of her magazine.

Clive retreats to the kitchen, sighs, thinks, Well, you can't expect *everything*, can you? You can't expect *perfection*. That's why there are all these unmarried thirty-something women around: waiting for *Mr Perfect*.

Gonna be a long lonely wait, sister.

Then he thinks of Amrita: the gold bracelet she wears, a ring of little gold discs. And her arms. So slim and brown! And those huge dark eyes, and her smile. He can picture exactly the way she smiles at him, the last time he took a mug of coffee to her desk and tripped over the extension cable to her fax machine and spilt half the coffee over a spreadsheet she had only just printed out. And she had looked up at him completely unfazed and said, 'Thank you, Clive.' So different from . . .

Then the milk boils over.

He springs across and lifts the saucepan off the ring so suddenly that he tips a lot more down the front of the oven.

Then as he is mopping up, Emma calls out from the sitting-room, 'I hope you haven't let the milk boil over, darling. You know what a horrid smell it makes.'

And Clive has to resist the powerful temptation to leap up and run into the sitting-room and wring the stinky old milk-sodden dishcloth out all over her. And then say something *silly*.

And then *BURP*.

Right in her face.

20

Only a few days later, Beth agrees to meet me for lunch. It may be all over between us, but we can at least try to behave like civilized human beings.

I'm there early, seated by 1.10 with a bottle of Sol. I want to see her coming across the piazza, her hips lightly swaying. I want to see what she is wearing, from head to toe. I want to see all of her.

Unfortunately it doesn't quite work out like that. The first I know is that someone has announced a jaunty 'Hello!' behind me, given me a swift peck on the cheek and sat down opposite.

'Appalling aftershave, by the way,' she says.

'I'm not wearing any aftershave.'

'God, even worse, then. It must be you. I never realized you smelt like that before.'

'I don't,' I say, smiling frostily. 'Are you always this personal?'

She waves her head airily about and lights a cigarette.

'It's the soap,' I add.

'Soap?'

'In the washrooms here. It's kind of . . . strawberry-flavoured, I think. Or maybe raspberry.'

'And ribbed for extra pleasure?' she asks, quite blank-faced. 'Anyway, what were you washing your face with soap for? It's so touchingly schoolboyish. Had you said a rude word, like "bum" or "willy"?'

'No. I had photocopier ink all over my neck. I'll explain another time. What would you like?'

Beth asks for a vodka with ice. Her eyes glitter at me. 'Always find they mix very nicely,' she says. 'Vodka and . . .'

'?'

'You don't, do you?'

'Not this early.' So that's where the self-assurance is coming from.

'No, never mind.' She tilts her head slightly to one side, quite insufferably kittenish and seductive – but she could be doing it for anyone. It's just an act, to a faceless audience, unseen because of the white glare of her own ego's footlights. She murmurs, 'I'm quite sure you wouldn't want me to corrupt you.'

Flirt, flirt, flirt, I'm thinking sourly. So, Beth, apart from trying to get as many men as possible to lust after you, what other interests do you have nowadays, if any?

And at the same time, '*Yes please!!!*' my treacherous, primitive reptilian back-brain is screaming, a libidinous grey globulous mess, fizzing axons and synapses routed directly to my groin, bouncing up and down and wringing its Jurassic paws together, '*Please, corrupt me, please!!!*'

'Is this what you call being good?' I say.

'Just flirtatious. Nothing wrong with that.'

'Well, anyway, no I don't want you to corrupt me, absolutely not. Although I wouldn't mind a cigarette. I'm clean out.'

'Of course, darling,' she says. 'Except I'm clean out too.'

'Oh, do you want me to . . .'

'No, don't worry,' she says, already on her feet. 'I've got to get some more anyhow.'

She's gone for a while. When she returns her vodka is on the table. She's bought a new pack of Marlboros, offers me one, extends a lighter towards me. I suck on the flame. She leans back, wiggles her glass at me. 'Chin-chin.'

'Chin-chin.'

She looks positively radiant, as beautiful as ever, absurdly happy in her own skin. Though sniffing a lot.

'Got a cold?' I ask.

She eyes me drily. 'Fool,' she says. Sips her vodka. 'Hm.'

'What are you doing this afternoon?'

She brushes her hair back with her hands. 'Well, I'll probably go and see my friends working on the jewellery stall. Just through there.' She points over towards the river.

'What, male?'

She hears the jealousy in my voice immediately and dislikes it. So do I, frankly. 'Both female,' she says.

I nod, relax.

'Lesbian,' she adds. 'Not Sam, Livvie. Lesbo Livvie. Always making passes at me. Think I might give in one of these days. Most girls give it a go at some time or another. Not surprising really, men being how they are. And you have to try everything once, don't you think?'

'Would have thought you already had.'

She smiles sweetly. 'My, my.' Looks away. 'But *men*. Once you've had one, you've had 'em all.'

'Do you really think so?'

She shrugs. 'They can be very unimaginative.'

'I'm not.'

She ignores me. 'I mean, is there *anything* more mind-bogglingly boring, anything more painfully unerotic, than the average porn film made by men, for men?'

For a while, as we discuss the pros and cons of pornography, things are a little less brittle between us. And she knows (oh, how knowing she is!) that for a woman merely to talk about sex is enough to make hordes of men fall for her.

'Well . . . porn films aren't supposed to be works of art.'

'They're just . . . well, fucking, aren't they?'

'Mostly,' I allow. 'The fucking element does tend to be fairly *pivotal*, yes.'

'Just in-out, in-out,' she says, lighting up another cigarette. 'I mean, *that* bit is the one bit that is exactly the same *every time*. That mechanical bit that finishes it all off – at least, for men. Women are just so much more imaginative. Find other things more of a turn-on.' She giggles. 'There was a girl at school who was famous for being able to –' she hesitates, a moment of uncharacteristic bashfulness – 'you know, just from snogging.'

'What, to . . .'

She nods. 'Yes, to . . .'

'Wow.'

'TO HAVE AN ORGASM,' she says very loudly.

I sigh. 'You're quite embarrassing sometimes.'

'I try.'

'So,' I say, 'let's get back to the foreplay.'

Her eyes glitter at me. 'Whatever you say.'

But after the flirting and the high comes the comedown.

The lunch hour is nearing an end when she casually says, 'Miles is off to Frankfurt again on Thursday.'

'Is he? Till when?'

She won't look me in the eye. 'Not back till Sunday.'

'Saturday too? On business? How come?'

'They've all got to go paint-balling in the Black Forest.' She giggles. 'Enhances team spirit, corporate morale, all that rubbish.'

'Miles'll love that.' I wish I hadn't said it: so matily.

She smiles, a fond, absent smile. 'He will.'

'But poor lonesome you, though. What'll you do?'

'Oh, I'll cope,' she says. 'Maybe I'll go and see my friend Livvie. Unless, of course –' tracing her finger through the spilt sugar – 'you want to come round?'

'So much for your resolution to be good.'

'Don't lecture me. Do you or don't you?'

'Just for the night?'

'Well, yes . . .'

I smile, shake my head. 'You just don't get it, do you, you stupid cow?' She looks startled. 'I'm not interested in a quick fuck any more – maybe I never was. I'm not available just to be your bit on the side. I'm only interested in *marrying* you.'

'Don't be ridiculous, you know nothing about me.'

'I know a fuck sight more than you do.'

Now it's her turn to get back at me. (The one war you have to win is the war with the person you love: we both know

154

that.) So she starts telling me about how delighted Miles was to see her home again when she got back from Cornwall, a.k.a. Edinburgh.

He went out specially to the local pie shop and came home with a rather pleased expression on his face and a steak and kidney pudding. When Beth saw the enormous pudding sitting on the kitchen table in its blue and white stripy bowl, so reminiscent of childhoods in warm kitchens, and happiness, and innocence, she felt close to tears and was possessed by the strange and almost irresistible desire to snatch up the bowl and (to the accompaniment of a song that has been going round in her head for days, *I don't want to change but maybe I should*) to plant kisses of love and remorse all over the vast white suety floury warm gentle dome that reminded her so much of Miles himself, even if it meant making it soggy with her tears.

'It's lovely,' she said, with a lump in her throat, and turning back to Miles she said again, 'It's lovely.'

She's telling me too much, I can't help feeling. She's talking to me like she talked to the WPC. Lynne Bunn. Or she's not talking to me at all, she's talking to herself. Trying to convince herself.

He saw that her eyes were watery with emotion and, taking her in his arms, he gave her a huge bearhug. 'God,' he said, 'if I knew you loved steak and kidney pudd'n this much I'd buy one every day.' He kissed the top of her head. 'So you missed me then?'

'Lots,' she said. 'Hugely.'

'Me too. So how was Auld Reekie?'

She wasn't sure if this was a street name or the city itself so she replied with a noncommittal 'Hm, nice shops.'

'And don't tell me, you saw some lovely little dress in the window that was *rather* expensive but you thought you just *had* to have it . . .'

'No, I didn't actually. All I bought was this scarf.'

He examined the scarf around her neck. 'Very modest,' he said. 'Royal Stuart. That's *really* all you bought?'

'Really.'

'What were you doing all the time?'

'Working. And sitting around waiting. You know, the usual thrilling stuff.'

'You'll have to take up knitting backstage or something.'

She smiled. 'Yeah, something like that.' She buried her head back in his shoulder. 'Knitting or something,' she murmured.

After dinner, Miles carried Beth to bed and tucked her up. She felt so tired. He gave her neck and back a gentle massage and then kissed her and whispered in her ear, 'Why didn't you phone?'

'What did you say?' I ask her.

'I just told him I was too busy. Sorry.' And she looks away.

I stub my cigarette out and glare out over the chill blue river and then back at her. 'Why do you even tell me all this? Maybe I don't want to know about the girl I love's blissfully happy relationship with my best friend.'

She looks apologetic but determined. Picks at her spaghetti vongole. Looks away.

The lunch is over, though it never really began. Her pasta is shaped and sculpted and uneaten.

When we get up to go, I move to give her a peck on the cheek and she turns towards me and gives me a rich, full-fat, dairy-cream kiss on the lips. 'Thanks for the drink,' she says. 'See you soon, gorgeous.' And sashays off with her fake self-assurance in the direction of Lesbo Livvie and her jewellery stall, the light breeze across the piazza flirting with her hair, her dress swaying carelessly around her thighs.

21

Sweet, single Kate, meanwhile, is not happy at all.

She's still brooding over Tom, can you believe. That total bastard. That smooth-talking, tall, athletic, successful, charming, arrogant, highly educated, two-faced BASTARD. She doesn't believe that he has ever had his heart broken in his life, and that is what he so obviously needs, to turn him into at least the *semblance* of a human being. She speculates that in some men, although they may grow physically (to an athletic 6 feet 3 or whatever, perfectly filling the immaculate contours of their Hackett suit), their hearts, or maybe their souls, have failed to grow much since they were a wailing, egotistical three days old.

The soul only grows, only becomes generous and wise and understanding and properly *adult*, under the stress of hurts and wounds. The soul is largely composed of spiritual scar tissue. And since *he* has never felt the wound, has even *boasted* that he has never given a girl the chance to finish with him, has always made sure to fire her first, his heart retains its original, babyish, *foetal* dimensions, metabolically effective but emotionally no larger than a full stop.

But what really makes Kate unhappy is the fact that, despite being able to perceive all this in him, despite her acute awareness that the man is a total, unadulterated shit, there is still a little part of her that remains desperately in love with him. This simultaneously baffles, enrages and depresses her. She feels betrayed by this pathetic, dependent part of herself that still yearns after him even when the more sensible, judgemental side of her knows perfectly well that a) he isn't worth it and b) she will never get him back anyway. How can this pathetic, dependent part of herself (represented in her imagination by a high-pitched, girlie, wheedling, masochistic, perhaps even *lisping* voice, saying, *Pleathe, Tom, oh pleathe won't you take me back? I'll do anything, I'll let you do anything, you can chathe other women if you like, I don't mind, only pleathe take me back into your life!* YUCK.), how can this part of herself still yearn after *that*, that bastard? How could she have such poor taste?

She's thirty-four years of age, single white female, attractive, witty, good career, single, slim, smoker, single, 34C, single, single.

'Oh, forget him,' I say. 'Just *forget him*. Get a cat or something.'

She scowls at me. 'It is a truth universally acknowledged that a single woman in possession of a cat must *not* be in want of a husband.'

When I was out 'on business' the other night, Kate put on a video of *Carousel* and started drinking a bottle of chocolate cream liqueur. It was the perfect combination, the creamy texture offering instant comfort and luxury, the alcohol dispensing numbness and oblivion. By the time she was three-quarters of the way through the bottle, however, the depressive effect had kicked in, coinciding fatefully with the melancholy course of the film, so that by the end she was blubbing hopelessly and crawling over to the cupboard to get out the bottle of Jameson's.

When she awakes it is daylight. The video has ended and rewound long ago. The bright-hued banalities of breakfast television wash over her. The blonde presenter gives a time check. 8.45 a.m. Kate sits up.

And immediately wishes she hadn't. Her mouth tastes foul. Like whiskey gone mouldy. Her head thumps. She feels like she has been sleeping under a pig all night, a 30-stone Tamworth sow. Also, a cigarette butt adheres to her cheek and she has dribbled in her sleep.

She stares at the TV. It can't be right. She stares at the

bottle of Jameson's. She drank more than half the bottle last night.

Oh, *shit*.

She sucks extra-strong mints all the way to work, but to little avail, since she throws up in the loos as soon as she gets there. When she finally collapses behind her desk, she is one hour and twenty minutes late, and convinced that she still reeks of whiskey. Suzie flicks her on the shoulder as she passes by and says, 'Hard night last night, gel?'

Just after 11, Hilary calls her into the office. Her expression says cross, but concern at the same time, which makes it ten times worse. Nausea rises in waves from her empty stomach, she feels icy sweat break out across her forehead and upper lip, and thinks that if she doesn't faint in the next few minutes, she'll throw up again.

'Coffee?' says Hilary.

'Yes, please,' she says thickly.

Hilary makes them both coffees – with her own fair hand! – and sits her down. And then she starts to address her lateness, her recent work record, her apparent difficulties in concentrating, her emotional outburst last week after the guest lunch.

Kate listens, only half taking it all in. Why are you telling me this? she thinks miserably. I know it all already. I was there too. She eyes Hilary glassily. If you're going to sack me, just get on with it. Then I can join Dan on the dole queue. But stop telling me what a disaster area I am.

Hilary she talks on. Kate has always been such a good employee, a joy to work with, so well liked in the company, a great team-player. But – these ominous buts – in the past few weeks, things have just got worse and worse. She isn't unreliable, she still meets her deadlines. But Hilary fears it is only a matter of time. Meanwhile, she does have a time-keeping problem, a bit of a sickness problem – five days off in the past month – 'And –' Hilary clears her throat – 'we think you may be drinking a bit too much.'

Kate says nothing.

Hilary adds that she is by no means a puritan in such things, she likes a drink herself. 'But if we were like one of these companies that nowadays insists on all employees being stone cold sober at all times, then I fear that you, Kate, would . . .' Hilary hesitates. 'How can I put this delicately? Fail by a mile? There is more than a whiff of eau-de-Famous Grouse about you this morning, my dear. Or did you really splash out, eau-de-Glenfiddich?'

Kate smiles politely and grits her teeth. Her loathing of Hilary is already producing an adrenalin rush that is making her feel better.

Hilary smiles back. She has made a little joke. There is considerable debate in the office as to whether Hilary actually has a sense of humour. She cracks jokes, certainly, but that is not necessarily the same thing.

'All in all, Kate, I'm very sorry about it. But I can't let it go on. It's unfair to the rest of the team, for one thing. And for another, we've got to give you the chance to sort yourself out. Forgive me for saying so but – well, word gets around – apparently you've had some man trouble?'

Kate looks up, startled. 'Man trouble' is such an unlikely phrase to be heard from Hilary's lips.

She swivels in her chair, takes some papers from the wire tray in front of her, plucks a couple of sheets out and pushes them across the desk. Kate looks at her without blinking, although she can feel her eyes beginning to smart.

'Just like that?' she says.

Hilary steeples her fingers and rests her chin on them and looks at her steadily. 'Just like that,' she says. 'Why not? You deserve it.'

She looks down, to hide her tears, and fumbles for a handkerchief. Too slow. A fat teardrop falls on her P45.

Only . . . when she dries her eyes and looks again, it isn't a P45. Some new document. She looks up stupidly, red-eyed.

'What's this?'

'Well – read it,' says Hilary.

She looks down again. It is a fax from a holiday company, confirming the reservation of a place in the name of Ms K. Luckett in a group of twelve on a spring-time Vineyards of Bordeaux Cycling Week. She looks up again, more stupidly than ever. Hilary continues to regard her blankly, secretly loving every minute. She feels like she used to when her children were young, and their eyes shone with delight on Christmas morning as they unwrapped their presents. She almost chuckles to herself. *The Modern Manager as Santa Claus*, she thinks. *How to Get the Most Out of Your Staff*. I should write a handbook.

Kate looks down again, re-reads the letter. Still her mind is flailing about in epistemic limbo, whirring and clicking and coming to no conclusions, like a logic machine wrestling with the statement 'This statement is untrue.' She flicks the letter up and finds stapled to its underside a return ticket on EuroStar, Waterloo to Bordeaux. She looks back at the letter a third time. At last it is beginning to make sense.

'I was going to chuck in a bit of spending money too,' says Hilary, 'but I thought that would just look too much like favouritism. Not that you must let any of your colleagues know about it, of course. Anyway,' she adds, 'there should- n't be too many extra expenses. The holiday includes half- board and lodging, so –' and at this point she begins to wave her hands around in an airy, Gallic, most un-Hilary-like fashion – 'you'll just have to fork out for the occasional three-course luncheon at some little *auberge* on the banks of the *Gironde* or the *Isle* . . .' She returns to normal and smiles at Kate. 'The Dordogne's lovely,' she says. 'And cycling with a small group like that will be great fun, I imagine. Today's Thursday. You go on Sunday night. You can have till then off, of course. Give you time to sort yourself out, buy some bright yellow Lycra cycling shorts or whatever.'

Kate is near to tears, but refusing to cry. 'Thank you,' she sniffs.

Hilary raises her hand. 'Not at all. You need it.'

Kate wonders whether to give her a big hug – Hilary! The Dragon! – but decides that it might look unprofessional.

She lurches out of Hilary's office and dashes for the exit. Wait till Dan hears about this.

22

Last night was a huge house in Hampstead and having to vigorously pleasure a twenty-something Swiss girl, *and* her unmarried sister, while her septuagenarian spouse watched us at it, as he squatted on a tiny gilt stool in the corner of the palatial bedroom suite, munching his way through – get this – *three whole tins* of salt and vinegar-flavour Pringles.

(Is there no perversion known to humanity that is not being performed, at any given time, somewhere in this great capital city of ours?)

Spectacularly weird, yes, and apart from it all taking place under the rheumy eye of the Pringle-addicted septuagenarian, I should have enjoyed it. Every young man's dream. They were lovely girls. And I hated every minute of it. Could it be that I am losing it? Could it be that I am turning into a *monogamist*? I didn't even enjoy it as some kind of revenge against Beth, that unfeeling unfaithful bitch whom I so hopelessly love.

But something strange, and indeed career-threatening, is happening to me: *I think I am going off sex.*

The next day: a knackered lunch with Clive in the usual cheap Italian.

On the telephone yesterday, Clive was jubilant. He had managed to effect a *rapprochement* between himself and Amrita, explaining that the reason he behaved so peculiarly over her spring water + peach juice drink recently was because he was on medication for Seasonal Affective Disorder. (Apparently, *she believed him.* She must be a lot more stupid than she looks.) And he discovered that she really is an Indian princess, even if they officially abolished it a few years before she was born.

Plus – their night out together at the Wigmore Hall last night apparently went very well. This is all my doing, too. Call me an old romantic, but *I fixed it up.* It went like this:

A few days ago, I received two free tickets for a concert at the Wigmore Hall and I couldn't make it, as I had a prior booking with the wife of an Indonesian rubber magnate. So early evening yesterday, before going home for a shower and then the long trek up to Hampstead, I went round to Clive's place and, Emma mercifully not around, I handed them to the little chap on a proverbial plate.

'Whassat?' he says, standing in his doorway clad in a claret-coloured bathrobe, drying his carroty locks and peering.

'Tickets for the Wigmore Hall.' I shrug. 'From a happy client. I mean, an *ex*-client, a business client, of course. Two tickets for a concert tonight.'

Clive opens the envelope and stares at the tickets. 'I dunno . . .' he says. 'Em isn't much into this stuff.'

'Not Emma, you fool,' I hiss. '*Amrita!*'

Clive gawps up at me. 'You don't like Em much, do you?'

I ignore him. 'Chopin, *Nocturnes*, a few *Mazurkas*. Everybody loves that stuff, and the Borodin and Liadov are OK too.'

'How do you know Amrita'll like it?'

'Course she will. S'culture, innit?' I nod down at the tickets vigorously. 'S'Classic FM, innit? S'Radio Free, innit? All the toffs like that stuff.' I talk normally again. 'I know it's short notice, but I think you should give her a ring.'

Clive considers, flapping the two tickets between forefinger and thumb. 'And what if she knows about it all already? I don't know anything about these people. Are they Russians?'

'They certainly are. Apart from the Chopin, obviously. Oh, just bluff it out. Mussorgsky was a bugger for the bottle, the Five, the Mighty Handful, Balakirev etc. I'm sure your natural eloquence will surmount all obstacles.'

'Don't you have one of your funny little rhymes about them?'

I frown. 'I'm afraid not.'

'Well, can't you make one up? She'll think I'm dead clever.'

'*You* try finding a rhyme for Mussorgsky. And anyway, Clive, as a high-flying freelance self-employed advertising copywriter and all-round creative whiz-kid, I really think I have better things to be doing than sitting around at home making up footling little rhymes about Russian composers, don't you?'

'Hm.' Clive broods. 'And what do I tell Em?'

'You had to work late. I'll cover for you if need be.'

'OK,' says Clive at last. 'Thanks.'

'No problemo.'

I decide to walk back to our pad in the Bush, get some exercise. And fresh air and exercise, of course, stimulate the lyrical and versifying faculties just as much as the digestive and the excretive. So that in no time at all I find that I have indeed invented one of those 'funny little rhymes' that Clive wanted, to impress his bird with. When I get home, I phone him on his mobile. He's already at the Wigmore Hall, waiting for his Indian babe. I begin without preamble.

> '*Modest Mussorgsky*
> *Drank more than he ought-sky,*
> *Especially claret and ten-year-old port-sky.*'

'Is that true?' asks Clive.

'Is what true?'

'That he drank claret and port?'

'Of course it's not true, you fool,' I snap. 'But it rhymes, doesn't it?'

'Sort of.' I must sound furious so Clive pacifies me. 'It's

165

very good. Amrita'll love it. But I thought you said you had better things to do than . . .'

'So I have,' I say briskly. 'And I must get on with them straight away.'

Five minutes later, I feel I have to phone him again.

> 'Which meant that he'd trouble
> In keeping his balance,
> And in consequence
> Never could manage to wat'r-sky.'

Five minutes, I try once more.

' . . .' I begin.

'Daniel,' says Clive, 'I really think that's OK now. She's here and the concert starts soon. Honestly. But thanks anyway.'

'Very well, then,' I say with dignity. 'I trust it will be a vigorous and passionate performance.'

So now, back in the restaurant, lunch time next day.

When he arrives at the restaurant – not with Amrita, I note with some vicarious disappointment, although they may just be covering their tracks, and it doesn't necessarily mean that they *didn't* spend last night making mad, passionate love until dawn – but when Clive comes in, his face is all aglow with a roseate lustre that I doubt a night in bed with *Emma* could give anyone.

'Well?'

'Well what?'

'Oh, don't give me that. How did it go?'

Clive smiles smugly.

'You didn't!'

'Didn't what?'

'Well . . . shag.'

Clive looks outraged. 'How dare you!' he hisses. 'You are talking about the woman I love! She's not just going to fall into bed with any bloke who happens to take her to a concert at the Wigmore Hall, you know.'

'No, no, of course not. But – it went OK, anyway?'

'Brilliant,' says Clive. 'Tum – tum te tum tum tum tum tum tum tum . . . *tum-tum* . . .'

'Ye-es,' I say. 'I think I prefer the orchestral version.'

'*And* she doesn't know diddly about classical music.'

'Really?'

Clive shakes his head. 'Not a sausage,' he says happily.

'And you told her the amusing rhyme about Mussorgsky?'

'Yep. In fact, I . . . I embroidered the Mussorgsky thing a bit.' Clive looks vaguely guilty.

I sigh. 'Go on.'

'Well . . . I told her I was actually a *descendant* of Mussorgsky.'

'You *what*?'

'Mussorgsky and a Russian princess. Well, she's got this true blue blood in her family, her dad was a small Raja, technically she was born a *Rajkumari*, and I'm just an Hon., so I . . .'

'And you're a woodcutter's son!' I interrupt.

'Hunh? Well, *sort* of.'

(Clive's father owns, among other things, 20,000 acres of prime timber plantation in Caithness and a couple of sawmills outside Dundee.)

'Oh!' I exclaim, clasping my hands girlishly together, 'It's so *romantic*!' Then more sober. 'But you've told her a pack of lies. You've told her you're descended from Mussorgsky.' I sit up very straight and stare out of the window. Clive blunders on.

'And . . . and that his alcoholism has been passed down through the family.'

'You told her you had a drink problem?'

'Not me,' says Clive. 'Olivia. My mother.'

'Oh, yes, Olivia. I remember her.' There is a long silence. Then I ask, 'Clive, why did you tell Amrita that your mother has a drink problem?'

Clive looks hunted. 'I dunno exactly,' he says. 'I got carried away.'

'You did.'

'I . . . I mean, everybody else's family life is so fucked up and angst-ridden and interesting, or at least it seems it, you know, their mother died suddenly, or eloped with the dog, or isn't their real mother or whatever, and so that makes them interestingly traumatized and all that, and mine are minor aristos and so ought to be lovably eccentric and always off hang-gliding in Tibet or whatever, and in fact they are just so *normal* and *sane* and just *averagely repressed* and I have no traumas and angsts at all. Except with the shoe-polish, maybe.'

'And except for the fact that you're a congenital liar.'

Clive brightens considerably at this. 'That's true,' he says. 'Perhaps I suffer from full-blown Munchausen's Syndrome. That would be quite interesting, wouldn't it?'

'Not really. *All* blokes suffer from full-blown Munchausen's Syndrome.'

There's no doubt about it, little Clive Spooner is a very rum chap. But so far, so good. The romance of the Princess and the Woodcutter's Son continues apace.

23

It's worse while Kate is away. I phone Beth all the time, far too much. She's so cool, I can't even tell if she's annoyed with me phoning so often or not. So then I don't phone, and she's still cool, which tells me nothing at all.

When Kate comes back, she has a mysterious glow. 'Tell me all about it, then,' I say.

The cycling group was comprised mainly of fit young men in shorts and T-shirts, to whom Kate's first reaction was a rather vulgar *Phwoaarr!!!* The only other people in the group were two middle-aged ladies who seemed to be very much 'together', and certainly eccentric, their cycling costume including long skirts and straw bonnets; and a puffing, balding, tubby man with curly black hair called Vernon.

In the end, she got on best with the two old batty-girls and Vernon, forming with them a slow, sedate and immensely dignified rearguard. And despite the drizzling March rain, Bordeaux was very beautiful, hills ribbed with ancient vines, hidden red-tiled villas, spring flowers. The fit young men were fanciable, but boring. And Vernon was great, but she didn't fancy him. So she had a fine, stress-free holiday. And she brought something home in a box.

I assume it's fine wines, cheese, charcuterie, all the full-fat *foison* of France, for my delectation.

'Wrong again,' she says. 'Take a peek.'

It's a fucking kitten. 'It's a fucking kitten,' I say.

'Well observed.'

'What . . . how . . . I thought you couldn't just bring them back like that?'

'You can now, thanks to the wonderful EU.'

I stare at the kitten a while longer, still wishing it was a bottle of Grand Cru claret. The kitten stares back at me, blue-eyed, silent, probably wishing I was a herring. 'What are you going to call it? You always said Socrates was a good name for a cat.'

'It's a him. Yeah, but he's very French. I thought Gaston.'

'You can't call a cat Gaston.'

'Why not? Here, chuck him over here.'

I lift Gaston out of the box, a limp hank of bone and fur, and pass him to Kate. She sets him on her lap, bends down, nuzzles him with her nose. Looks up at me, as if issuing a challenge. 'Well?'

On a sudden impulse, I lean down and give her a kiss. 'Gaston it is, then,' I say. 'It's a good name.' After a moment, I add, 'I think I might be getting a cat myself soon.'

Kate laughs.

'Um,' I say. 'Well, we can be politically active or whatever. Join the Lib Dems.'

'And do we?'

'Um . . .'

'Do you know *anyone* our age who is "politically active", as you so quaintly put it?'

I'm round at Miles's pad, Upper Chelsea. Only Miles is in the Black Forest, popping off paint-balls at sweaty-faced German financiers called Hans and Willi. So I'm round there with Beth. And no, we're not going to go to bed together. I'm round for tea and then I go home. Like I will continue to do. We meet for lunch now, we talk, sometimes we go to the cinema together. Sometimes in the cinema together, or walking in the park, we hold hands. But she's in love with Miles, my best friend, and she's not going to leave him.

If this is an affair, it's a chaste one.

She doesn't ask me about work and I don't tell her. She did say to me, when I first arrived on her doorstep, 'Ah, so you're still alive then?'

'Hunh?'

'Haven't died of AIDS yet or anything?'

Which I took to be a very Beth-like joke about my chosen profession. In revenge, I did start to tell her about my night in Hampstead, jovially, lecherously, to make her feel jealous, but she cut me short and said she didn't want to hear about it. Which is a good sign, I guess.

Now I look at her and see something surprising, intense, ardent in her face, something combative. She stands leaning against the kitchen cupboards, one leg crossed before the other, brushing her hair back from her face.

'Er . . . well, no,' I say. 'What's all this about?'

She doesn't answer directly. 'We must be the least politically active, least ideological generation since – when? People first got the vote? Maybe we bed-hop not because of totalitarian repression, like all those introspective bores in Kundera novels, but because there's fuck all else to do.' And with that her combativeness evaporates and she laughs, a little embarrassed, as if she has given too much of herself away, and relaxes and gazes to one side. 'Oh, I don't know either,' she says. 'We're a pretty useless bunch, aren't we? I mean, we don't believe in *anything* nowadays. We really are *true* nihilists, to the marrow.'

'I believe in *lurve*,' I say in a stupid accent, and immediately wish I hadn't. Wish I'd said it straight. Oh, the curse of irony, ubiquitous irony, irony always triumphant.

Never say what you mean. *So-o-o* uncool, darling.

She flashes a smile. 'OK,' she says.

When Miles is away, she says, she completely falls apart. Nothing gets done. The house turns into a pigsty within hours. The way she tells it, it's quite funny. But what she's really trying to tell me is what a nightmare she would be to live with. Don't worry, darling, I'm thinking. I know that well enough already.

As soon as the door shuts behind Miles's broad unburdened shoulders, all Beth's energy leaves her. She doesn't bustle around the house sorting stuff out or paying bills. Sometimes she does manage to strip off the bedsheets and pillow slips and pile them in the middle of the bathroom. And then she sits on the edge of the bath and stares at them. Just stares. For five or ten minutes. An immense weariness seems to have come over her. Eventually, with an inner struggle, she gets up and lugs the bundle into the kitchen and stuffs it into a plastic binbag. She pauses then to consider if she ought to wash it all immediately. Of course I *ought* to, she tells herself snappishy. I *ought* to, I *ought* to, so much that I *ought* to.

She catches sight of herself in the mirror: her tousled hair, the perpetual shadows under her eyes, the last of those bruises still showing, and again she thinks what the hell and bundles everything up and stuffs it unwashed into the back of a bedroom cupboard. Sluttishly, she thinks. *SLUTTISH-LY*.

And the rest of the day opens up before her like a yawning abyss, like a wolf's maw, and she wanders around the flat for a while and eats a kiwifruit and starts to make another coffee but then sits catatonic at the kitchen table and doesn't drink it. She could ring Charlie. She could ring Lesbo Livvie. See what they are doing tonight. While Miles is quaffing steins ruddy-faced with his workmates in some Bierkeller. Or else she could call up an old friend. Not Charlie, she thinks sourly to herself, charlie. Or the other one, the one for empty days.

And every day feels like an empty day nowadays, days like these. *Every day is like Sunday*, she sings softly to herself as she reaches for her mobile. *Every day is silent and grey*.

At that moment the phone trills in the sitting-room. She goes to answer it, and I hear her voice, sounding pleased about something. She says she'll have a G&T ready and waiting. I hear her coming back.

'It's Miles. He's in a black cab, stationary in the King's

Road, but he'll be back in five minutes.'

Time for me to go.

Standing at the bus stop waiting for a number 11, I thank God that Miles phoned ahead. Thank God, too, for mobile phones. Otherwise he might just have come striding in, like Odysseus back from his wars and wanderings, and fingered me as an evil suitor, standing in his kitchen drinking his coffee, eating his chocolate bourbons and flirting with his Penelope. And in a trice he'd have whipped a bow and arrows from his executive briefcase, and I'd have been pinned back against the stripped-pine kitchen units, stuck full of arrows and looking like a fretful porpentine.

As it is, all will be well. I see Miles coming in the front door and setting his case down in the hall, and then standing there capaciously, plump and sleek and happy to be home, arms akimbo, and Beth running to him and leaping into his arms and hugging him about the neck and . . .

The number 11 is only fifty yards away when my mobile goes. It's Beth, whispering. 'Can you come back?'

'Why, what's wrong?'

'I don't know yet, but something's up. He's just in the loo, so I'm whispering. I sort of feel it would be easier if there was someone else here too. I don't think things have gone so well. Can you just pretend to drop round by chance?'

'On my way. I know, I'll pretend to be dropping in the book I'm reading for you.'

'Which is?'

'*The Children of Green Knowe.*'

She laughs. 'Read it already, but I don't think he'd realize. OK, see you soon.'

On the way back, I think how I only really love people who love children's books. And I only really love people who love animals. And I only really love Beth.

Beth must understand him better than I do, because at first

he seems fine to me. He sits there on the sofa, G&T in hand, and says he's had a great time. He had been dreading it but actually it was all rather a laugh, even if their German colleagues did take the paint-balling terribly seriously and insisted on playing by the rules and looked puzzled and then offended when Miles's team had started shouting, *Jawohl mein Führer!* and Don't Mention The War! He chuckles to himself, so sleek and plump and cheerful, the chuckles like pure oxygen bubbling through honey. Later that evening in the Bierkeller, Heinrich and Willi had explained very solemnly that, although the English could joke about the war and such things, in Germany this was still hardly possible.

So after that they all bought more drinks and talked instead about beer, football, cars and women. The general consensus was that, English ale aside, German beer was the best, but Czech could be pretty good too; that no Italian player was any good once he was transferred to an English club side; that Mercs probably *were* the best cars in the world; and that Liz Hurley had yet to find a film role that, *Austin Powers* notwithstanding, would really make the most of her thespian talents.

Beth smiles at all this and says she's glad that he's had a nice time. He gets up to go and refill his glass, and passing by her he bends and kisses her lightly on the forehead.

While he's in the kitchen getting ice, I whisper, 'Not being rude or anything, but – why am I here?'

Beth won't look at me. 'Trust me,' she says. 'Something's happened.'

I don't see it. I don't see him as *disturbed.* Miles, more than ever, seems to have about him a halo of contentment and self-confidence, essentially benevolent but bordering on the complacent. He has the same plump, sleek sheen as the Merc. His shiny red cheeks and shiny well-brushed hair and clean blue eyes and barrel chest and aura of physical stretch and competence and effortless 5-litre, V-12 Oxbridge intellect . . . and all of it just right. Rightly judged and distributed, prudent and correct, like every other aspect of his life. Just right. And what is wrong with that?

And I reckon I understand what Beth likes in Miles. It's the security he gives her. When they go away for weekends, I can picture all too well what it's like for her, when they're cruising down the motorway to visit his parents or for one of his shooting weekends down in Hampshire – 'Gotta get out of the big smoke now and again,' Miles says. 'Too much London can drive you mad.' She presses a pad in the armrest, the window slides down, she hears the wide tyres on the tarmac below: they whisper of status, the cushioned susurrus of wealth. She shuts the window again, nestles in the passenger seat of the big Merc, something mellow and ambient on the multi-CD and no road or engine noise audible at all now, and feels so aware of Miles's steady bulk beside her humming along tunelessly, wearing his awful shapeless baggy bottle-green corduroys and a faded rugby shirt that he's probably had since *school*, completely styleless, completely oblivious to fashion (which is exactly what she loves so much, she says). And the way his large fleshy hands hold the steering wheel, lightly yet firmly, relaxed but alert, just like you're supposed to be (rather than exhaustingly tense but totally unalert, like Beth usually feels), everything rightly judged, prudent, correct, just right . . . I do understand how she must *love* those times, all that, those long, cocooned car journeys. I see them cruising along at a steady 90 or so and feeling like they are hardly moving, and then an ancient, bouncing 800cc moke will come alongside them and painfully overtake, its engine gasping, the whole car bouncing from corner to corner, kids in the back, Dad hunched grimly over the wheel, eyes on the road ahead. The knackered moke, exposed to the elements, unsheltered and unprotected, full pelt, teetering on the edge of a smash-up from which no one will survive . . . That's how Beth would

175

be, without Miles. For her, it's like looking in the mirror. But safely tucked up in Miles's Merc, insulated and secure, she can believe that she is no longer like that, she has changed. Now she rides in a big Merc with its plethora of safety features. And she has Miles by her side too, with *his* plethora of safety features: the ABS of his unassailable equanimity, the driver's airbag of his fat salary (+ bonuses), the crumple zones of his happy family life, the side impact bars of his . . . well, whatever. I guess he makes her feel safe. And compared to him, what do I have to offer? Obsession, jealousy, arguments, insecurity – and quite definitely no V-12 Merc.

I'm wrong about pretty well everything, as usual.

He perches on the edge of the sofa, drink in hand, and I suddenly register that he *is* edgy. And he starts straight in.

'Then yesterday afternoon, it all went pear-shaped,' he says. Sips his drink. No, gulps it. 'It was our last paint-ball session and we were all really up for it, really hyper and into the game. Heinrich and Willi's teams were based in the trees opposite, and there was this open heathland between us, and then in our sector were my team, and a Dutch team under a guy called Peter. Anyway, I said we should go round the back and outflank them. Classic military manoeuvre, yeah? Come up behind them and splat them in the arse. So I led a small contingent round to the left, and we were hiding behind a clump of gorse, really chuffed that we had got so near to them without being seen, when Heinrich himself comes running straight out of the trees and at us in this mad death-or-glory charge.' Miles laughs. 'It was still really funny at that point. But then he caught his foot in a root or something and it just stopped him dead. He gave this big lurch and flipped over on his side and started screaming. Turned out the silly bugger had only sprained his ankle, not broken it or anything, although I guess it was quite painful. Anyway, he was only a few yards in front of us, pinned down, and I thought this was just like that scene in *Full Metal*

Jacket, you know? You get an enemy soldier pinned down in your sights, injured, and the rest have to come out and rescue him? Anyway, that's all I was thinking of: Heinrich was like a bargaining counter at that point. So I lined up my gun on him and called out to the rest of his team still in the woods that if they didn't all march out and surrender in ten seconds I'd start firing off pot shots at Heinrich. I mean, they're only *paint-balls*, for Christ's sake.'

I see that Miles's hand is shaking. He isn't looking at us. His account is one of self-justification now. Something bad has happened, is going to happen. Beth is right.

'Anyway, as soon as I shout this out, I hear his team all shouting No! No!, which I take to mean that they're refusing to surrender. In fact, as they said later, they were protesting at me shooting Heinrich when he was lying out there injured. I suppose it was a shitty thing to do, but, you know . . .' Miles sighs. It's like he's wrestling with something he doesn't understand, someone whose face he can't see. 'In the heat of battle and all that . . . Anyhow, I count to ten, and they're all shouting from the trees at me, and the guys with me said they were protesting too, though *I* never heard them. Anyway, none of the Germans are coming out in surrender, and when I get to ten I feel so pissed off with them and hyped up and stuff, I just let Heinrich have it. How was I to know that it would hit him in the face?'

It crosses my mind to point out to Miles that he *is* a regular on shooting weekends down in Hampshire and he can hardly claim to be a poor shot. But he goes on. 'Yellow paint all over his physog. But I knew something had gone really wrong and maybe I'd overdone it, because Heinrich was really howling now. And then –' he waves his hand vaguely in front of his face – 'the yellow paint started getting all streaked with red . . .'

I feel slightly sick, but from the look on his face, so does Miles.

'Jesus,' whispers Beth.

'Was he badly hurt?' I ask.

Miles sniffs, rubs his nose, looks away. Long silence. Eventually he says quietly, 'The paint-ball broke his nose.'

'Oh, it was the *paint-ball* that did it, was it,' snaps Beth, 'not *you*?'

For a moment then I'm really frightened. Miles leaps to his feet, his face puce, screaming, 'Don't you fucking start in on me, you're supposed to be on MY side!' He stands glaring furiously at her for a moment and then subsides. Sits back down again. Sighs, strokes his big hand back over his hair. Slowly, like plants uncoiling in the sun, Beth and I relax. I realize that I have been gripping the edge of the drinks table, ready to pick it up and defend myself and Beth if things should get really ugly.

Another long silence. At last, Miles adds, even more quietly this time, 'Oh, and there might be some problem with his eye. But they don't know that yet.'

I feel so sick. Beside me, Beth has curled up like some primitive animal going into defence mode. I'm freezing up too, suddenly remembering a brief incident, a non-incident as I thought at the time. A few weeks ago, I had a quick lunch-time drink with Miles. We sat in a wine bar and had beers and gossiped and then, when he reached across for his bottle at one point, I noticed he had blood on his shirt cuff. I pointed it out and he glanced at it and then said, 'My watch caught, just nicked the skin.' But he spoke distantly. I thought he was bored or even embarrassed. He resumed the conversation, gossip, future plans, the rugby, his voice as distant as ever, his clear blue eyes small and serene.

Now Miles gets to his feet, slams his empty glass down and announces that he's going out. Beth calls after him, but he ignores her. The front door slams.

We look at each other. 'Bloody hell,' I say.

'I don't want to stay here,' she says. 'I don't want to be here when he gets back.'

'*You're* not scared of him, surely?'

She laughs. 'No, of course I'm not. He's fine with me. But he does get in such moods . . .'

'I'm sure he never used to. I mean, he was always competitive and stuff, but . . .' I shrug. 'Not like that. Must be all the stress or something.'

'Some excuse.'

I look at her. 'You're being pretty hard on him.'

'I am?' She shakes her head. 'I don't know. *Poor* Miles.'

'I do think you'd better stay with him, though. Really.'

She nods, slowly. 'Maybe you're right.'

We kiss goodbye in the hallway, *before* we open the front door. Look at each other, both smile. We each know what the other is thinking. If we kissed in the open doorway, Miles might see us. From where he is standing on the other side of the road, under the sodium haze of the streetlight, waiting for me, an iron spike in his hands . . .

But I make it OK.

I hope Beth does too.

A few days later I meet up with Miles for a game of squash and we studiously avoid any mention of Germany, paintballing or outbursts of violent psychotic behaviour. In fact, I end up talking about her. To *him*! Just can't help it.

The squash is good, though Miles wins, as usual.

'So *eighties*,' he sighs, swiping the sweat from his forehead. 'But I still enjoy it.'

Afterwards we sit in the cafeteria gorging on orange juice and Danish pastries.

'What are you doing this weekend?' asks Miles.

'Masses of work to do,' I mumble through a widely diffused spray of pastry flakes. 'I'm not going to go out of the house for forty-eight hours. I'm going to live like a hermit, eat toast and get it all done. I'm way behind.' I gulp my orange juice. 'And you and your bird?' (Any excuse.)

Miles shrugs. 'Just a quiet weekend *à deux*. Nice really.

Might even get out into the country. Too much London . . .
And Beth's had a cold. Poor lass, she was really quite poorly.'

'I heard. But she's better now?'

'As better as she'll ever be.'

'And what does that mean exactly?'

'Oh, I don't know,' he says. He hunches forward and
stretches his arms out across the table, toying with the styrofoam cup of orange juice between his fingertips, staring
down. 'Beth's not normal, I'm beginning to realize. I mean, I
like it really, I know. That streak of . . . *lunacy* in her.' He grins.
'You know, she's not *boring*. But there are times when . . . there
are times when I just don't have a clue what she's thinking, or
even *how* she thinks. You know?'

'Don't you think we all, blokes I mean, have this problem
with our other halves?'

'Any other human being is a mystery,' he says. 'Damn
sight easier, though, being a poove, all the same. And with
Beth especially . . . Chalk and cheese, we are. I mean, maybe
it's not really a Big Problem that you don't understand each
other in the slightest, maybe it's a good thing: it keeps the
mystery alive or whatever, the Great Unknown, lying there
next to you in bed night after night. But there are times with
Beth when – I wish she'd tell me more, when she just seems
plain secretive. Not that I don't trust her, of course I do. But
she doesn't open up to me as much as . . . well, as much as
you expect girls to, about how they feel and all that.'

I nod sagely. 'Maybe she will in time. It's not been long
yet, has it? Seven months?'

Miles ignores me, or doesn't hear. 'Other times I feel like
. . . Like she's putting on a performance. She's doing it all for
my benefit, but it doesn't mean anything to her.'

'What about between the sheets?' I ask boldly.

Miles gives a sly grin. 'Between the sheets,' he says, 'on
the floor, under the table, in the bath, over the bath, on the
washing-machine (on fast-spin cycle: that was the best, I
thought she was going to wake up the whole street), on the

180

roof, in the car, over the bonnet . . .' My mouth begins to gape. Miles reaches out a hand and shuts it for me. 'No, there's no problem there.' He frowns. 'Except, again, I suppose I get the feeling sometimes that she's just putting on an act, a performance for my benefit. You know?'

I know. 'I shouldn't worry about it. With performances like that, I really shouldn't complain.'

'This is true,' says Miles. 'And anyway, I do all the stuff that girls in turn are supposed to find a turn-on, strange creatures that they are: flowers, unexpected presents, mystery weekends away in luxury hotels, that awful wet weekend back in June when I said fuck it and flew us both to Capri and got a local restaurant to bring us dinner down on the beach by moonlight. All the same, I think . . . I think Beth knows all about pleasure, but I don't know if she really understands happiness.' He looks up and fixes me with his searching clean swimming-pool-blue eyes. 'I don't know if she'll ever be really *happy*.'

And I shake my head and look away. Then look back, say, 'There's nothing really wrong, is there?'

A pause and then a tiny sigh. Such a small sigh from such a large person is poignant. But there is always something revolting about that kind of self-protective pity for the person you've just kicked in the balls. It's the executioner apologizing to the corpse after the act. It's an added insult.

Miles sets his glass down. 'I . . . I think she's seeing someone else.'

I say nothing.

'On top of that, I think she's – I think she's mad. *Really*. In fact I think she's stark staring bonkers. No, I mean it, I'm serious. I don't think she even knows truth from lies, I don't think she's even on this planet half the time.'

'She's a daydreamer,' I say, stopping abruptly. Careful now. I don't know *too* much about her, after all, do I?

Miles looks up at me. 'She's a fuck sight more than that. I mean, I know her work and all that whole world, that fashion and acting thing, is totally unreal, but I always thought she knew that too. You know? And of course there's bound to be drugs and stuff all tied up with it, and . . . but she's not even *into* it that much these days. She jokes that she's too unreliable for them.' He lets his hands fall on to the table. 'I don't know. I'm at my wits' end, Dan.'

I place a peanut neatly between my lips. 'So what's this about her seeing someone else?'

Miles struggles for a moment and then says, 'She told me she was popping back to see her mum last Friday. Then Friday night her mum actually *phoned*.'

'Did you say anything?'

He shakes his head. 'Managed to hold my tongue. I just said she was staying the night with a girlfriend and her mum says she'll phone again tomorrow. Then when Beth gets back on Saturday I ask her how her mother was and she says fine, and goes into this long and highly convincing spiel about how they went round a craft fair together and I asked her if they'd bought anything and she was caught on the hop and looked away and then said, "Oh, Mum bought some honey."' He sucks some orange juice from the glass, swallows bitterly. '*Honey*, for fuck's sake.'

'So you haven't said any more to her?'

'Not yet,' says Miles. He sighs. 'I can't. I don't want to lose her.' He shrugs tiredly. 'I don't know. I don't know whether I'm shocked or not, in a way. It's more – I just wish she'd settle down. Like I say, it's more like she's *mad* in some way. This self-destructive streak she has. Don't you think?'

'Has she? I . . . sort of. A lot of girls have it.'

'Why though? Is it our fault? My fault?'

'No,' I say firmly. 'No way is it your fault. I just think – I mean, Beth is still pretty young, after all.'

'Really? You think that's all it is?'

'It could be. Couldn't it?'

'Yeah. I suppose so. So I shouldn't say anything?'

I consider. 'Probably not.'

24

Our chaste affair continues. Chaste, but intimate. We have no secrets.

One day I ask her, 'So how many men have you slept with then? What's your magic number?'

She laughs, with startled eyes. 'Blimey, that's a bit direct, isn't it? No girl can count beyond three anyway.'

'Oh, come on.'

She closes her eyes and raises her nose in the air and folds her hands in her lap and tries hard to look demure and discreet, although it doesn't really work.

'OK, but would you *need* to count beyond three, if you *could*?'

She opens her eyes and avoids looking at me and smiles to herself, an evasive, elusive, slightly uncertain smile. 'Um . . . well, ye-es,' she says at last.

'Go on then,' I say. 'Name the number.'

She tells me what she *thinks* it is.

'Nearly thirty partners,' I say. 'Not too bad.'

'Nearly thirty *men*.'

'Hunh?'

'You asked how many *men*.' She grins lopsidedly. 'You've established how many *men* I've slept with, not how many *partners*.'

'You're teasing.' I stare at her. 'You're not, are you?' She shakes her head. 'Livvie?'

'Maybe.'

'How many others?' My voice betrays such an urgent need to know, is so intensely, schoolboyishly comical.

'Well,' she says, 'if you're going to include women, what constitutes *sleeping with*? How far do you have to go?'

'Well, if I was adding up the *blokes* I've slept with –'
adding with scrambling haste – 'which of course I'm not,
never having in fact slept with any blokes, obviously –'
(thinking: apart from that unfortunate incident, more of a
misunderstanding really, with Byles in the tent on CCF exercises in the fourth form; and that strange, dreamy, almost
romantic summer of the Lower Sixth, when I was so friendly
with Hamilton-Dalrymple . . .) 'then I'd define *sleeping with*
as . . . well, penetration, I suppose. You know. With his knob.
Or mine.'

Beth raises her eyebrows.

'Not just the sort of minor fooling around that went on in
the showers after rugby. Or,' I add very quietly, 'on CCF
exercises, say.'

'I see.'

There is an embarrassed silence. (Embarrassing for me,
ticklishly hilarious for Beth.)

'So,' I resume. 'Girls. Well, *sleeping with* must mean . . .
um. Attaining, or, OK, coming close to, the point of orgasm
because of what someone else is doing to you in bed.' (Jesus,
I never realized that defining *sleeping with* could be so
tricky.)

'Or wherever.'

'Or wherever. I guess you'd have to say that *that* constitutes full-blown *sleeping with*, no? Anything else might just
be . . . y'know. A friendly cuddle or something.'

'OK then,' she says. 'I've slept with enough women to
take me over thirty.'

My eyes sparkle. I wish they didn't, but I can feel them.

'Although,' she goes on, 'if the definition of *sleeping with* is
simply – what was your charmlessly clinical phrase? –
"attaining the point of orgasm", and incidentally that is such
a *male* way of thinking about it . . .'

'Well, I *am* male. I can't help it, it's just the way I was born.'

'Thinking of orgasm as a *point*, for instance. It may be just
a *point* to a bloke, but for a girl it's a . . . *ideally* it's a . . . if your

184

lover's any good at all, it's a . . . a *zone*, a . . . you know. A *plateau*. A *point* makes it sound like about half a second. So – as I was saying. What was I saying?'

'About girls,' I remind her, perhaps a little over-eagerly. 'You and other girls. In bed. Together. *Naked*.'

'And your definition. Yeah, well, like I say, if orgasm is the definition of sleeping with someone, then I really can't remember. I mean, there must have been one or two drunken flings . . .'

I steeple my fingers. 'Sleeping together, male/female, denotes penetration. That much is evident.'

'What with?' she giggles.

'Oh please.' But I'm flummoxed again. 'I suppose you could define sleeping together, female/female, as implying either lingual, digital or . . . artificial penetration.'

'These definitions of yours,' she sighs, 'are possibly the least erotic musings about sex that I have ever heard. Men are so *fixated*. Female/female sex, as you call it, is not just about using your finger as a willy substitute, you know. You're trying to define the indefinable. Just as defining your exact sexuality in terms of *straight* or *gay* is impossible.'

'Yeah. Maybe. Still . . . these girls of yours.'

'It was . . . interesting,' she admits. 'OK. Once at school – although some of my friends, the boarding-school ones, say that that doesn't count, *everyone's* gay at boarding-school.'

'I don't know what you mean,' I snap.

'Several, casual. Once, with a close girlfriend when we were both miserable and recently maltreated by men. And once – with a married friend.'

'Married! What . . . you mean she was a secret lesbo?'

Beth sighs.

'Oh, sorry, I forgot, you can't define the indefinable, I'm being too crude, we're all about 20 per cent *really* etc. Did her husband ever find out?'

She hesitates. 'Um . . . he knew about it quite quickly, actually.'

'Really?'

She nods. 'Well, he would, wouldn't he? He was watching at the time.'

The sick feeling, the helpless fascination, the hopeless jealousy. She has done it all, she'll do it all again, there is nothing I can give her. I feel like I'm looking into an abyss and the abyss is looking into me and there is nothing I can do but slide helplessly towards the dizzying edge in lust and fascination. And wish she was different. And hope she stays the same.

'This married couple,' I say. 'Tell me about it.'

There must be something else other than, on the one hand, the consumer dream and, on the other hand, heroin. There must be another way, with a greater complexity of relationships and burden of responsibilities and a pleasure in doing the right thing the right way, and always guided by a bracingly pessimistic sense of the fragility of human things.

But Beth . . . She's *happy* with this? Could she be? With this . . . *mess*, this *trash*. She sang it to me last night, sad-happy, '*We're tra -a -ash, you and me . . .*'

And still I feel it, all the same: what it must be like to live in her world, and still I yearn for it: *nostalgie de la boue*.

One inebriated afternoon, after a long lunch in Old Compton Street, Beth suddenly says, 'Right, it's my turn to embarrass *you* now' (although I don't remember that I had been embarrassing her in any way), and grabbing me by the hand she drags me into a sex shop.

When we reappear fifteen minutes later, I'm as flushed as fuck. Beth has been unbelievably explicit in questioning this sad, myopic assistant (nylon shirt, faint whiff of stale, lonely semen, a philosophy graduate no doubt, no cash, no girlfriend) about the quality and longevity of his merchandise. I've also shelled out nearly £60 smackeroonies.

'OK. You win,' I say. 'You are more embarrassing than I am.'

I can't keep up with her. I will never be able to keep up with her. She will skip on ahead, laughing, in a halo of perpetual sunshine, clasping her hands together delightedly like a careless little girl, troubles falling on her head like rain on glass and trickling hurtless away; and I will be left far behind, helpless, sinking, drowning.

Ah God, ah God, that night when we two . . .

Daniel, Daniel. O my prophetic soul. Dithering Hamlet and his country matters.

And Beth too. Beth's burdens. She knows them all too well, she tells me. Women have to do a lot, lot more these days: they have to be top executives at IBM *and* wear a different Nicole Farhi suit every day *and* drive a growling Porsche, FAST, *and* have three immaculate kids called Elizabeth and James and Jessica (all doing terribly well at school and very happy there), *and* stay slim and cool and have the complexion of a *Vogue* cover girl, an airbrushed *Vogue* cover girl at that, and a lovely house in the country with inglenook fireplace and oak floorboards as well as a bijou pad in Belsize Park, *at the very least*, and if they don't make the grade then they better fucking get their act together now.

And men too, I tell her, have to stop acting like men and doing the stuff they enjoy and must lose their love of adventure and learn to think of all that as just juvenile and laddish and they have to *grow up*, i.e. be more like women.

Familiarity and adventure: yes, that's it, those are the cruxes (the cruces?), I've decided. Familiarity we hate and adventure we love. It's a boy's thing – no, fuck it, it's a man's thing, there's nothing wrong with it, that love of adventure. That stalwart soldier in his red coat kissing his pretty young wife goodbye at the garden gate, the babe in arms looking up at his bobbing shako and crying, that quintessential, immemorial Homeric moment, and the redcoat soldier turning and marching off to join the regiment, to go to war against some other men far away whom he neither knows nor cares about . . . There is something in that man's heart at that moment that feels that even if his chances of coming back alive are only moderately good, and his chances of coming back missing a limb or two are uncomfortably high, nevertheless there is, far greater than these fears, a feeling of absolute and pure head-rush exhilaration and happiness. Adventure! Travel! Fighting! Facing down death and surviving to tell the tale! Testing yourself on a man-size knife edge! Nothing else comes close to that. Nothing. But it's not available any more, that buzz, so we have to make do with football. And women even sneer at our taste for that, the last place where the old male virtues of loyalty and determination and physical courage and daring have any role to play at all. That's what we're reduced to.

And that is something the pretty young wife weeping at the garden gate will never understand. Although at least if she didn't understand it she used to accept it as the way things are. If it was hardship for her, it wasn't exactly a fucking picnic for us either, but it was the way things were. The only alternative is . . . this. I scowl ferociously around the park. I see thirty-something dads with fifty-something paunches straining under pastel-coloured V-neck pullovers, pushing the kids round the park on a Sunday afternoon while worrying about their health, mummy sitting at home frantically checking the figures for tomorrow's meeting on her laptop. And Jesus H. Christ, *doesn't it make us happy*!

At which I do something I've never done before: I spit, a bitter gob of caffeinated mucus, hitting the tarmac with a definitive splat. *Fuck*, I think.

I think all this is called 'Trying to Intellectualize Your Way Out of a Problem That Only Has an Emotional Answer'. And the *energy* I expend, desperately trying to persuade myself that I am not naturally monogamous!

Ironic, really.

'Isn't it? Hey? Isn't it? It is, isn't it? Hey?'

A few days later I am trying these ideas out on Clive, with much insistence and finger-jabbing. Clive becomes annoyed, in his mild way.

'No,' he protests. No, he doesn't feel 'absolutely sickened' by the idea of spending the rest of his life with the same woman.

No, I didn't mean that exactly. That is not what I meant at all.

I can't help noticing, incidentally, that Clive doesn't say 'with Emma', he just says 'with the same woman', so it could well be that little Clive is deceiving himself after all. Perhaps Clive's 'a woman' represents in his mind some composite, idealized version of the less-than-perfect realities on offer? Some chimerical, DIY female of the imagination's prosthetics, made up of Liz Hurley's body, Marie Curie's brain and the soul of Abbess Hildegard of Bingen.

'You really mean that? You could quite happily settle down? Not be tempted?'

'Not not be tempted,' says Clive. 'I didn't say that. But I wouldn't be *sickened* by the thought of it – you know, life-long monogamy. Which was the word you used: *sickened*.'

I nod. I did.

'Will you please take your partner for the next dance?' I say. 'But what if you were told, "Will you please take your partner for the *one and only dance*? After that we are all going to die"? That's what life is like, isn't it?'

'Very deep,' says Clive. 'Very philosophical.'

'I think so.'

Clive considers for a moment. 'What would the dance be?'

'Hm?'

'What would the last dance be? The music?'

'The *only* dance, not just the last one. Oh, I don't know. "Moon River"?'

'Really?'

'Why not?'

'That's quite a good one. *There's such – a lot of world – to see-ee-ee,*' warbles Clive.

'But you're only allowed one.'

'One world?'

'That too, but no, one partner.'

'Oh, I see,' says Clive. Then again, 'Yes, I *see*. There's only one dance, and one partner.'

'In a room full of beautiful, kind, sweet-natured girls.'

'God, rub it in, why don't you?' says Clive.

I shrug. 'I didn't make it that way. But that's the way it is.'

'But,' says Clive, after further rumination, 'is it? I mean, if all these girls are *equally* beautiful, kind, big-breasted . . .'

'Um, *sweet-natured* was what I actually said.'

'OK – if they're all equally *attractive*, for whatever reason, whether character-wise or jubblie-wise, then why do you want them *all*?'

'In the genes,' I say lamely. 'Actually –' after a pause – 'I think you've put your finger on it.'

'I have?'

'Yes, indeedy. The whole point is, as you say, that they're *not* all the same. In fact, they're all different. This is the whole point. One girl is attractive because she's this gorgeous blonde. Then another 'cos she's a dark, exotic – Indian, maybe, and a true-born princess . . .'

'You leave her alone.'

'Maybe another's attractive because she's very together, very confident, elegant, etc. So you go for her. Then halfway through the dance you suddenly see this other girl across the room, who's equally attractive because she's all over the place, absolute boiling chaos, dangerous even. Drunk as a skunk, dancing on the tables, shaking her long hair, arms in the air –' (Not that I'm thinking of Beth here, of course . . .)

'I don't like those kind,' says Clive. 'I mean, I know the *type* I like. Surely you must have an ideal, and when you meet a girl who fits it near enough, you think, Bingo! Sorted. Result. Otherwise – I mean, otherwise you're saying you want every girl in the world. And that's just greedy.'

'Yeah,' I agree. 'It is. Like one of those revolting middle-aged politicians with their fading hair and committee-room pallor who have to prove themselves not only through political power but also by shagging their research assistants, wheezily and joylessly, across the desk in their poky House of Commons office. It's so . . . *demanding*. Like a baby, only a lot less endearing. Grab grab grab.'

Clive and I even formulate a new type: Supermarket Man. Supermarket Man demands his right to Perfect Love and Sexual Satisfaction like they're stuff on a supermarket shelf. You can have it all – look at those people in the adverts! – if only you know where to look. Supermarket Man expects it to fill all the gaps left by those wacky hopes of the sixties that went with flared jeans and iron-on sunflowers on the holes, and further back, I suppose, the end of the Empire and the death of religion and all that. Nowadays there's not much room for such things, and to the ones with brains and a sense of irony existing religious forms remain woodenly unappealing, if not actually embarrassing. Even I find them pretty embarrassing.

To Supermarket Man, everything is a commodity. The shelves groan under the weight of exotic air-freighted fruit with unpronounceable names, and organic ostrich steaks, and Algerian Shiraz. Yet Supermarket Man is still dissatisfied, and hunts up and down the aisles looking also for designer religions (to tell him he'll live for ever), or at least designer babies (to tell him that, even if *he* doesn't live for ever, his genes will). And, of course, perfect designer lovers. Because Supermarket Man is an idealist and that's all he's asking for, really. Perfection.

And that's Supermarket Man: lovelorn and heartsick and self-obsessed and idealistic and deluded, poor li'l orphan in the lonely dreamworld of the universal supermarket.

Have I no discernment?

But I return to the fray.

'OK, greedy, but in what way? You're saying it's just lust. But what if at the heart of it is actually an *intellectual* or even a *spiritual* greed or appetite: a desire to know the world. That's very human, isn't it, that's our great characteristic as a species, this lifelong childlike curiosity? And what if one way, the best way even, to *know*, to find out stuff about the world, is to sleep around? Hunh?'

'Hm.'

'And what if this ideal is never found? I mean, you never find your *ideal*, do you?'

'I have,' says Clive dreamily.

'You think you have. Just wait a few weeks or months and you'll start to look at other girls.'

'You're just a sexual pessimist.'

'I certainly am.'

'You just think there's this incurable gulf between the sexes . . .'

'You can't cure a gulf. An *unbridgeable* gulf, maybe.'

'And that men and women want different things, and no relationship lasts for ever, and that passion is always short-lived, and monogamy is a comforting delusion, and nobody understands you.'

'Well,' I say, 'yes. I think that just about covers it.'

Clive smiles. 'Well, I'm going to marry Amrita.'

'You are? What, you mean, you've actually . . .'

'Not yet, no. I've got to get rid of Emma first, for one thing.' He broods. 'Oh, and we've all got to go to a Hunt Ball at my place in a couple of weeks.'

'What, at Castle Clive?'

'Castle Clive,' he says.

I watch no news, or if I do I take none in. The plight of the Kurds, the Sudanese, greenhouse gas legislation, the NHS, Europe . . . My world has shrunk to myself and my love. The outer world could burn away and I wouldn't care, cocooned there in the darkened room, tightly wrapped in the delirious selfishness of lovers, free radicals in the body politic, free agents oblivious of our duties and our passion's damage, our passion burning in the dark room with a violet glow and reaching out to consume the fabric round us. Politics doesn't matter, doesn't even exist. Love and death are all that matter.

It is a chaste affair but a careless one, the risks we take only augmenting our pleasure, skipping, hand in hand, giggling, collapsing against railings, eliciting looks of envy or resentment or baffled amusement from the lonely, the not loved, the not in love.

We go to an exhibition of German Romantic Art, mostly Caspar David Friedrich, but some other stuff as well: some Nazarenes, Cornelius, Overbeck. Beth doesn't often go to art exhibitions. 'At least,' she says, 'not art this old. I'm not much of an exhibitionist.' I raise my eyebrows.

Inside, I proceed to lecture her on Romanticism: the French Revolution and the Liberation of the Bastille (net result, seven prisoners: four forgers, the incestuous Comte de Solages, a lunatic and an Irishman who believed he was Julius Caesar). Then back to Rousseau, and then forwards to Mary Shelley and Frankenstein and Vampires and Byron and Galvani, and then Joseph Wright of Derby, and then back to Caravaggio and then forward to Friedrich himself and then (rather vaguely skated over) Goethe and Schiller and Kant and Hegel and then Schopenhauer, from whom I can even quote: *Want and boredom are the twin poles of human life.* Then I am just getting into Heine and Mendelssohn and Mahler, with a digression on Jewish Romanticism, when Beth interrupts.

'Daniel. Daniel. Would you mind shutting up for a *little* while, so that I can just look at the pictures?'

I subside into an injured silence.

Because of course I *love* being able to tell her things she doesn't know. But I didn't really mean to lecture her, certainly not to prove my superiority over her in any way. I would hate her to think that all I was doing was bullying her into a sense of her own intellectual inadequacy: where would the pleasure be in that? No, this intellectual turkey-cocking is in fact something quite unintellectual and far more deep-rooted and instinctive: it is a manifestation of the innate urge to protect. This ring of words and facts and cultural offcuts that I offer her might *appear* to be no more than a crude form of courtship display – look, aren't I clever? So my genes are clever, so our kids will be clever, and you know how important brains are going to be for the coming generations, so please please *please* can't I sleep with you?

But no, in addition to this there is something else quite different. I'm offering her a kind of protective umbrella, to protect her, to protect both of us, from the storms of indifference and stupidity all around us.

But it is just one of the many incommunicable things between us, forever not understood. But then again, if there is often this intellectual discontent, this hopeless and everlasting disjunction, there are times when it is overruled by a pure emotional trust, by a sweet and childlike unspoken pact between us. Nothing is said, everything is understood.

Beth then admits that she doesn't actually *mind* being told stuff about why two-stroke engines can't run in reverse, or about how MagLev trains work, or that steam engines were first actually invented in Alexandria around AD 50. She doesn't actually *mind* being told all this stuff, and certainly doesn't remember any of it a week later. But what she positively likes, she says, is the look on my face, the flush of enthusiasm, the gestures of my thin hands as I set off on some new topic-for-the-day. Then she smiles and I apologize for talking too much and she says she doesn't mind, she likes it really, and loops her arm through mine, and we walk closely side by side, my greater height protecting her a little from the wind and rain, our umbrella protecting both of us, and it is at such moments that intellectual discontent and

194

suspicion and all the irremediable failures of human under-standing are suddenly outweighed by that pure emotional trust, that sweet and unspoken childlike pact between us.

'You can be in love with two people at once, can't you?' I quiz her.

She draws deep on her cigarette and speaks as she exhales, her gaze fixed on me under half-closed eyelids, and in her best Dietrich drawl, and with that tantalizing, unfor-gettable smile of hers, full of sad regrets and reckless promises, hovering on her lips, she says, 'Oh, yes. I do it all the time.'

I know that it's still pure unmixed, blind, half-ignorant adoration that I feel for her at this stage, the besotted-ado-lescent stage, but soon it'll be the more lasting, dancing double-helix of love + resentment-that-I-should-love-you-this-much that spirals steadily at the heart of permanent relationships.

And I find I can't read any more. I've lost all imagination, all easy sympathy with merely fictional characters. Because suddenly reality is far more interesting than imagination, my own life more dramatic than that of any fictional charac-ter. I try to read *Anna Karenina* for the second time, and the *Princesse de Clèves*, and *Adolphe*, and *The Rainbow*, and *The End of the Affair*, in a half-hearted attempt to find guidance and wisdom from those who have gone before. But I never get further than the first few pages before my eyes begin to swim with boredom and longing and the book drops back into my lap defeated and my gaze falls on the window-pane and I listen to music instead. There's always music.

And it's springtime, when the world is puddlewonderful, and all the peeplies etc., and in the park there's spring sun-shine that dyes your eyelashes golden, and sauntering beneath the horse chestnut trees you see the *purple-headed crocuses thrusting their way up into the fecund lap of the moist, vernal earth* and chuckle lewdly to yourself. Horse chestnut trees and voracious squirrels and starlings and the foxy babes you always see in Ken High Street and Church Street and I don't look at them, any of them, because they are not Beth.

Never mind what you can do in life, it's all the other things, the infinitely more things, you will never do that horrify. I find it almost unbearable. Already I can make a list of things that I will never do. I will never be a student at the Sorbonne, never live in the Latin Quarter and wear a little beret and smoke rollies. I will never be a rock star. I will never join the army, never be a soldier or fight in a war. I am already too old to do any of these things.

It always amazes me that other people don't seem tormented by this, by the limitations of the single life. They even seem *contented*, for fuck's sake.

It's the small hours, I'm very drunk, I'm on my way back from an assignation with a client in St John's Wood and I couldn't get it up. This is the worst thing that can befall a male prostitute. Humbled in the act of love. Tomorrow she – by no means the most monstrously hideous crone I've had to deal with – she'll weepily phone Caroline and tell her. And Caroline will phone me and remonstrate gently, '*Dar*-ling . . .'

And I'll be finished.

So I'm lying down here on Primrose Hill, in my dinner jacket, drunk, the grass damp and comforting beneath me, tears on my cheeks – *tears*, for fuck's sake – and looking up at the stars, piercing the darkening sky, brilliant incisors, diamond-head drills coming through the velvet, and thinking, some of us may be looking at the stars, but we're all still lying in the gutter. Stars light years away and fading fast. Imagine the future up there, infinite and high-tech and dazzling between the colder, lonelier stars, and the people of the future too, and their gene-perfected bodies manicured and pedicured, censed and toned, miracles of prosthetic art and cyberhuman handiwork, spiralling for ever in the zero gravity of their sad starlit domes, making random love to whomever, human or machine, polymorphous, perfect and perverse. Strange, starlit and sad.

So never mind all the parallel lives you'll never live. Imagine all the past lives – and all the infinity of future lives too! Whole worlds that you'll never know, whole galaxies yet unknown, for you forever unknown. This urge to know: explore/have/possess. It is unbearable. So unbearable that you have to laugh.

And laughing I arise and wander home.

25

'I've been sacked.'

'What – as a prostitute?'

'As a prostitute.'

'God, that's awful. What a colossal *failure* you are.'

'Thanks.'

'You can't even make a career for yourself as a *prostitute*!'

'Like I said, thanks. Actually, I was on the verge of resigning anyway. But . . .'

Beth smiles down at me from the top step of Miles's luxurious, fabulously expensive, egregiously-unlike-my-own-sock-in-the-Bush Chelsea terraced house. 'You'd better come in.'

We're lying on the sofa drinking tea, fully clothed, making spoons. I have suggested that she should take her top off so I can give her a thorough but entirely asexual back massage, but she's adamant that she won't. It's mid-afternoon. It's what we do. We don't have sex, but we do this a lot. One day Miles will come home early and find us and disembowel us both with a paintbrush.

I stroke her hair. 'So. How many men have you *really* slept with?'

She sighs. 'Oh, I don't know, Dan.'

I sit up on one elbow. 'Whaddya mean, *you don't know*? You've lost count?'

A ghost of a smile. 'Yes, I've lost count. Not *too* many.'

'How many's not *too* many?'

'Well – not more than . . . not a *lot* more than . . . a hundred?'

There is a profound silence.

'Not more than a hundred?'

'Not a *lot* more than a hundred,' she corrects me. She twists round on her back, her hands fluttering free ready to protect her face, because among those 'not a lot more than a hundred' there have no doubt been a few who have enjoyed hitting her when they have felt, according to their own stern consciences, morally entitled to do so. She knows I won't hit her, I hope, but it is a reflex action by now. 'And I don't know what that expression of yours is supposed to mean,' she says. 'I've never claimed to be anything other than a useless tart.'

'A hundred,' I'm saying softly to myself, 'over, what . . . you're twenty-six now. Over eight years?'

'More like nine or ten,' she says.

'Even so. That's like a different partner every . . . month.'

'Exactly,' she says. 'It's not *that* much when you think about it, is it?'

'Excluding steady relationships.'

'Well . . .' she says, fiddling with the corner of a cushion. 'Um . . . sometimes.'

'What times? What about now? Is there anyone else? Has there been?' She doesn't answer. 'Beth?'

'Oh, for God's sake. Who, what, when? Jesus, talk about *hypocrisy*. Coming from a professional *whore*.'

'*Ex*-whore.'

She ignores me. 'Yes, there have probably been a couple since I first slept with you, OK? So what?'

'But . . . but . . .' I feel desperate and helpless. Stupid. 'Why?'

'Why?' Her voice softens again when she sees my puzzled hurt. 'I don't know why. It just happens. What reason do you need?'

'You . . .'

'Lust. Loneliness. Boredom. Worry, even. It happens, darling.'

'But . . . *a hundred*.'

I want to tell her that there are different kinds of promiscuity. There is the life-loving, fun-loving, irresponsible, generous, Casanova, perpetual-adolescent kind, and there is the more despairing, pleasureless kind. A prostitute knows all about the second kind. And so, I think, does Beth. But I can't tell her this. I can't tell her anything.

Her eyes are deep wells of hurt and she freezes up a little further and repeats that tedious mantra I've heard before. 'You don't own me, nor does Miles. Nobody owns me.' Then she relents a little and offers an explanation of sorts. 'For a long time I was – OK, promiscuous, and just wanted someone to look after me and make me feel safe. Then I found Miles, or rather he found me, and I thought, At last! And then . . .' She struggles. 'I don't know. It wasn't right. It never is. I never find it.' She doesn't look at me. 'Some people,' she says, after a long pause, 'are occasionally unfaithful. Me, I'm occasionally monogamous.' She turns and kisses me lightly on the cheek and springs off the sofa. 'But not very often,' she adds. 'More tea?'

'He said to me not long ago that he thought you were seeing someone else. I said I was sure you weren't.' She says nothing. 'God, what would he do if he found out?'

She smiles. 'Probably kill me.'

26

Well, if I can't sort my own life out, at least I can interfere in Clive's.

After all, we're all supposed to be going up to Castle Clive next weekend for this Hunt Ball, and by *all* I mean Emma too: still Clive's tenacious consort. And I, for one, do not fancy being stuck in the back of a minibus for eight hours with Emma. For that reason alone, I think it is high time he ditched the bitch and got it together with Amrita.

I suggest a dinner party for Clive, Amrita, Miles, Beth, Kate and me, round at our place. Clive accepts with alacrity. He tells Emma it's a work thing. Amrita can only make it for drinks, then she has to go on somewhere else. But that will have to do.

Kate and I cook together – so sweet, so touching. Back at the table, I murmur, 'Such a shame Emma couldn't make it tonight too. Still, it'll be fun up in Scotland, won't it? The more, the merrier!'

Clive shoots me a venomous look. Amrita sees it and raises her glass to hide her mouth.

Later, Amrita says it's time for her to go off to her lecture at the RGS about the funeral rites of the Toraja peoples of the Sulawesi highlands. There is really no answer to this, so we say goodbye and each give her a kiss on the cheek, and I say, 'So, we shall see you again soon?' And she nods and smiles. As soon as she's gone, Clive lays into me.

'I'm *not* a bastard,' I protest.

'Oh, he *is* a bastard, I promise,' puts in Beth.

Kate thinks this is hilarious. I think it's positively dangerous. Beth is knocking back the wine and although she doesn't get drunk, she gets risky. And when people start being rude to each other in just that particular way, everyone knows that it's really flirting. Miles says nothing.

'So what was all that about Emma?' Clive goes on. 'And "the more the merrier"?'

'Nothing. I mean, you are still *with* Emma, aren't you?'

'Oh, leave him alone, Dan,' says Kate. 'Never you mind him,' she says to Clive.

'He can't help it,' adds Beth.

Clive says nothing, continues to destroy the remains of the bread roll beneath his nervous fingers. At last he says distantly, 'I'm crazy about her.'

'*Emma?*' I say, aghast.

Clive looks at me as if I'm quite the stupidest person he has ever encountered. 'Not Emma, you twit. *Amrita.*'

I smile smugly. 'I know, Clive old chap. I'm only teasing. Of course I know you're besotted with your Indian princess. It's all too evident.'

'God, you're insufferable sometimes,' says Clive.

'Most of the time, in fact,' says Beth.

I ignore her. 'I understand,' I say to Clive. I wonder whether to reach out and pat Clive on the back of the hand, but decide that this might just be *too* provocative. 'You're only annoyed because you thought your unrequited love for your Dark Lady was a secret.'

'Unrequited?' says Clive. 'How do you know?'

'Well – I mean, I *assume* . . .' I'm already backtracking, realizing I may have gone too far and actually hurt Clive's feelings. I fumble in my jacket pocket.

'You really are an A1 bastard,' says Clive.

I extend a grubby plastic bag towards him.

'And no,' he spits, 'I *don't* want one of your stupid fucking "I'm so endearing" mangy scrofulous fucking mint humbugs.'

'Go on,' I say, adding with reckless generosity, 'take two if you like.'

Clive gives me a long cold stare and then snatches a mint humbug from the bag and viciously bites its head off.

'Hey hey hey,' says Kate, coming in with a dish of poached salmon. 'No sweeties between courses. Disgusting habit.' She waggles her head. 'This one always was a terrible one for the mint humbugs.'

'Always was a *cunt*,' hisses Clive.

Everyone is really quite shocked.

But, you see, you have to be cruel to be kind.

It's a successful enough dinner party, though Miles is very quiet. Clive whispers to me on the way out that he has changed his mind about Beth, whom, he admits, he previously didn't like that much at all.

'She's wonderful,' he says. 'And . . . and you do that thing, don't you?'

'What thing?'

'Just you and her. That special wavelength thing that leaves everyone else out. It's not deliberate, I know, it's quite touching. And that slagging-each-other-off-the-whole-time thing as well.'

'I don't know what you mean.'

'I do,' he grins. 'Don't you know *Much Ado About Nothing*?'

Seen through a window in Greek Street, on a balmy April evening:

A couple are dining together in a restaurant. She is an Indian beauty in a sari and a cashmere shawl, with a single gold bangle on each wrist and earrings of gold and topaz. With her kohl-rimmed eyes and red lipstick, she's a tantalizing mix of East and West, and she knows it.

Her dining partner is a lucky man.

Especially given certain physical disadvantages under which he labours: he is perhaps two inches shorter than her; he is carrot-haired and plentifully freckled; and he looks abjectly nervous. Other men in the restaurant have clocked him and thought, Not a chance there, mate. Way out of your league. Nevertheless, he obviously has one big advantage, for every now and then he appears to say something, expressionlessly, that has the Indian beauty throwing back her head and shaking her long raven hair and laughing with resonant full-throated laughter that sets her gold earrings dancing and glittering. Jewelled fruit on a dark tree, turning in the breeze. Her dining partner looks faintly surprised and pleased and dares to think that perhaps the humble woodcutter's son is in with a chance after all.

After the meal, Clive drives Amrita back to her studio flat in Bethnal Green, trying to imagine how she would look fumbling for her keys at the front door and then turning round to him and murmuring, 'Well, you better come in for a coffee, darling.' Waiting at the lights on Old Street, he is appalled to see his pump-action water pistol still lodged in the driver's door. If it begins to leak, it could be disastrous. Water, OK, but this isn't just water. And thereby hangs a tale.

Only this morning, Clive had to drive out to somewhere called Ruislip to see a client, and on the way, the traffic on the Westway stagnant in an appalling traffic jam, he was seized by the terrible need for a pee (as one invariably is in stagnant traffic jams). He held out for twenty minutes or so, but at last he knew that he *just had to go*. Fingers skittering around the various compartments and map pockets of his car, the only container they encountered was this pink and yellow pump-action water pistol. Saying a quick prayer of thanksgiving for the fact that there was no sweaty trucker high in his cab alongside him looking down and watching every move he made, he had unscrewed the pint cylinder that sat on top of the weapon and relieved himself into it with a rapturous sigh. Then he screwed it back on to the pistol to stopper the cylinder, resolving to empty it as soon as he parked at work. Then he forgot all about it.

And now he remembers it. Now, of all times, when he is driving home the most lustrously beautiful, intellectually formidable girl he has ever met in his life – now he remembers that he is carrying a pink and yellow pump-action water pistol brimming with his own pee, lodged in the door pocket of his tinny little 900cc 'car' designed by midgets in pebble glasses and built under licence in Mongolia.

And there has already been an unfortunate pee-oriented incident between himself and this young lady, from which he only narrowly escaped with his reputation intact.

For fuck's *sake*.

He drives grimly eastward, knuckles white on the wheel, eyes flicking nervously between the rear-view mirror, the road ahead, the door pocket with its heinous contents and Amrita's slim brown arms (so slim! so brown! so beautiful!).

Then she cries out, 'Left here!' And too late. He has shot past her turning and is trapped in the baffling one-way system around Columbia Road.

'Oh, hell,' he says. 'I'll drive round again.'

'No, don't worry,' she says, leaning forward already, clicking out of her seat belt and reaching for the door handle. 'Just pull over here and I'll walk back.'

'You sure?'

She nods.

He pulls over to the left and stops the car. She leans swiftly over and kisses him on the cheek. 'Thanks, Clive,' she says. 'That was a lot of fun.'

'It was? So you might care to repeat the experience some time?'

'I *might*,' she says with a smile. 'Yes.'

And then she's out of the car and shutting the door behind her and bending down to blow him another kiss through the window and moving round the back of the car and crossing the street. He waits to see her safely into Columbia Road, gazing adoringly into his rear-view mirror, adjusting it slightly to follow her round the corner and out of sight.

Then he picks up the two youths sitting on a low wall where she has just passed by. One black, one white, both baseball-capped, baggy-trousered and enormous: raised since infancy on a high-protein diet of crunchy chicken mega-nuggets and three-pound burgers. One of them follows Amrita with his eyes and then slaps the other on the arm. They both stand and follow her round the corner and out of sight.

Emitting a strange succession of yelps, squeals and gurgles, Clive is out of the car in a trice and halfway across the road, straight into the path of an oncoming transit van. The driver of the van is asleep at the time, having driven from Newcastle since noon, and so Clive would certainly have died had he not, with a further strange yelp, spun around and run back to the car to retrieve his water pistol, unwittingly managing to avoid the transit van in the process. Then he scampers over the road again, water pistol pumped up and ready to shoot its unhygienic load, succeeding in colliding only with a taxi this time, barrelling over the bonnet and back on to his feet on the other side in immaculate TV-cop fashion. He hares around the corner and sees . . .

Tableau: Amrita tugging at one end of her handbag, the black boy tugging at the other end, and the white boy raising his right fist preparatory to smacking this dumb Paki bitch in the mouth for givin' 'em such dis. Before his fist can land home, however, Kurt (for such is his name) feels an extraordinarily acidulous jet of water hit him across the eyes and he steps back aghast, crying out, 'Ar've bin blinded, man, viss fucking bitch maced me!'

Milton (for such is his name), always confused when more than one thing happens at a time, releases his grip on the Paki bitch's handbag and turns in puzzlement towards Kurt, only to feel himself being punched in the back of the head.

"Ave 'im, Milt, fuckin' 'ave 'im!' roars Kurt, shaking his head violently and rubbing his reddened eyeballs like a tearful little boy.

Without another word, mute, inglorious Milton turns and is about to punch a startled Clive on the schnozzle, when he feels a much harder and altogether more authoritative blow to the side of his head, struck by a foot rather than a fist, which sends him sprawling sideways against the wall. Kurt, more enraged than ever, advances on this Paki bitch who thinks just because she's been to a couple of karate evening classes at her posh local gym, she's now Brandon Fucking Lee. He'll show her. He'll mash her fucking face in.

Kurt doesn't show her, however. Instead he feels his advance curtailed by her foot landing firmly in his midriff, bending him double and sagging like a windless sail. Milton, meanwhile, is having another, rather half-hearted go, but she dissuades him with a gentle and regretful cuff that puts him down again. Kurt retreats and finally sits down in a puddle, head bowed.

Clive drops the water pistol that he is still clutching and turns to Amrita. 'Are you all right?'

'Of course I'm all right.' And to his surprise and delight, she bursts into tears and falls into his arms, burying her face in his shoulder, her hair soft and dark and spicy against his freckled cheek.

Half an hour later they are sitting on the sofa in Amrita's small but exquisitely furnished flat, drinking Lapsang Souchong tea. She has repeatedly said to Clive, 'I'm sorry, I'm so sorry,' until he has had to be quite severe with her and tell her off for being apologetic.

Clive, meanwhile, is feeling rather sorry himself, for having punched an underprivileged and probably unemployed member of the working classes. Clive's good like that.

'It's just –' He shrugs. 'I feel so guilty. But then, you could have got badly hurt. Not that you did, with all that karate stuff you know.'

'Thai kick-boxing. Well, so could you. And it was my fault.'

'Yeah, right. You were just *asking* for it.'

'No, I don't mean that, it's just that – I mean, this part of town is actually really safe.' She does a passable E2 accent. 'We look out fr'each uvver round 'ere. S'a community, innit?' She sighs. 'I don't know.' She looks at him again. 'Thank you anyway. My hero.'

He gazes into his teacup, eyes swimming with pride. 'Oh, really,' he murmurs. 'Hardly.'

'Well, you did fight off two hulking great thugs single-handed who were much bigger than you. Not that you're particularly short or anything,' she adds hurriedly.

'Yes, I am,' he says. 'Short and carrot-haired and freckled and fairly ridiculous all round really.'

'Aw,' says Amrita. 'Poor, poor Clive.' She leans across and hugs him, then sits back. 'I feel totally sober again now. How about a bottle of wine?'

She goes and retrieves a bottle of bubbly Provençal pseudo-champagne from the fridge. They clink glasses. 'Cheers.'

'Cheers . . . my hero.'

He can't tell now whether she is teasing him or seriously flirting. But from little signs – the way she crosses her legs, the purse-lipped smile, the way she flutters her hands – he is beginning to suspect, thrillingly but terrifyingly, that this might be *serious flirting*.

'By the way,' she says, 'what *was* in the water pistol?'

'Er. Soapy water,' he says. 'Washing-up liquid. And water.'

'Oh, right,' she says, and pauses for thought. 'And . . . why?'

'Um. To clean it.' He makes desperate, entirely meaningless hand movements by way of illustration. 'When the nozzles aren't working, you see.'

She isn't convinced, he can tell. And already, on date no. 1, he is lying to her. He takes a deep breath and tells her the truth.

'I see,' she says. There is a long pause. At last she says, 'Clive?'

'Hm?'

'You haven't . . . I mean, you haven't got a serious pee-thing, have you?'

He assures her that he hasn't.

'Only – you know, I consider myself broad-minded and all that, but I really do draw the line at . . . you know. Water sports.'

'Well, quite,' says Clive, not at all sure what she is talking about.

'Well,' she laughs. 'OK.' She sets her glass down and stands. 'I'm going to have a quick shower. Have another glass of wine. Oh,' she calls from the bathroom, 'and stick some music on if you like.'

Amrita has a dainty little midi system, speakers encased in red-brown cherrywood, and her CDs are stored not in a functional metal rack but stacked in a walnut box, carelessly yet tastefully. In fact, now that Clive has time to look around, the whole flat is designed in the same insouciant but tasteful fashion, with a scattering of kelims and a rich blue Indian cotton cover draped over the back of the sofa, every piece of furniture of dark polished wood, two table lamps (one of which looks hand-painted, red and green), an ornately carved wooden mirror, Indian surely, an alabaster Ganesh doorstop, Pre-Raphaelite pattern curtains that should have clashed terribly with the rest of the room but didn't, fitted bookshelves to the right of the fireplace, loaded with neatly sorted books: groupings of orange-spine, green-spine and black-spine Penguins; a shelf of white Picadors, with a preponderance of travel writers; an entire set of Macmillan Kipling in fading red leather; *Tristes Tropiques*, Claude Lévi-Strauss, *in French*; lots of other stuff about Polynesia; and then of course loads of stuff about India – art and architecture, anthropology, botany, even military history, *A History of the Mughal Empire* in twelve daunting volumes. Crikey, thinks Clive. But he finds the collection, like the room, like Amrita herself, impressive without being overbearing or pretentious.

He returns to studying her CD collection. This is more eclectic than the books, everything from Palestrina to the Chemical Brothers, by way of Ravi Shankar and Django Reinhardt. He briefly considers putting on some Ravi to show how multiculturally aware he is, before thinking, Don't be an idiot. Then his tripping fingers pause over Ravel's *Boléro*.

After the first few bars, Amrita pokes her head out of the bathroom door, her raven hair hanging wet and heavy, and says with a smile, '*Cheeky!*'

Crikey, thinks Clive again.

When she reappears, Amrita is wearing a dark red silk dressing-gown and her hair hangs loose and tousled around her shoulders. She sits down beside him and he hands her a glass of wine. They talk, about her books, her CDs, parents, siblings, deceased pets, surgery, osteoporosis, cheese, France, seaside holidays, sand, fossils and Darwin.

After a lull in the conversation, Amrita asks, 'Just one thing puzzles me, Clive, my hero. Why were you carrying a water pistol in your car in the first place?'

Clive looks puzzled. 'I always carry a water pistol in the car,' he says. 'You must have toys to play with.'

Amrita nods her head carefully. 'OK,' she says. 'Being grown-up is internal. You can still play with toys and trains and stuff – God knows, my older brother does – and it doesn't mean you can't be adult about the serious things. Toys,' she muses, 'the earliest human artefacts?' Then she smiles and sets her empty glass down on the carpet and stands up and goes into her bedroom. A few seconds later she comes back and stands in the bedroom doorway with something in her hand.

Clive looks up. 'You've got a water pistol too!' he cries joyfully.

Amrita looks ceilingwards with a patient smile.

'What is it then?' he asks.

'This is one of *my* toys,' she says, and stretching out her arm – so slim! so brown! so beautiful! – she beckons him towards her bedroom with curvaceous forefinger.

Crikey! thinks Clive.

The next morning, Clive goes home, all ready to tell Emma to pack her bags and go. If she protests, he'll threaten her with a water pistol. But it seems we all misjudged Emma in the end. Especially me.

'I let myself into the flat and called out her name,' he tells us. (Scene: kitchen, coffee, Clive, Kate and me.) 'She was upstairs. She called back, but her voice sounded funny, muffled. For one mad moment, it crossed my mind that she was upstairs in bed with someone else, which would really give me the excuse I needed to ditch her. But then, if I found her doing something so wildly unpredictable, so out of character and shocking . . .' Clive gives a sad little laugh, at the fickleness of the heart's affections. 'I'd probably suddenly feel like not ditching her after all.

'But anyway, she wasn't in bed with someone else. She was bending over a suitcase on the floor, packing. She looked up at me and she'd been – Emma, ice-cold, heartless Emma had been – crying. For the first time in weeks, I felt at that moment that I was in love with her. Like, all over again. Do we only like our women when they're suffering?'

I say nothing. Kate reaches out and squeezes his hand. 'Some men do,' she says. 'Not you, I don't think, Clive Spooner.'

'Well. So, she looked away again, carried on packing. Walked over to a chest of drawers, started pulling out knickers and tights and stuff. I just stood there, unable to speak. So she started speaking for me. Not looking at me, rummaging through the drawer, she said, "I'm leaving you, Clive. I'm sorry, but it's not working any more. You know it's not as well, but you're too feeble to do anything about it. But that's OK, you're only a boy, you can't do stuff like reality."

Still the acid-tongued bitch, for all the tears. But for once I didn't resent it. I thought she was probably right. At last I managed to ask her why now? Why today? She said I'd had a phone call this morning from a friend at work wanting to speak to me about something I did wrong yesterday, and she'd said, Well, didn't he see me at the works thing last night? and he said, What works thing? The usual, feeble, give-away story. I told her it wasn't like that, that I wasn't with anyone in particular, that she's just a good friend . . . "Oh, so there *is* someone in particular, is there?"' Clive grimaces. 'She won every round. She might have been crying but she was totally in control. I was getting more and more panicky by the minute. But I knew I'd blown it. When Emma decides on something, she doesn't change her mind.'

'So she's gone?' I ask.

'She's gone,' he says. 'I stood and watched her pack her suitcase, and she said she'd be back to get the rest of her stuff in a few days, and she swept off down the stairs. I followed along behind her, unable to think of a single thing to say. And at the door she turned and looked at me straight, and just said, "I still love you, Clive. But you don't love me any more. That's why I'm going." That was the worst part. And I still couldn't think of anything to say. And then she went.'

It does, I admit, look like I seriously misjudged Emma all along. Tart and cold and unlikeable she may have been. But maybe at heart she was a better, stronger person than all of us.

Clive's low and depressed but not tearful. Kate makes him another coffee. I offer him a jelly baby. He tells me to fuck off. The usual stuff. I think he'll get over it.

27

So there we are in the minibus, at 6 a.m., bouncing up the M1 on the way to Scotland: Kate (at the wheel), Gaston (in a box – Kate refused to leave him), Clive, Amrita, me, Clive's older brother Hector and his boyfriend Edward (yes, Hector's a poove, and no, Lord Craigmuir doesn't know about it, of course he doesn't, but we're not going to go into that now). Miles and Beth went up the night before in the Merc, staying over with friends in York.

Hector keeps us all entertained for a long time, along the lines of 'Well, *she* was the mistress of Duff Cooper, who was of course the *most* terrible sort of Edwardian *roué,* but then *they* were a quite *dreadful* couple anyway, Nancy Mitford used to write *the* most dreadful letters about them to Evelyn, her husband was some Greek *shipping* magnate would you believe, who had the barstools on his yacht upholstered with the penises of *sperm* whales . . .' But eventually, somewhere around Worksop, even he starts to flag. So we put him on driving duty. In the back, the rest of us nod off on each other's shoulders like children.

Most of us have been to Castle Clive before. It is an incredibly bleak place, even by the usual standards of Scottish baronial. The beds are made of granite, the towels are made of sandpaper. Breakfast is raw boar. Dinner is porridge and boiled bracken. The newspapers are printed on slate. Pyjamas must be made of tweed, no heating is allowed (in case it makes you homosexual) and shoes must be kept highly polished at all times.

You think I'm joking.

On the other hand, though, as always with Scotland, in

the morning you step outside the front door and the view makes you sob and shudder with a kind of aesthetic overload: the green lawns, the silver loch, the roan mountains on the other side. The silence.

We arrive after midnight. There is no sign of the joyless, brooding presence of Lord Craigmuir. Clive shrugs and plies us with tea and whisky in the kitchen and we huddle round the range. We start to wake up then and chatter excitedly. A few minutes later, the kitchen door creaks open and it's Beth, tousled and sleepy-eyed in a woollen dressing-gown. I'm on my feet and halfway across the kitchen towards her before it occurs to me that my delight at seeing her might seem a bit excessive. So I slow down as I near her and say, gawkily, 'Hi. Is, er, is Miles still asleep?'

She nods, tilts her cheek very slightly. I give her a light kiss and we go back over. I try not to catch Clive's eye, but he catches mine anyway. Sly smile into his whisky. Then I see that Amrita is looking at me too. What does *she* know?

We finish our drinks and then rinse out our mugs and glasses and then we unpack our suitcases and put on all the clothes we can wear without suffocating and make our way up to bed. We have to avoid holding on to the banisters going up the stairs, in case our hands freeze over and stick to them. On the wall at the top of the stairs is a huge stag's head, with about sixty-four-point antlers. Its teeth are chattering.

We say goodnight at the top of the stairs and head off to our separate rooms. Beth waggles her fingers at me over her shoulder and vanishes down a dark corridor, gliding away from me as silently as a ghost.

The view from my window is spectacular, moonlit Highlands and a glassy loch, though the room is freezing. And my bed is far too big for one. My feet keep pressing themselves against my legs to warm themselves, at which my legs snatch themselves away. But my feet always follow on closely behind. Just can't seem to shake them off, the little fuckers. Sleep fitfully, trying not to picture Beth warmly asleep in Miles's powerful arms.

At about 7 a.m. Hector is striding around waking us all up, rattling his claymore against his buckler or whatever they do here. By 8 we're up and washed and sitting around the table in the breakfast room, eating porridge and kippers and drinking tea. Amrita has never had porridge before, but claims that she likes it very much. Clive asks if anyone saw the ghost.

'What ghost?' says Kate.

'Oh, I *thought* it must be a ghost,' says Beth, pouring more cream on to her porridge. 'The woman standing at the landing window?'

'Dah,' says Miles, 'you've been reading the guidebook.'

'No,' says Clive, 'there isn't a guidebook. Never has been. She's quite right. What colour dress was she wearing?'

'Green.'

'Is the right answer.' Clive sits back, nods slowly. 'Well, well.'

'Go on then, who is she?'

Clive looks very proud and proprietorial. 'Nancy, supposedly. A daughter of the house, in the early eighteenth century, I think. There's several places you can see her. She fell in love with a local sailor called William, but the match was disapproved of. They must have sworn true love and all that before he went off to sea, and he didn't come back for months and years. And Nancy used to stand all day, every day, there at that window, looking out to the mouth of the loch and the sea beyond, waiting for her William. She also used to sit down in the cove, on a rock called Nancy's Rock. One moonlit night, an old woman saw her sitting out there, with the tide beginning to rise and a storm coming. But Nancy seemed oblivious. At last the woman was about to go

215

and get help, when she saw that Nancy wasn't alone after all, but some sailor was sitting beside her, with his arm around her.'

'This is *so* cheesy,' says Miles.

The rest of us are absurdly spellbound.

'But as the old woman watched, still the pair didn't make any attempt to move or get back to shore, and the seas rose and rose around them. Finally, a great wave broke over the rock, and when it had gone, the rock was bare. Nancy was never seen again, and the next day word came that William's ship had foundered in last night's storm, with all hands.'

'This is a great story,' says Amrita, after a pause. 'I love this story.'

'And last night,' says Clive, 'Beth here saw Nancy in her sea-green dress.'

'Yeah, dripping seaweed too, no doubt,' says Miles. He looks sidelong at Beth. 'What were you doing up in the middle of the night anyway? Where did you get to?'

'Nowhere.' She shrugs. 'Just stood on the landing and watched this woman. I couldn't sleep. She went away after a while.'

There's something awkward in the air now, so Clive starts talking briskly about the walk we're going on after breakfast.

We go for a walk along the lochside and see brown trout jumping, and then round the south-west end and up into the hills beyond. Clive claims to have seen a red deer, just for a moment on the skyline, but the rest of us miss it.

Amrita says Scotland is like the Punjab. Edward says it reminds him of Hampstead Heath. Hector does some funny voices. Beth looks beautiful, wearing ancient cords and a Shetland jumper. Miles looks rosier than ever. We walk nearly twelve miles.

*

In the afternoon we doze in front of the fire – OK, there's *sometimes* a fire – and at teatime other people start to arrive who are staying the night. Most of them seem to be related to Clive in one way or another. It's still very tribal around these parts.

There's still no sign of Lord Craigmuir.

Around 6 we grit our teeth and go upstairs and dress for the ball.

I wear my new DJ, bought for me by a grateful Caroline before I lost the meretricious art and was humbled in the act of love. Everyone says how smart I look. Even more, everyone says how stunning Beth looks. She is wearing a very straight, ankle-length emerald-green dress – perfect with her auburn hair – and dark green high heels. 'Manolos, darling,' she tells me. Round her neck is a broad jade choker. Oh, and she's wearing long green evening gloves that come right up over her elbows. And I know why: the stupid, junky bitch. But I can't say anything to her now, so instead I just needle her (if you'll forgive the pun).

'All in green, like Nancy.'

'*Don't* say that.' She doesn't look at me.

'God, you really are superstitious, aren't you? I bet you read your star signs, *and* believe them.'

Now she looks at me, a hard, green stare. 'And what do you believe, Daniel Swallow?'

'Oh, I don't believe anything. Which of course I wouldn't, being a Leo, a very pragmatic sign.'

She sneers. 'That's just the sort of shallow wit I'd expect from you.'

'Better shallow wit than profound stupidity,' I riposte, thinking what a truly shallowly witty, and indeed virtually meaningless, riposte that is.

'I quite agree,' she says. 'Though I'm sure you're just as capable of profound stupidity too – if not more so.'

Clive and Miles have both been standing there listening to

217

this exchange, laughing, and now they both butt in simultaneously, 'Come along, that's enough of that, we're here to party,' and other platitudes.

Miles is in a kilt (his mother is half-Scottish or something), and so is Clive. I'm not sure this is wise. I know Clive is fully Scottish, but he does have very freckly knees. Still, he and Amrita are obviously, happily, sickeningly besotted with each other. Bastards.

There is still no sign of Lord Craigmuir, but just before we are about to go in to dinner, the doors are flung open and in a cloud of cigarette smoke and air kisses and swathes of black silk Olivia arrives.

I do hope she doesn't say anything embarrassing.

Dinner is magnificent. Venison and braised red cabbage, really good Burgundy, and marmalade pudding soused in whisky and custard. Just the thing before some vigorous Scottish reels.

Conversation centres around the rather philosophical question, Is Happiness a Respectable Goal in Human Life? I don't know how it came up but it really gets people going. And I thought it would all be just gossip about who knows whom.

Amrita defends Hinduism against the charge that it's unworldly and looks forward only to extinction. 'So much of Hinduism is actually directed towards sanctifying and beautifying the ordinary pleasures of life: marriage, sex, food . . .'

Edward modestly inclines his head. 'I stand corrected,' he says. 'So religion, properly understood, does often tally with our modern obsession with earthly happiness.'

'I doubt if our modern obsession is about the same sort of happiness,' says Amrita. 'More about . . . pleasure, as derived from possessions, money, status. I think the pursuit of true happiness is the one thing we are really useless at now, incredibly ignorant about. Our daily lives are de-sanctified, de-ritualized, and we are so much the poorer for it.'

'Which makes us, by definition, a very stupid people, a very stupid culture,' says Edward. 'The business of a wise man is to be happy, like Dr Johnson said.'

'What . . . *my* Dr Johnson?' queries Clive.

Everyone looks bemused.

Clive colours and reaches for his glass. 'Oh, never mind,' he says, his puzzled expression betraying that he is still thinking secretly how peculiar it would be if he and Edward had the same GP.

'Hm,' says Amrita. 'I suspect Johnson was adapting a line from Montaigne, *De l'Institution*? *"La plus exprèsse marque de la sagesse, c'est une esjouïssance constante."'*

She's just too perfect, isn't she? Thai kick-boxing, half a dozen languages, palaeo-anthropology, beauty, elegance . . . There must be *something* wrong with her.

'But but but,' says Kate, feeling perhaps that the conversation is becoming just a little *too* ostentatious, 'people still undervalue contentment as a goal though. It sounds so . . . puddingy.'

Edward grins. 'It's the end of the story,' he says. 'After all the trouble and strife, everything comes to an end with happiness, stories end with lovers' meeting, and the curtain comes down.'

'But it's true,' says Kate. 'People think happy endings are for fairy-tales, kids' stuff and trashy novels. *Serious* novels have to end *seriously*, with the heroine ODing dramatically or slashing her wrists or whatever.'

'And yet to think of happy endings as kids' stuff is such a crude misunderstanding,' says Amrita.

I listen dreamily while she talks about the archetypal heroic myth of death and rebirth, adventure and return. It does all make a kind of sense to me. Indistinct, but a kind of sense. I pour myself another glass of wine. It'll fade, I console myself. This feeling, this ache, this emptiness when I think of her – her, sitting opposite me now at this very table beside Miles, my friend and the man she loves – this permanent absent-mindedness – it'll fade in time. Everything fades in time. And then I'll look back and see in it a pattern of some kind, an adventure. Beth was my adventure. Now I've gone round and come back to where I started, to . . . well, wherever.

I'm not the first to have gone through the mill and I won't be the last. Soon I'll be back in London, striding across Albert Bridge to a party in Battersea or somewhere, the river wind strong in my hair, a smile on my lips, thinking how lonely and intoxicating it is to be free again. And I'll stop halfway across the bridge and lean on the railing and look down.

The film's closing shot: pan back – I'm left alone now, a figure solitarily gazing out over the water, my reflection below only a small shadow, while all along the Embankment the lights are on, the cars shine red and gold and the lights of the City towers swarm across the river downstream and from the surface the first hint of mist arising. The wise river that's grown old and seen it all before through all the centuries: the Gaulish archer and his dark-eyed girlfriend, the tow-haired mercer's apprentice and the Lord Mayor's daughter (their trysts on London Bridge, beneath the Lollards' heads on pikestaffs at Drawbridge Gate!), the young baronet who seduced the kitchenmaid and accidentally fell in love . . . The river's seen it all before and sees it all again. Beyond me are many millions more human souls like me, most of them, like me, yearning for life and more life and being given no more life than is allotted to the human frame or that can be weathered by the human heart, and so, all heroes and heroines of novels forever unwritten, like me making of what brief life they have what life they can.

Later the music starts up and I dance with Olivia. Across the room I can see Beth dancing with Hector. She's flirting outrageously. She doesn't quite know what she's doing in the reels, much like the rest of us. But whereas we all look gawky and gauche, she still manages to look perfect. Hector is flirting back. He may be a poove, but like so many pooves he's damnably good-looking, and loves flirting with women at any opportunity. In fact, he may not even be 100 per cent poove. Clive tells me that Hector confessed to him just recently that he was getting worried about how much time he spent looking at girls these days, and even thought he might be *turning back into a heterosexual*.

At first I can see no sign of Miles. Ah, well, he never was much of a dancer. He's probably over at the bar, talking about rugby with the boys. Then I glance up and see him standing in the gallery above our heads, leaning forward over the oak balcony. And the look on his face chills me to the bone. I don't think Beth has realized he's up there. If she did – if she saw his expression – she might not be flirting so much with Hector.

'So,' says Olivia, as we spin about the floor, her forearm resting lightly on mine, 'how is your career going?'

I tell her the truth. She looks rather disappointed in me. 'Oh, well, it can't be helped. I suppose no one can go on doing that sort of thing for ever.' We dance a little longer, and then she says, 'I'm off to the Middle East in a couple of weeks' time.'

'Lucky you.'

'Business, not pleasure. You'd be amazed how many nineteenth-century watercolours by British artists you can still pick up in Damascus.'

'I would.'

'The trouble is, Davina's gone and got herself preggers, silly girl. My gallery assistant. I don't suppose you'd be interested in . . . I wouldn't expect you to do it for ever. But it would be a great help. The money's awful, obviously.'

A Pimlico art gallery assistant: it's a job, I suppose.

'And of course, darling,' she adds, leaning up to my right ear, 'there's less risk of getting the clap in this line of work.'

*

'What were you two talking about?' asks Clive, mopping his brow with a scarlet handkerchief.

'Business,' I say. 'Business.'

Another reel, another conversation.

'So,' says Olivia, 'and what about your love life?'

'Ah. Well, it's a bit complicated.'

'Don't tell me,' says Olivia. 'The girl over there in green.'

'How . . .'

'You can't take your eyes off her.'

'No one can take their eyes off her.'

'Yes, but when your eyes are on her, you look . . . as green as her dress. Like you're going to be sick.'

'Thanks.' I smile, don't know why. 'Anyway, she's not available.'

'She and Miles are happy?'

'Blissfully, I'm afraid.' I twirl her round under my right arm, with no timing whatsoever, but with a certain angry flamboyance that I feel justifies the manoeuvre. 'As are Amrita and your third one.'

'Amrita,' says Olivia. 'Now she is quite charming. I think she's marvellous.' She scans the room. 'I do hope he turns up soon. I can't wait to see his face. The Grand Master of the League of the Defenders of Albion.'

A couple more dances, with Kate and Amrita, and then the girl whose dress matches my face.

'So,' I say, spinning us round, 'you look like you're getting pretty hot. Why don't you take those gloves off? Or are you ashamed of what's underneath?'

She scowls at me ferociously. 'You know nothing, Swallow.'

'Oh, you always say that. I know a lot more than you realize.'

'Is that so? And what else do you know?'

I glance up at the gallery, but Miles has disappeared. Beth is about to start yammering at me again, so I get in first with, 'I know that the best way to stop someone talking is with a kiss.' And in mid-twirl, I plant a kiss full on her lips. 'And I know that I love you.'

'Now is not the time or the place,' she says, stopping the dance and detaching herself. 'You don't know what sort of trouble you could get me into.'

After that, I dance with a very tall, thin, needle-nosed girl called Veronica, and I'm so hot that I have to retire to the library.

There I encounter a pig-faced youth who is furtively helping himself to an entire box of the finest Monte Cristos. He looks up and sees me and snuffles slightly through a gormless grin, 'Just, ah, just seeing what's what, you know, what's on offer!'

I regard him coldly and then say, 'Do you know who I am?'

He is so alarmed by this that he slaps the cigar box shut and scuttles crab-like for the door, although still clutching half a dozen Monte Cristos in his piggy little fist.

Greatly elated by the success of this, my first attempt at aristocratic impersonation, I pace around the library as if it is my own demesne.

Much of the shelf space is taken up with bound sets of back copies of *The Field*, and *Blackwoods Magazine* and the *Edinburgh Review* and the *Gentleman's Quarterly*. But there are some interesting old books too, seemingly untouched (and undusted) for decades. Down at the far end the light is bad, and I have to squat behind the sofa to examine them. I wonder if anyone would notice if I half-inched a few?

No sooner am I down than the door opens and some people come in. I can't see them, but from where I am it sounds like it's a snogging couple. Who can it be? Surely some revelation is at hand?

It's fierce, passionate snogging too. They don't say a word

to each other, it's all primal grunts and gasps and weird ejaculations that make no sense. Any minute now they might repair to the sofa and start going at it hammer and tongs while I'm stuck down here like a lemon or, even worse, like Hugh Grant in that scene from *Four Weddings*. Soon there'll be an elephantine thump from next door and Simon Callow will have suffered a bowel-emptying infarction.

Then I recognize the girl's voice. It's Beth. The fucking slut. At a party with both her serious boyfriend *and* her sometime lover, and she still can't resist the chance for a quick snog, maybe more, with some passing wanker in a kilt. Maybe it's not just a snog, maybe it's more. I can feel my insides boiling with jealousy, and bewilderment too. Do I have any right to intervene?

'No, no,' she's gasping, and it crosses my mind that maybe the oaf is taking it further than she meant. Though why did she sneak into the library with him in the first place?

Cautiously I peer round the corner of the sofa.

It's not at all like that scene from *Four Weddings*. And it's not some passing wanker in a kilt, either. It's Miles. It's Miles and Beth. And if she's enjoying what he's doing to her, as a sign of his affection, then she's even more screwed up than I thought she was. He's got her pressed up hard with her back against the library stacks. With one hand he has pulled her dress off her shoulders, and even from where I am I can see that her bare shoulder is covered in bruises. Her long gloves have crumpled down around her wrists and I can see, too, that her arms are similarly multicoloured. No needle did that. She is bleeding from nose and mouth where he has been hitting her, little bunched rabbit punches at close quarters. He's forcing her legs apart with his own chunky thighs, pinning her up and off the ground, his left hand reaching down and wrenching up the hem of her skirt. And, just so that she gets the message, he now has both his hands locked around her neck and he's strangling her.

In the three seconds and eight paces it takes me to get to him, my skin is drenched in freezing sweat and my brain has whirred and clicked and worked everything out and I've understood what has been going on and I am very frightened. I am very frightened for all of us.

Beth is pressed back against the bookcase, her eyes closed, and Miles is facing her, his face almost touching hers, his hands around her throat, his face puce. He is talking to her, in a low growl, but I can't hear what he's saying and I don't want to hear. He may be telling her that she's a fucking slut, a whore, that he'll teach her, that he'll show her what happens to whores who fuck around with other men at parties . . . But I've got a horrible feeling that what he's actually saying to her, while he kills her slowly, is, 'Forgive me, my darling, I love you, I *need* you, oh I love you so much, and I can't live without you, my darling Beth . . .' And that, I don't want to hear.

Beth's hands are on his arms but they are already limp. I come up behind him and loop my right forearm round his neck and close my left hand about my right wrist and draw it back tightly. Immediately Miles lets go of Beth and she falls to her knees, choking softly. Locked together, Miles and I stagger backwards, and then he stamps his left foot on mine, heel first. That is the most painful bit, by far. I don't think I've ever felt anything so painful as that. I can dimly feel the ends of my socks turning soggy as they fill with blood from my split toenails and my burst toes, but I don't mind that, not at all, I just wish the pain would go away. And however fuelled up with anger I was until this moment, it has now been hopelessly outmanoeuvred by the pain. I can't concentrate any more. I just want to crawl into bed. Is this what cowardice is?

After that, the pain doesn't get any worse. I wish he would stop hitting me, certainly, but it doesn't hurt any more. I've reached my maximum pain level already. It's just that the pain is more evenly spread, more widely and fairly diffused.

My tongue and lip are bleeding copiously from where he has punched me, but it's my jaw that really aches. Being punched in the stomach is more acutely uncomfortable than painful, and makes me feel that my insides have been folded up and crushed together for several days, and I need to be stretched out on a large rack to recover. Then there is the comforting smell of cool leather, and the feel of it against my damp cheek, as I kneel there by the side of an old armchair, one arm on the floor to support me, and I know Miles is standing back a pace or two so he can kick me, as hard as he can, in the face or maybe the stomach again, and this time it won't just hurt a lot, it will probably injure me quite seriously. If only Amrita was here, with her remarkable Thai kickboxing skills. She'd soon sort him out.

'Stop,' says Olivia. Just that: stop.

Miles stops.

Olivia walks over to us. She takes hold of my left arm and pulls me up. I'd rather not get up, frankly. I'd much rather lie down. But it seems impolite to refuse the arm of your hostess, so I lurch drunkenly to my feet. It is the most abject cowardice, I know, but for some reason I keep my eyes closed.

'Get out of my house,' says Olivia. 'Never come here again.'

There are a few seconds of hate-filled silence, and then I hear Miles's footsteps across the library floor and out of the door.

I open my eyes. Or at least the one that will open. Olivia lets go of my arm and goes over to help Beth to her feet.

'I'm so sorry,' Beth starts to say. 'I can explain.'

'I don't want to hear any explanations,' says Olivia. 'I don't want to hear anything.'

And without another word she leads us out of the library and up the stairs to the bathroom.

She massages Beth's neck very gently, and peers down her throat, and hugs her when she starts to cry – her sobs so eloquent against the background noise of a car engine violently revving up and fat rubber tyres grinding across the gravel. Definitely a Merc – and Olivia carries on hugging her even after she has stopped crying. And then she whispers something, some private joke in Beth's ear, and Beth manages a soft laugh. Then they turn on me and undress me completely, and they both whistle and start to joke about my injuries – although the sight of my pulped and mashed-up toes rather halts them in their tracks. Olivia says I'll have to go to hospital. I nod, suddenly feeling very tired.

'I'm sorry I was such a coward,' I mumble.

Beth sits down beside me and slaps the back of my hand. Actually *slaps* me. After what I've just been through. 'Don't be ridiculous,' she says. 'You saved my life. *Again.*'

'Hunh?'

'Well, I'll leave you two to finish cleaning up – but do make sure you come down again. No sneaking off to bed now, for *whatever* reason.' And Olivia departs.

We sit side by side in companionable silence for a while. At last I say, 'I know my brain isn't working very well just at the moment – but I'm just sort of running the reels backwards and trying to make sense of it all. You've lied to me so much . . .'

She sighs. 'I've lied to myself too. To everyone. If that's any consolation.'

'Hm. Not really.' More pause for thought, then I say, 'So, OK, you were wearing the gloves because of the bruises. And you had the bruises because of Miles.'

'Because of Miles,' she confirms. 'That's one way of putting it.'

'So – so you're off the drugs?'

She nods. 'I've been a good girl ever since you, and still got – *punished* for it.'

I shake my head. 'Why on earth . . . So, yeah, now I think about it, I haven't seen you wearing a T-shirt or anything for a while, you've always been covered up. Is that why?'

227

A soft laugh. 'I might have gone to bed with you again, after Cornwall, except that you'd have seen the bruises. It was one way of keeping me chaste, I suppose. In a weird way, I think I was trying to protect yours and Miles's friendship.'

'What about protecting yourself?'

'Oh, but I have a big strong knight in shining armour to do that for me, don't I?' she says, giving me a painful hug.

'Some knight.'

'Ye-es,' she allows. 'Your fighting skills do leave *quite* a bit to be desired.' She gets up and runs some cold water into a glass. Sips and hands it to me.

'And, obviously, when you were beaten up and turned up on my doorstep that time – that was Miles too?'

'Obviously.'

'I knew you were lying to the police. Just couldn't figure why.' I sip some water. 'Weren't you ever – I mean, *afraid* of him?'

'Why do you think I asked you to come back that time, when he got home from Germany?'

'Oh, shit. But I left later that night. Did he . . .'

She nods. 'The usual.'

'That *bastard*. I'll kill him.'

'Don't be ridiculous, you couldn't kill a mouse. Anyway, it's all over now. Come on, let's head back downstairs.'

Still reeling with confusion and nagging pain, I stumble along after her.

Downstairs, people initially think we've been fighting each other and Beth has completely trashed me. But Olivia has been discreetly spreading the word, and Clive guesses what has happened, and before long I am regarded as something of a hero, even if totally crap at fighting. I sit there in the corner by the booming fire, beneath the walls decorated with monstrous claymores and halberds, a patch over one eye, my left foot shoeless and hugely bandaged, the size of a baby in swaddling clothes lying in a manger.

'I never did like him,' says Clive. 'Those small eyes.'

I shake my head. 'I don't feel anything just now. If anything, I'm worried for him.'

Beth is sitting the other side of me, cradling a whisky. 'Just think,' she says, 'just think what he'd have done to you if he'd known *everything*.'

'You mean . . .'

She nods. 'Oh, yes. That was just him being jealous about me dancing with Hector, and then turning on you for interfering. If he knew we'd slept together he'd probably have killed you.'

I sip some of her whisky, dribbling most of it down my front. 'He was never like this at uni. The stress of work excuses everything nowadays, I suppose.'

She shrugs. 'People change. He knew something when I got back from Cornwall,' she says. 'But not about you.'

I look at her. 'Tell me.'

She got back from Cornwall, and he cooked her that steak and kidney pudding, and he put her gently to bed because he could see she was tired.

And then he leant down over her and whispered in her ear, 'So why didn't you phone?'

She froze. Tried not to, tried to stay relaxed and fluid under his hands, loose-muscled in case the blows came raining down upon her. 'I . . . I was so busy . . .' she stammered.

It was all so unlikely, she knew. Not one phone call. Her disappearing after the violence of last weekend. Of course she just ran off. He leaned even closer to her, and said softly, so tenderly, 'You lying fucking slut. I don't believe one word you say, you lying fucking slut. You bitch. Who was he? Or maybe it was she? Maybe you've taken to fucking your girlfriends too now, just for a bit of variety. Yes?' And he was lying on top of her now, holding her wrists down deep in the pillows so that she couldn't stir an inch, face buried, speechless, dumb.

Miles hurt her a lot again the following night. It started with a childish spanking session, Beth wearing her school uniform for him, but it soon grew crueller. As she writhed on the bed, pulling against the silk cords that held her down so tightly, Miles kept his eyes fixed intently on hers, as if unable to tear his gaze away, as if she were the centre of his whole universe. And that is what he told her. That she must never leave him, that he could never live without her, he would die without her, that he was nothing without her, she was his whole world. 'I love you so much,' he said.

And afterwards, when he ungagged her and peeled the constricting ropes away from her reddened limbs and rubbed antiseptic cream into her cuts and bruises and followed it with healing kisses, he whispered softly to her again with such tenderness that he loved her so much. And she was so exhausted and bewildered that she could no longer say whether she loved him or not. Even whether she liked it or not. Maybe, she thought, I really do deserve it.

And after, Beth whimpered fitfully through the usual dreams: landscapes of midnight forests, trees wintry and bare, a chill blue river embroidered with flowers of ice – and the wolves in the dark caverns, the endless dark caverns through which she wandered sorrowful and lost . . .

I'm too angry to sympathize. Too angry with both of them, contemptuous almost. What has she been *doing* with him? Is happiness really so unfashionable?

'And the time you came round to mine, having been beaten up by Miles, who did you say it was, your dealer . . .'

'Stan.' She almost laughs.

'Stan.'

'Stan couldn't beat up a midget. Stan couldn't even beat *you* up.'

I don't laugh. 'So you lied to the police massively as well. And the time before *that* . . . when you called me round to the hotel, as an escort, a *whore*, and had me fuck you . . . that wasn't just a coincidence, and it wasn't just because you thought it would be a jolly jape either.'

She lowers her head. 'No. I'm sorry, that was really – really cruel. I did it as revenge against Miles. A bit convoluted, I know, but I thought, You beat me up, I'll fuck your best friend. And you *were* a prostitute. I mean, it was your job.' She sighs. 'D'you remember I told you about my friend Alex, a male model, who does male escort stuff on the side when he's short of work? I was actually looking him up on the website, just for a laugh, and there were you, on the same site. You both work for –' she puts on a smoky, nightclub voice – '*Grosvenor for Ladies.*' She smiles weakly. 'I'm sorry. I didn't know you were going to . . . I mean, we were . . . you know. Get so *romantic.*'

'You just used me.'

'Oh, for Christ's sake. I *don't* think you have much right to . . .' She breaks off as Amrita comes to join us, but she sees that we're having some kind of heart-to-heart and slips gracefully back into the throng.

'Come and live with me. Me and Kate.'

'No. I can't do that.'

'Where, then?'

She smiles. 'Weird, isn't it? Not so long ago I had my boyfriend's million-pound house in Chelsea, and sometimes even a West End hotel, when I was filming in the role of the new Amañuna girl. Now I have absolutely nowhere to lay my poor head, though the birds of the air and the foxes etc. . . .' Sips some more whisky. 'I'll stay with Lesbo Livvie for a while, and then next week I get a free apartment while I'm filming *No Mercy*. After that, I have to get somewhere of my own.'

'Marry me.'

'Daniel, you're . . . OK, you're not drunk, I admit, but maybe you're concussed or something . . . I mean, that would be *mad*. I'm twenty-six, for God's sake. I won't be getting married for *years* yet, and when I do it'll be to some gormless billionaire.' She looks hard at me. 'You don't really mean it. You don't really love me. You certainly couldn't cope with living with me.'

'We could be happy together for the rest of our lives.'

'That would be about, hm . . . two months? Then we'd be found dead across the kitchen table with steak knives stuck in each other's backs.' She says again, 'You don't really love me.'

'Oh, and Miles did love you, I suppose?'

'You don't know why . . . You don't know . . .' She despairs of explaining. Instead she flaps her hand half irritably, half sadly about her bruised neck. 'You think he would do this to me if he didn't love me?'

'Oh, I *see*. They're signs of his *love* for you, are they? I'm so sorry. And here was me thinking that they were just signs that my pal Miles is a complete fucking bullying violent *bastard*.'

She shakes her head. 'You know nothing.' After a while she says, 'You don't know what I did to him. I'm a bad person.'

'What did you do? I *know* what you did, you've already told me. So what?'

'They were bad things. Bad enough things.'

'You're justifying him now?' I'm incredulous.

'I'm not . . . For God's sake, no, I'm not justifying it, I'm just saying . . . you don't know, you don't understand, and you have no right . . .'

We sip our drinks, brood. At last I say softly, 'OK, I know I'm not really one to judge anybody. I mean, look at me: I'm a fucking prostitute.'

'*Ex*-prostitute.' She smiles. 'In fact, *failed* prostitute.'

I reach out and take her hand and am suddenly serious again. 'We both need rescuing, though.'

She pulls her hand away. 'It's not like that,' she says. 'It's really not like that.'

We're talking with Kate, Clive and Amrita, and Edward, when Olivia wafts over to us, bringing a couple more people with her: some woman called Venetia, and some bore with a brick-red face. We all pause to admit them to our circle.

'I'm so sorry that my beloved husband is laid low this evening,' says Olivia, 'although he may yet manage to join us later on. But I think it has been a wonderful party, despite the absence of his celebrated *bonhomie*.' We laugh. 'And, of course, the unfortunate outbreak of extreme violence in the library.'

Only Beth and I laugh, slightly uncertainly. I know at once that the couple she's brought along are just stooges for Olivia's evil sense of humour.

'Now, my dear friend Daniel Swallow,' she says, taking my hand demonstratively and looking around the group, 'broke up with his girlfriend nearly a year ago now, and since then he has, I'm afraid, been a bit of a tart.' Hearty laughter at this, pierced by an unattractively nervous and high-pitched titter from myself. 'Well, you *have*, darling,' she says, fixing me with her brilliant blue eyes. 'You can't deny it!'

What is she *saying*? I knew she'd get embarrassing. Beth squeezes my other hand, greatly amused.

'But I am delighted to say that he has now seen the error of his ways,' Olivia continues to the group in general, 'has abjured such behaviour, and in a week or two's time, he will start work for me in my Pimlico gallery.' Polite grunts all round. 'As for his tortuous love life, it is really not for me to say. Although I do have a *shrewd suspicion* . . .'

Beth lowers her gaze to the floor, although to be fair does-n't actually detach her hand from mine.

'And now Edward here – Edward and my oldest son, dear Hector . . .'

It must be at about this point that Lord Craigmuir, recent-ly risen from his sickbed, pulls up behind us and begins to listen in, quite unnoticed.

'Hector,' Olivia goes on, 'as all those close to him know, has been going out with Edward for *years* now, and I am very pleased to say that at last Hector will be making a respectable man of him. And next month they're flying out to California to have a Proper Gay Church Wedding – to which you are all of course invited!'

From somewhere nearby comes a low, subterranean moan, but none of us take much notice at the time.

'Last but not least – it gives me great pleasure to introduce you to the new girlfriend of my third son, Clive: the Princess Amrita!'

Amrita, charmingly shy suddenly, does a graceful little curtsy, unfortunately marred by a thunderous cry from behind Olivia. 'But she's a black!'

And turning round, we are just in time to see the seventh Baron Craigmuir, fourteenth Grand Master of the League of the Defenders of Albion, clutch at his chest and slither to the floor in a deep swoon.

After that there is a thrilling ride in a helicopter ambulance over the snow-bound Cairngorms to hospital, with Lord Craigmuir lying there blue-faced in an oxygen mask and Olivia flirting outrageously with the dark-eyed, softly spoken medics. She insists I go along too, in case I've broken any toes.

I *have* broken some toes, as it turns out – or rather, Miles has broken them for me. The doctor on duty looks wearily at them, stubby and stamped on and terracotta with dried blood. His panda eyes are ringed with tiredness, trying to twinkle with amusement and failing.

'So what do you want me to do about it?' he says. 'We don't make splints that small.'

He tells me that people break their toes all the time, stubbing them against furniture, getting stamped on by psychotic ex-best friends, etc. There's nothing that can be done. They'll mend themselves eventually. Rest up for a while.

Lord Craigmuir, on the other hand, has to stay in hospital. He's not at all well.

There's a long and tedious taxi ride back to Castle Clive, and when we get there the party's pretty much over. I suppose it wouldn't be entirely polite, anyway, to carry on reeling after your host has just had a massive coronary owing to his oldest son coming out as a poove and his third having carnal relations with a black.

Clive makes tea for us and we go up to bed. On the stairs approaching the landing, I ask Beth if she can see anything. She shakes her head. 'No,' she says. 'She's gone now.'

The moon has set. The loch below and the mountains beyond are an inscrutable black. We stand side by side by the window for a while, both shivering, from cold, from whisky, from emotional trauma, I don't know what.

Finally I put my arm round Beth. 'Come on, you,' I say. 'I'm buggered if I'm going to sleep alone after a night like tonight.'

The big bed is still cold. But not as cold as it was.

She's almost asleep, I know, but I can't resist it: this dangerous question, propped on one elbow, looking over her, her face childlike and characterless, as everyone's is in sleep. 'What did you think of me when you first met me?'

'Mm?' She rolls over towards me, eyes tight shut. Eventually she says, 'I knew I wasn't indifferent to you.' Just as I'm beginning to smile complacently in the darkness, she adds, 'I always knew you'd be some sort of significant disturbance, some major irritation in my life.'

Ah. 'Like . . . like the pearl in your oyster.'

'Don't push it.' She opens her eyes. 'You were funny and charming and flirtatious and all that, but I've met all that before and it doesn't go that deep.' She thinks. 'You were quite lost, but not too little-boyish. I kept wanting to disagree with you but actually found that I thought the same as you on a lot of stuff. Your favourite film being *Kind Hearts and Coronets* really irritated me, because it must be my second or third. And you were *sort of* grown up. I don't mean you're *outstandingly* mature, don't get ideas, you're just *acceptably* mature, unlike most men your age. Or world-weary, anyway, and the world-weariness wasn't just faked and adolescent, it was real. That was good.' She sighs. 'I thought I'd always feel strongly about you – one way or another.'

'And now?'

'I still feel strongly about you –' cautious smile – 'one way or another.'

I lie back down again. After a long time, she stirs again and I feel her hand on my shoulder. She murmurs, 'And I always will.'

Sunday is slightly weird. A phone call earlier has informed his sons that Lord Craigmuir passed away peacefully in the night. Olivia arrives back, and clearly everyone feels they should be in deep mourning, and aren't. I half expect Olivia to propose a champagne breakfast.

Hector is now Lord Craigmuir, with a castle to boot. Odd thought. And he is full of plans to have the place renovated from top to bottom, and turned into Europe's finest gay golfing centre. Egged on by his mother, he even proposes having the vast, neglected Victorian hothouses behind the castle turned into steam rooms and saunas.

He may be on to something.

Meanwhile, Kate keeps giving me odd looks. Eventually I ask her why.

'It's that joke Olivia made in her speech last night . . . twice, in fact,' she says to me. 'You know, about you being a tart recently and all that. I mean – I hope you don't mind my asking, but she's not serious, is she? I mean, you haven't *really* been working as a prostitute all this time, have you?'

I sigh, lay my spoon down in my porridge, look soulful and hurt. 'Kate – surely you know me better than that?'

'The trouble is,' she says slowly, 'I don't think I do.'

*

236

After Sunday lunch, we all pile into the minibus and head back to London. Including Beth. But she's adamant she won't stay with me tonight. She's staying with Lesbo Livvie for the time being. Next week, she starts filming her shlocky blockbuster – *No Mercy*, for fuck's sake – and she gets an apartment of her own in Cumberland Terrace, no less, for the duration of filming, even though she only has a small part and gets wasted, *Peckinpahed*, in the first five minutes.

It's a long way back to London. And we can't think of any stories to tell, to beguile the time, like we did on the way up with Clive's. At least, no one else can. I can think of a story I could tell – but I don't know if anyone would believe me. And I don't know whether or not it has a happy ending either. And that's clearly what everyone is in the mood for.

28

Two days later, Beth asks me round to Lesbo Livvie's to read a letter she's had from Miles. It's long and rambling and seems to be about a failed suicide attempt, and I really don't know what to make of it. Along with his letter is a scruffy little scrap of paper bearing the words, *Don't waste it*.

> *Dear Beth*
>
> *I am sorry for everything, but I know I can never be sorry enough. I'm putting in for a transfer to the NYC office, and I'll probably be there in a fortnight, and stay for a good long while.*

He then swerves off battily and starts describing a fresh spring wind blowing in from the sea, the sea lightly bumpy with lone white horses breaking here and there, far out. High white clouds, the wind in the coarse grass, young sea kale appearing on the cliff tops, the buffeting wind funnelled up the cliff sides, clumps of thrift nodding furiously, eagerly, and the gulls riding on the updraughts for no better reason than it's fun.

He was parked up there in the car, thinking about life and death, he says, when he met a guy called Greg. Greg came stumping up the hill to the headland, sweating profusely, his square steel specs continually sliding down his shiny, stubby nose. He pushed them back up with a bunched fist, squinting as he did so. He had wiry ginger hair and a slightly darker, unkempt beard. His whole appearance was just a little eccentric, a little makeshift. He carried an enormous rucksack, wore baggy beige shorts revealing very cylindrical, hairy, white calves. He muttered to himself frequently. He snorted at times, loudly. He stopped and stared at the gulls, squinting into the sun, as if he had never seen anything like them before in his life.

'Why is he telling you all this?' I said, looking up. 'I mean, it's all very amusing, I'm sure, but what's the bastard on about?'

'It sort of makes sense in the end,' says Beth. 'Go on.'

When he got to the top of the headland, Greg stared across at me sitting in the car, and then came over and told me off. How many birds' nests had I run over on my way here, how many fledgling larks had I crushed? His glasses steamed up with heat. Habitat, flora, he muttered furiously, his mouth working, birds, wheatears, scabious, the delicate rich eco-system, the biodiversity of coastal chalk downland getting just squished *under the fat tyres of your fat car . . . He was folding away this big clasp-knife while he ranted.*

And to top it all, I still had my engine running, staring gormlessly out to sea. To Greg, though, I was just another fucking jumper. Another depressed Londoner come down here to chuck himself off the cliffs.

'Ah, diddums,' I say to Beth. 'It's an almost-suicide note.'

I must have looked like shit, I know. Dinner jacket and bow tie in disarray. Unshaven. Depressed. Greg made a window-winding motion. 'Engine off, mate, surely,' says Greg. 'Some people come up here to get some fresh air.' I turned the engine off. Greg must have seen clearly then how miserable I looked. But he walked on. Five hours later, getting dark, he came back. Saw me still there. He rested one arm on the roof of the car. Gazed out to sea. 'Been lovely weather today,' he said. 'Lovely weather. You can see France sometimes.' Then he said, 'I came up here to get some sea kale. Ever had sea kale?'

The weirdest thing. Anyway, he ended up taking me off to the pub. He just made this decision, snatched my door open and said, "'Ere, budge over.' I stared at him briefly but then, because I didn't care any more either way, I shifted over to the passenger seat. In the pub, he bought us each a pint and handed me mine. Later he bought supper too, but I couldn't eat it, so he ate shepherd's pie, potatoes, carrots, peas, followed by half-cold cod and chips and peas. We had some more drinks. He kept buying them. Then he said I could crash at his place.

'Don't tell me Miles is going to come out too?' I say. Beth smiles, doesn't answer.

Greg's place was a spartan cottage just over the road. In the kitchen there was a rancid, meaty smell, and a swathe of fresh blood across the cross-hatched pine table. Greg said that he'd been gutting rabbits that afternoon, though I couldn't see any rabbits. The sitting-room contained nothing but a sagging sofa, a guitar and an ash-sprinkled hearth. 'You kip there,' said Greg. 'I'll get a blanket.' I could hear him grubbing around outside, chopping logs, which seemed weird this late, but all the same I was past caring. I went fast asleep.

In the morning I left before he even got up. I pulled the Merc out into the lane and turned left. North to London. After a few miles I had to stop for petrol. Fumbling in my jacket pocket I found a bar of chocolate and a note. The note said simply Don't waste it. I stared at it for a long time. Then I folded it and put it back in my pocket. Later that day – today – I wrote this letter, and I enclose Greg's advice too, for you. (Because after all, sometimes people with big knives in their pockets are not psychotic killers. Sometimes people who invite the lonely and fucked up back home with them and get them drunk and then, when they've fallen asleep on their sofa, start fumbling around outside for an axe only

mean well. Sometimes people are good and kind to each
other. Even these days, strange days like these.)
    Love, Miles

'Do you get it?' asks Beth.
I stare at the letter, the little scribbled note, at her. 'Sort of,'
I say cautiously.
    'I do,' she says. 'I get it.'

29

Two weeks later: a sun-drenched day in May, but the roses in Regent's Park are obscured by snow. Fake snow.

'Come along and see me filming,' Beth has said to me on the phone. 'You won't be able to come too near.' She smiles. 'You might get burned by my sheer, incandescent star quality.'

'Ye-es.'

'No, really, you won't get a set pass. But you can come and see me from afar.'

'So gracious. Thank you.'

And so here I am, circling around the periphery of things like an absent-minded electron, while gangs of fat, bearded men in T-shirts and baseball caps lug around trunks of equipment and swear a lot, and camp production assistants and girls called Katrina punch their mobile keypads and twitter joylessly to each other, and the director (also fat, bearded, T-shirted etc.) shouts at people through a loud-hailer.

Ah, the glamour of the movies.

After a while I get bored and try to sneak in past the security guards, but it's no go. So I go out and round the corner to Cumberland Gate, and when the guard patrolling that side isn't looking, I slip over the fence and wince with pain when I land – it's surprising how much my toes still hurt – and sneak back and go and find Beth.

She's even got a little trailer. It's not exclusively her own, she has to share it with a couple of other actresses who are similarly gunned down in a later scene, in a scorching firefight between the playboy-turned-killing machine hero and the Latin American bandidos. They're both wearing micro-dresses and they've just finished having a whole set of exploding blood capsules secreted about their persons for a dummy shoot.

'Brian likes blood,' Beth explains. 'Brian de Plasma, we call him.'

Brian is the director, I assume.

The actresses flash us goodbye smiles and slip out of the trailer. 'Candy and Sandy,' she says, 'honestly. They've both been under Brian's desk, given him blow jobs.'

She's sitting in front of a mirror in the trailer, wearing a gorgeous wedding dress, smoking a joint.

'I suppose you're covered in little exploding blood capsules too?'

'I sure am, honey.'

'Don't you . . . I mean, it *is* all crap, isn't it? If you don't mind me saying so. I'm not trying to dis your career, really I'm not, but it's . . .'

'*Everyone wants to use you,*' she sings softly, '*everyone wants to abuse you.* It's life, sweetie. Now don't be so naïve. At least *I* haven't had to give Brian a blow job. Not yet.'

'You'd better fucking not.'

'So *jealous*, darling!'

'And don't call me *darling*.' I scowl at her.

She smiles serenely back, exhaling dope smoke.

'Should you be doing that?'

'No, for two reasons. One, anyone using drugs on set is immediately fired. After filming, fine, but not during. And two, I'm pregnant.'

'What?'

'And it's yours.'

The trailer gives a violent lurch, as if a fat, bearded cameraman has just bumped into it. 'You're . . .'

'Pregnant. And it's yours.'

'How do you know it's mine?'

'Because I haven't slept with anyone else in the last three months.'

243

Yeah, like I really believe that. For God's sake, she told me *herself* that there had been 'one or two' . . . And what about Miles? I don't believe her. I can't believe her . . . can I?

'I . . .' I have to sit down. After a while I say, 'What are you doing smoking?'

'What else am I supposed to do?' She looks at the clock. 'I'm on in five minutes. I've had to have the dress altered in secret but . . .' She stands up and smooths her hand over her stomach. 'Do I *look* pregnant? Please say no.'

'No.' But she is, though. She's *pregnant*. 'I don't know what to say.'

'There isn't much to say, is there?'

Not now there isn't. I can't even see straight, let alone think straight. I reach out and take the joint from her and have a deep lug. That'll help me think more clearly.

Finally I exhale and say, 'We've done everything backwards, it seems to me.'

'?'

'First we fucked.' I glare at her. 'You couldn't call it any more than that: just fucking. In an anonymous hotel in the West End.' She doesn't argue. 'Then we went on some kind of romantic honeymoon together: Cornwall. And first kissed, and made love. Then I proposed to you. And then . . .' I frown. 'The trouble is, you're getting pregnant doesn't fit in at all. That should have come right at the beginning, if these things are going to be properly reversed.'

What am I *talking* about? Theorizing in this cool way when she's sitting there with my offspring in her uterus. *Our* offspring, supposedly. Another lug. Another think.

'Well,' I say. 'You'll have to marry me now.'

She pats me on the head. 'You're stoned already, sweetie.'

I swivel towards her as she heads for the door. 'Fuck you.'

'Fuck you too, sweetie.'

So that went well.

On the other side of the park, where I climbed in over the

fence from Cumberland Gate, there's a balloon. It must be meant. A hot-air balloon, tethered up but all ready and straining to get up into the London sky and start advertising toothpaste or life insurance or life or whatever.

It's a crazy idea, but it might just work.

On the way over, I pause to swipe a bunch of dark red roses from a flowerbed. My thumb bleeds.

In my ending is my beginning. The last time I had any business with balloons, it almost resulted in the deaths of three minor but much-loved television personalities. That was . . . nine months ago, almost to the day. O prophetic term, pregnant with omen!

But what will come of this latest balloon encounter? Precisely this, and no more: three minor but averagely much-loved non-television personalities will return to earth, one of them still *in utero*. That is my fabulous plan.

And then I realize that that isn't the plan at all. That is not what is meant at all. Scrambling into balloons, flying away, fleeing . . . the high jinks are finished and the farce is over. From now on it's serious. We're not in the movies now. And our final scene is destined to be played out with our feet planted firmly on the ground. No running away any more.

I turn away from the balloon and walk over to the film set and the glare of lights.

Ahead of me, I can see a wedding service about to take place, in a welter of roses and snow. This will allow for some beautiful, cinematographic shots, when Beth gets gunned down by the Latino bandidos, of rose-red blood blooming against white. How will they explain roses in wintertime? I don't suppose they will. It's *film*, innit? It's *art*, John.

The bride is radiant in white lace and muslin, and the groom is broad-shouldered and pretty, though I can't help noticing that his head is about the size of an orange. They're

245

just about to shoot the scene where Beth gets shot. In the crowd around her, I can see a gang of swarthy Latinos in black suits and shades, and then an outer circle of cameras. The wedding is about to turn into a blood bath, whereupon her hitherto spineless, limp-wristed faggot playboy of a husband will vow vengeance over her dying body, before turning into a remorseless killing-machine hellbent etc. Only I'm going to mess it all up first.

Security is surprisingly lax. I veer round to the side, between groups of people milling endlessly about, even as the cameras are rolling. Step between two colossal gantries bristling with lights, like watchtowers from the Berlin Wall. Up ahead, I can see Beth, her arm on the arm of her new spouse, shielding her eyes, staring out. I keep walking steadily, eyes fixed on her, clutching my purloined bunch of dark red roses in my hand.

The Latino bandidos are just pulling their guns, and the technicians backstage are about to pop those radio-controlled blood capsules all over her body, when I reach her side. I seize her in my arms and put myself between her and the guns, glaring back over my shoulder and into the blinding lights. The bandidos hesitate, fatally. I look back at Beth. She stares at me in complete bafflement. I am a walking category error. Here she is, in movie world, and suddenly someone from Real Life butts in. It just can't happen like that. A girl could get quite confused.

'What the fuck are *you* doing here?' she blurts out.

'I'm saving your life, *again*,' I say. 'You're about to get shot.'

'I *know* that, it's in the script.'

I hear a dim directorial roar from far away – 'Who's the fuckin' banana?' – but I ignore it. Nearer to us, the bandidos have their fake guns still trained on Beth, the muzzles wavering uncertainly.

'Do you know this guy?' her groom with a head the size of an orange demands of her. Then he leans behind her and asks directly of me, 'Does she know you?' I ignore him, which only serves to anger him further. 'Hey, pal, I'm talking to you.'

'But I'm not talking to you, I'm talking to my fiancée,' I say. Then, looking up at him very briefly, I add, 'And anyway, you have a head the size of an orange. Now look, Beth . . .'

'Security!' yells the groom, moving away from us, by now thoroughly panicked.

Film people, including the Latin American bandidos, start to circle around us.

'OK, buddy,' says a fat man with beard, 'I don't know who you are, but will you just let go of the lady, move to one side and put your hands up.'

'Never!' I cry, glaring around. 'The broad is coming with me!'

'Whaddya mean, *broad*?' hisses Beth in my ear.

She looks great in a wedding dress. A long, silent stare. In the distance, there is a lot of shouting going on, but it is far, far away.

'Marry me,' I hiccup. 'I'm not asking you again.'

She pats me on the back. 'God, you're such a pain.'

'OK, I'm giving you till ten, buddy, then we're coming in!' shouts the fat man with beard, almost in my ear. 'So if you don't want any trouble, I advise you to *move away now*.'

'Don't be so ridiculous,' Beth snaps back at him, 'you're talking to my fiancé.'

I smile. 'I knew you'd give in eventually.'

'Don't push your luck, you smug bastard.'

'And you'll really have to learn to keep a civil tongue in your head.'

'Up yours.'

'Up yours too, sweetie.'

As we push our way back through the surrounding rings of people, arm in arm, the fat man with beard murmurs to us, 'You two are getting *married*?'

*

On Marylebone Road, the traffic is frantic and foul. It has begun to drizzle, and we have no umbrella. Soon, the drizzle will turn to heavy summer rain and we'll be soaked. Beth has just walked out on her first ever proper movie role, wearing a wedding dress still loaded with radio-activated blood capsules. And I have an exciting job as a Pimlico art gallery assistant to look forward to. She's pregnant. We've no money, no careers, no status. No mortgage, no health plan, no life assurance. We stand at the side of the road, getting splashed by passing buses, gazing foolishly into each other's eyes. Her grip on my arm tightens. I lay my other hand over hers.

It's fine. This will do just fine.